Death in a Crowd

The Avenue's parade of people rivaled Easter Sunday.
The crowd waiting for a downtown bus convinced me
to walk a few blocks. Near Central Park's 85th Street
transverse, I joined a large group of would-be passengers. A bus pulled in, filled up, and departed leaving
twelve or fifteen of us behind to wait for the next one.
The cars and cabs whipped by. I felt two firm hands on
my back, then I was pushed, headfirst, into traffic. A
taxi barreled down on me, hitting me on my thigh and
spinning me around in the middle of the onrushing Fifth
Avenue traffic. Tumbling, I slammed my elbow and
forearm against the car's bumper and then hit the
ground. The last thing I saw before I lost consciousness
was an address on the green canopy—1040—the apartment house where Jackie Kennedy had lived and died.

MORE MYSTERIES FROM THE
BERKLEY PUBLISHING GROUP...

CAT CALIBAN MYSTERIES: She was married for thirty-eight years. Raised three kids. Compared to that, tracking down killers is easy . . .

by D. B. Borton

ONE FOR THE MONEY	TWO POINTS FOR MURDER
THREE IS A CROWD	FOUR ELEMENTS OF MURDER
FIVE ALARM FIRE	SIX FEET UNDER

ELENA JARVIS MYSTERIES: There are some pretty bizarre crimes deep in the heart of Texas—and a pretty gutsy police detective who rounds up the unusual suspects . . .

by Nancy Herndon

ACID BATH	WIDOWS' WATCH
LETHAL STATUES	HUNTING GAME
TIME BOMBS	C.O.P. OUT
CASANOVA CRIMES	

FREDDIE O'NEAL, P.I., MYSTERIES: You can bet that this appealing Reno private investigator will get her man . . . "A winner."—Linda Grant

by Catherine Dain

LAY IT ON THE LINE	SING A SONG OF DEATH
WALK A CROOKED MILE	LAMENT FOR A DEAD COWBOY
BET AGAINST THE HOUSE	THE LUCK OF THE DRAW
DEAD MAN'S HAND	

BENNI HARPER MYSTERIES: Meet Benni Harper—a quilter and folk-art expert with an eye for murderous designs . . .

by Earlene Fowler

FOOL'S PUZZLE	GOOSE IN THE POND
KANSAS TROUBLES	DOVE IN THE WINDOW
IRISH CHAIN	

HANNAH BARLOW MYSTERIES: For ex-cop and law student Hannah Barlow, justice isn't just a word in a textbook. Sometimes, it's a matter of life and death . . .

by Carroll Lachnit

MURDER IN BRIEF	A BLESSED DEATH
AKIN TO DEATH	

Ghostwriter

Noreen Wald

BERKLEY PRIME CRIME, NEW YORK

GHOSTWRITER

A Berkley Prime Crime Book / published by arrangement with
the author

PRINTING HISTORY
Berkley Prime Crime edition / June 1999

The Penguin Putnam Inc. World Wide Web site address is
http://www.penguinputnam.com

ISBN: 0-425-16947-2

Berkley Prime Crime Books are published
by The Berkley Publishing Group,
a division of Penguin Putnam Inc.,
375 Hudson Street, New York, New York 10014.
The name BERKLEY PRIME CRIME and the BERKLEY PRIME CRIME
design are trademarks belonging to Penguin Putnam Inc.

PRINTED IN THE UNITED STATES OF AMERICA

10 9 8 7 6 5 4 3 2 1

Ghostwriter

One

"You could kill Wagner in the kitchen," my mother said, "that way you could throw the bloody clothes in the washer and clean up everything in the sink. You know, use lots of Clorox. And don't forget the dishwasher's good for any weapons stained with clinging body tissues." Mom: the meticulous murderer.

"We'll talk about it after the company leaves," I said. She looked disappointed. I gave her a hug. "Let's not mix business with pleasure. Right now, why don't you mix me a martini?"

"Okay, but let's work on it later tonight for an hour or so." Mom headed to the dining room bar. Over her shoulder she added, "Oh, Jake, some guy called while you were at Gristede's. He wanted to discuss hiring you for a job, so I told him to drop by the party." That's my mother, hustling business in front of twenty guests.

. . . . .

"The thing of it is, you see, it's a delicate matter; my employer would need the arrangement to be handled in the best of taste."

The fop irked me. Who was he and what did he want from me? And why couldn't he get to the point, if there was one?

"I represent," he hesitated, brushing an invisible fleck from his well-cut Ralph Lauren jacket. I just knew he'd paid retail. No upstate discount malls for this fine specimen. Seventy-second and Madison—Polo's flagship—would be his store of choice.

"Yes," I prompted.

"Well, as I was saying, it's a tad difficult to be discreet and . . ."

"Forget discreet, try forthcoming." My voice had acquired a less-than-gracious edge. Not good. After all, he did represent a possible client and a cash advance. God knows I could use the business.

I flashed the full set of my just-bleached teeth—good thing today's dentists took VISA—and motioned to the white leather couch. Rooms-To-Go . . . no payment till January 2001. By then, I could be dead or rich or anywhere in between. Credit, the American way. My instant attitude adjustment seemed to relax him. Smiling back, he pulled a slim gold card holder from the inside pocket of his navy jacket and handed me a cream-colored engraved card.

Clinking cocktail glasses and high-pitched chitchat surrounded us. Jonathan Arthur, I read, thinking, "Beware of men with two first names." His address was on Sutton Place. "Hello, Jonathan." I held out my right hand as my left tucked his card in my blue blazer pocket. It occurred to me that Jonathan and I were dressed like twins: gray gabardine pants; white linen collarless shirts and black loafers. He'd added a tomato red scarf to his blazer's breast pocket. Two dapper dandies. "I'm Jake O'Hara."

"Indeed, you are." He sat, then primly arranged his trouser folds.

Mom passed by with a tray full of drinks. I grabbed my long-overdue martini, mumbled thanks, took a gulp, plopped into the Casablanca chair next to the couch and gave Jonathan my full attention. "What can I do for you?" I suspected it was going to be a long night.

The cocktail hour was my mother's longtime ritual. The third Friday of every month, she invited the lesser-literary-lights of our acquaintance—we knew few bright lights—to our big prewar co-op on 92nd Street. Mom still believed that 1957 had been the last great year for songs. "Stars Fell on Alabama" filled the room as the lesser-literary-lights discussed their yet to be published manuscripts. Everyone had a work-in-progress, some for as long as thirty or forty years.

Mr. Kim, the local greengrocer cum poet, and I had been comparing the patriotic verse of Walt Whitman and Rupert Brooke, when Jonathan Arthur had waltzed in, and Mom had two-stepped him over to me.

Graceful carriage in motion, military posture in repose. No slouch. Jonathan sat straight and tall, knees together, hands folded in his lap. Sister Mary Alice would have awarded him an "A" in deportment.

What can I do for you? had sounded like a reasonable query, worthy of an answer, but Jonathan appeared stumped. I tapped the rattan arm of my chair and drained the rest of my martini. Still smiling.

"This will be confidential—I need to know straight away, you don't discuss your clients or your contracts?"

"Jonathan, I don't do guest shots on *Rosie*. If I blabbed, I wouldn't be in business." Of course, at the moment, I had neither a client nor a contract. That's why Jonathan, however annoying, was being offered a cordial shoulder and another drink. He warmed to both.

"Let me be candid, Jake."

Thank God! "Please do." My smile would have to be chopped off.

"I'm familiar with some of your work. Oh, not from you, of course! But in our circle, the word gets out. My employer is most impressed with your "reported" body of work. She thinks you kill cute."

"I never thought of it that way. Jonathan, just who is your employer?"

He checked over both shoulders to make sure he wouldn't be overheard; then in an awestruck tone, he whispered, "Kate Lloyd Conners."

I, equally awed, said, "Wow! Cool!" America's Queen of Mystery apparently wanted to hire me as a ghostwriter. Wait till my mother heard this!

. . . . .

Mom and all lovers of the murder-most-cozy genre adored Kate Lloyd Conners, panted for her next release and had turned her into a multimillionaire, best-selling author. Her heroine, society sleuth, Suzy Q, was the widow of a wealthy, Irish-American senator. Any resemblance to Jackie O—definitely intended. Suzy's murder suspects skied at Biarritz, sailed the Aegean, gambled at Monte Carlo and shopped at Bergdorf's. Her victims included a reigning monarch's secret mistress and the secretary of state's former husband. Wherever the international jet set met death, Suzy-on-the-spot solved the case. The cookie-cutter formula, illogical plots and stereotypical characters were a lot of fun. I'd never confessed to mom that I loved them, too. Reading Kate Lloyd Connors, like devouring Milky Ways, was a secret vice.

. . . . .

"Well, Jonathan, I'd be delighted to have a chat with Ms. Connors."

"She's most anxious to see you. Is luncheon at one, tomorrow, too soon? The address on my card is Kate's townhouse. I live there."

"Fine, I'll see you then."

Jonathan Arthur rose, almost clicked his heels in a half bow and forged his way to the door.

Jeez, I thought, does the great Kate Lloyd Connors need a ghost? Has she used ghosts before? And why me? Our styles were as disparate as our incomes. I looked forward to our meeting.

The party dwindled. I kissed Mr. Kim good-bye on my way to find my mother.

My mother had missed being Miss Rheingold of 1961 by twenty-seven votes. Finished second in a field of six fresh-faced beauties. All the contestants, on their ballot and billboard photographs, looked as if a glass of beer had never touched their virginal lips. Deciding that she'd lost her one shot at fame and fortune, Maura Foley married my father, Jack O'Hara, an ex-marine, equipped with a dress uniform and the requisite tall, dark and handsome looks. The wedding at St. Patrick's included six bridesmaids in pink and white polka dots and organdy picture hats. Two hundred guests attended the reception at the Park Central, hosted by my party-giving maternal grandparents. The bride went back to college. The groom went to work as a salesman. After twelve totally incompatible years, they divorced. The first in her family. My mother often referred to my father as the Irish Willie Loman, but they were more than civilized when they met at wakes or weddings. However, when Dad died of cancer in 1980, Mom, if not the Church, canonized Jack O'Hara. Right up there with Jude and

Anthony. I, on the other hand, always had thought he'd been perfect.

I'd arrived five years into their marriage, after Mom's countless visits to gynecologists, a minor, mysterious fertility operation and a miscarriage. An Irish-American princess—with the most expensive baby carriage in Queens—christened Jacqueline Grace O'Hara, after Jackie Kennedy and Grace Kelly, my mother's heroines. Honest to God! My dad had the good sense to call me Jake, and it stuck—much to my mother's chagrin. Mom had hoped for a girly-girl to dress in lavender and lace; she got a tomboy, who by four had beaten up all the little boys in nursery school and cut off my much fussed-over long blonde ringlets. We've worked out a deal. She doesn't harp on curls and ruffles; I wear a dress on national holidays.

Just after my parents' divorce, my mother's maiden great-aunt conveniently up and died at ninety-five, leaving Maura O'Hara her grand old co-op: high ceilings, oak floors, chair rails, and moldings on the walls—tucked between Madison and Park, in Carnegie Hill, Mom's and my most beloved neighborhood in the entire city, plus fifty thousand dollars in cash. We were out of Jackson Heights and across the Triborough Bridge in a New York minute. The fifty thousand covered our expenses for the first few years. Living happily-ever-after among the wealthy while living off credit cards can be tricky, but Mom managed to send me to the Convent of the Sacred Heart, a couple of blocks from our apartment building, and to pay the co-op's maintenance and taxes for the next twenty years. A frustrated writer, Mom worked in the Corner Bookstore and did freelance editing.

Museum Row became my playground. On Sundays, we went to mass at St. Thomas More, occasionally sitting in the same pew as Jackie O—that made my mother's day—visited the zoo at Central Park, fed the seals, rode the merry-go-round and got our exercise walking through the park to the Museum of Natural History to see the dinosaurs. Then Mom and I would have tea at Sara Beth's Kitchen. Or we had picnics in Andrew Carnegie's former backyard, now the garden of the Cooper-Hewitt Museum. I had to sneak hot dogs in Central Park. They were on my mother's forbidden list, one item below "Don't talk to strangers." One item above "Always wear gloves on the subway." Mom worried about where, and if, the vendors had washed their hands after going to the bathroom.

Summer weekends, Mom loaded the wicker basket with cold chicken and a big thermos of Welch's grape juice and we'd ride the Long Island Railroad to Long Beach or Point Lookout. Even as a kid, I knew: It's a wonderful life.

"If you're going to college on credit cards and student loans, go for the gold . . . the Kennedy women's alma mater, Manhattanville. Jean Kennedy Smith fixed Ethel up with her brother, Bobby there," my mother had said. "It's co-ed now, you might get an MRS. along with a B.A." Sometimes my mother just sucked me into Camelot. I did get my B.A.; however, I'm still single.

I watched my mother stacking the last of the stemware gingerly in the dishwasher, thinking that she hadn't changed a hell of a lot from her Miss Rheingold second-place finish, almost forty years ago. Mom bubbled. "Oh, Jake, this is great. You might make some real money, giving you a chance to fin . . ."

"It's just a meeting, Mom, don't count . . ."

"But darling, I've suspected Suzy Q wasn't herself in the last book. I'll bet a ghost . . . maybe Emmie . . .

wrote them. Like Emmie, the plot was a little light on logic.''

Emmie Rogers was one of my closest friends as well as the daughter of Linda and Mike Rogers, childhood friends of my mother's.

I handed Mom the faux crystal candy dish, ''Can you fit this in there without endangering Nana's Waterford? Where was Emmie tonight? She hasn't missed one of your cocktail parties in years.''

''Emmie's still sleeping with that Hungarian waiter in Yorkville. She's flakier than ever. Served paprika on yogurt at lunch last week. But I'll bet that's why Suzy Q chased around Budapest in the last book. Kate Lloyd Connors would never be so . . . so Bohemian.''

''Come on, Mom, a little goulash and a lack of logic—never Kate's strong suit—doesn't prove a ghost wrote *Death on the Danube*. I thought it was vintage Kate Lloyd Connors.''

My mother's brows flew up under her ash blonde bangs. ''What a sneak! You're a closet cozy, pretending all these years you wouldn't be caught dead with a Suzy Q murder mystery.''

I threw the dish towel at her. ''Let's order a meatball pizza and watch *Casablanca*.'' This offer—two of Mom's favorite things—was ignored.

''A dishonest daughter is sharper than a serpent's tooth.''

''Call me Goneril. I just didn't want to admit I've inherited your taste for trash.''

''One woman's trash is another woman's opportunity. I'd decided on a Kate Lloyd Connors murder marathon read tonight, to get you up to speed, but since you've been such a sneak, maybe we can watch *Casablanca* instead.'' Mom flipped the switch on the dishwasher, surveyed the kitchen for crumbs or an unaligned canister and added, "Or, we could rent a Suzy Q murder mystery. Three of them have been made into movies, as you no doubt are well aware."

"I've only seen two. Let's get *Murder in Madrid*. And I want sausage on my half of the pizza."

"Really, Jake, you know how that ruins your digestive system. You need to watch that cholesterol, too. You're not getting any younger, dear."

"I know the facts of my life according to Maura O'Hara: Christ died at thirty-three; I'm not even engaged; my baby clock's on double time; and my arteries are aging. Okay, okay, no sausage and a double feature: Rick and Ilsa and Suzy Q does Spain."

As much as I loved Carnegie Hill, our apartment and even my mother, I had to ask myself for the thousandth time: Why is a woman your age living with her mother? The short answer remained money—or lack thereof—but comfort and no serious relationship were other contributing factors.

"Your deception's forgiven. Can we walk over to Lexington for the pizza? I like the crust better there and the oil is lighter, and—oh—on the way we can discuss your fees. You're now a ghost in demand."

Heading for the door, I took a last look around the kitchen. "Mom, you may be right about killing Wagner in here. Of course, I'd have to make the murderer as big an anal-retentive pain in the behind as you are."

TWO

Mrs. McMahon had turned doing the laundry into her life's work. At nine o'clock Saturday morning, I bumped into her and her ever-present plastic tub, filled with dirty clothes and the tools of her trade: Tide with bleach, Clorox, a favorite of Mom's, too, and a packet of bluing—that my mother said she hadn't seen the likes of since the end of WW II when she'd been a young child. Very young.

"You're up and about early, Jake. And all dressed up. Did you get a real job?" Her tone implying that I usually slept till noon. Her avocation was resident busybody, and she threw herself into it the way she threw the wet wash into the dryer: with a vengeance.

"I'm going out on an assignment this fine morning, Mrs. McMahon; however, I do have a job . . . writer, it's even listed on my 1040."

"But you have no books in B. Dalton's. Not a one, Jake. I had them check your name in the computer. None. Zero. Not under Jake O'Hara. Not under Jacqueline O'Hara. Zip. Nada."

"Ghostwriters are seldom seen on book jackets. Our

names are unknown, our faces are invisible; that's why we're called ghosts."

I'd like to read just one thing you've written. Give me a title, I swear I won't tell a living soul."

"Not a ghost of a chance, Mrs. McMahon. My contracts demand that I remain anonymous. Sorry."

"Well, Jake, if you ever want a career change where you would get some recognition, my daughter Patricia Ann's running a very successful operation." She plunged deep into her apron pockets, stretching its fabric tight across her hips, and came up with another packet of bluing. On the second try, she handed me a card. "I'd bet you'd make a great Mary Kay rep after Patricia Ann got finished teaching you how to line your eyes."

Patricia Ann should have started with her mother. Mrs. McMahon had florid skin that a beige foundation could have covered, her pale eyes were circled in black, matching a bad dye job on wispy hair, and her lips were magenta. Hard to believe that she and my mom were the same age. I took the card and put it in my briefcase next to Jonathan Arthur's. It was nice to know, on this beautiful June morning, that I now had two job offers to consider. Who knows? If it didn't work out with Kate Lloyd Connors, maybe I'd be driving a pink Cadillac. "Thanks, Mrs. McMahon."

"Give my best to your dear mother."

My dear mother believed that Mrs. McMahon gave the arcane term "shanty Irish" new life. But I just smiled and said, "Will do," as I wriggled around the basket.

As I walked by Mr. Kim's fruit display, on the corner of Madison and 92nd Street, he popped out of the store, "Looking spiffy, Jake. Eat this on the way to the subway." He waved a banana at me and sang, "Yes, we have no bananas, we have no bananas, today!'' Off-key but enthusiastic.

"I love New York in June . . ." I began.

"How about you? . . ." we harmonized.

"You two better keep your day jobs." Dennis, Mr. Kim's oldest son and a successful entertainment/literary attorney, appeared in the doorway, holding a cup of coffee, and laughing at us.

"See if we retain your services when we're a famous duo," I said. There was something about Dennis that made me edgy. Like my Jockeys-For-Her were too tight and my voice, too high. He had bronze, tight skin and long lashes, and his teeth were whiter than mine even after my $350 bleach job.

"Dad's right, Jake, you do look spiffy, today. Book deal?"

"Maybe. Wish me luck. How come you're not out in Quogue on this lovely June weekend?"

"Had an important meeting last night and missed the last jitney. But there's a great party tonight at Scull's in Southampton, I may head out later this morning. You've never seen my beach house. Interested in joining me?" Dennis asked this last question in a teasing tone, as he twirled a nonexistent mustache, while leering at me like Groucho Marx. He couldn't be serious, could he?

"Sorry, tomorrow, I have a date with death in—thank God—the final chapter—of an overdue manuscript."

His gold fleck eyes stopped smiling for just a second, then he laughed. Low and sexy. I squirmed inside my beige linen slacks but hopefully looked calm on the outside. I continued on my way downtown as the Kims said good-bye, serenading me and all of Madison Avenue's morning shoppers, "I'm mad about good books . . . how about you?"

· · · · ·

At 90th Street, I turned toward Fifth Avenue, taking me a block west and out of my way, but I wanted to check out the park on my power walk downtown, not the Madison Avenue shop windows. I passed the Cooper-Hewitt gardens on my right. The grass as green as it ever grows in the city and the white rosebushes like huge bridal bouquets. The summer solstice—the longest day of the year—and it was a pip. Turning south, I crossed Fifth at the southwest corner of 89th Street. Used book dealers lined the sidewalk outside Central Park, drawing a clique of semiserious walkers, probably glad for the break in their routine. The park was alive with the sounds of roller blades and the thumps of Nikes hitting the pavement. The city even smelled good today. God, I love New York in June. Dennis jumped back into my mind. I'd planned to use this time to decide where to murder Wagner, but all I could think about was Dennis Kim's unsmiling gold-flecked eyes.

· · · · ·

Mr. Kim's grocery store had been a fixture in Carnegie Hill for twenty-five years. He'd opened his store the same year Mom and I moved to our co-op. I'd been eight and Dennis, twelve. It was hate at first bite. The neighborhood boys were playing street hockey on roller skates. I wanted in and had my new skates on, ready to be goalie. Dennis had put a big-brotherly hand on my shoulder and said, "Go home and play with your dolls, kid." I'd brought my head down to his hand and bit him as hard as I could.

Our relationship hadn't improved much in the ensuing quarter century.

He'd married Victoria Wu, American News Network's

top anchor, three years ago. They had a messy, public divorce this past winter, each accusing the other of breaching their prenuptial contract. Vicky had revealed pillow talk, exposing one of Dennis's famous television star clients as a transsexual. It had been juicier than either Marv or Monica.

I'd spent a lot of time and emotion over the years deciding what I really felt toward Dennis. If I could get honest—as my program advised me—I'd probably admit it was lust and that I'd like to take another bite.

. . . . .

The regular ten o'clock, Saturday morning group of Ghostwriters Anonymous met at the Jan Hus Lutheran church on 71st Street, steps west of First Avenue. It was a support group—a twelve-step program—for those suffering from anonymity. There were ten charter members; I was one of them. We'd been meeting for almost two years.

I picked up my pace. Barbara B would be speaking on the first step: We admitted we were powerless over anonymity and our lives had become unmanageable. I needed to hear it; I enjoyed the fellowship of meetings more than process of recovery, achieved by working the steps. Listening to Barbara B would be good for me, especially today, when I would be lunching with the most famous writer in the country, Kate Lloyd Connors. No anonymous initial for her.

Unlike an alcoholic, who would relapse by taking his or her first drink, the ghostwriter's first credit on a book jacket would be a stepping-stone to recovery from his or her anonymity. A slip in AA is falling off the wagon. A slip in Ghostwriters Anonymous—we couldn't use the initials GA because the gamblers already had them—is breaking your promise to a client or your contract and taking public credit for a book you'd ghosted. A really sick recovering ghost is one who returned to ghost-writing after having published a book of her own. With her/his name under the title! We had two such sad incidents in our group, sending the ghosts in question flying back to step one and dramatically pointing out to the rest of us just how addicting anonymity can be.

Despite those differences, our adopted—and adapted—twelve-step program worked well for us ghostwriters, both in dealing with our anonymity and identifying with each other's feelings of inadequacy and rejection. I though Jane D had said it well at the last meeting: "Every time I finish a book and it goes to the publisher, it's as if, after a long labor, I gave birth to a baby, who's stolen from me in the delivery room. All the world will forever believe someone else wrote that sucker." When Jane didn't snooze during a meeting, she was right on.

A couple of the ghosts had wept when Jane D suggested using step three to deal with delivery dates: We turned our will and our lives over to the care of God as we understood Him. As for me, I thought it might be nice if God's will and mine coincided a little more often.

The smell of designer coffee filled the air. The second floor meeting room had twelve-foot-high ceilings, three couches, about thirty chairs and a buffet table now serving coffee, tea and homemade scones. The room was much too large for our group, and AA or NA, both drawing much bigger crowds, usually filled its space, but Saturdays at eleven had been open when we'd begun our recovery, two years ago. Some of us hadn't missed a meeting since. The Jan Hus church elders liked us ghosts because we tithed ten percent of our advances and left the room without a trace of evidence that we'd ever been there. Far tidier than the other addicts.

Ginger S, this month's chair and a well-paid cookbook ghost, only used beans flown fresh from Colombia's outback which she then ground with a cinnamon blend from Sri Lanka. She brought her china cups and linen napkins from home whenever she chaired. Said paper cups were plebeian. Ginger's table arrangements could make Martha Stewart's look sloppy; I gratefully grabbed a scone, smearing it with Ginger's homemade strawberry jam, and poured a cup of tea.

Ginger oozed capability. If she hadn't been so warm and funny, she'd have been totally annoying. A tall cool blonde, with shoulders made for the '40s retro suits she favored, Ginger had glorious skin, a sunny smile and a throaty Lauren Bacall voice. We'd known each other for years, were good friends, and both Mom and I adored her.

Where was she? I looked around the room and saw Ginger deep in a private conversation with Jane D. I'd devoured the scone and reached for a second, when Modesty M, an aspiring romance writer, who churned out potboilers to pay the rent, while she completed her 1,000-page gothic novel, joined me at the hospitality table. A small redhead with an outlandish wardrobe, Modesty was dressed like a mini monk this morning. She wore a long brown cotton tunic with a cowl neck, belted with what looked like—but I prayed weren't— rosary beads.

"I'm going to kill her, Jake. Then the tabloid headlines will read, 'Ghost-For-Hire Kills Employer From Hell!' That oughta sell a few books and my name will be under the title."

"Modesty, think this through." Program speak came in handy. Whenever you couldn't come up with any tangible advice for a fellow ghost, you could always resort to a slogan. And in this case, it was a good suggestion. What did Modesty have to kvetch about?

"The lady paid you fifteen thousand dollars for two hundred measly pages. You said last week that you only had twenty pages to go. Isn't the manuscript finished yet?"

"No, but she is. She just doesn't know it yet." Modesty stomped off and took a seat in the circle. I poured another cup of tea and, clutching my scone, I sat 180 degrees away from her. Grim and intense at best, Modesty could be murder when her client turned out to be miserable. And she had ghosted for some real bitches. The Ghostwriters Anonymous consensus was that Modesty was really a closet misogynist who deliberately chose wicked women-would-be-writers as her employers to substantiate her feelings.

Barbara B took her place in the circle's center and Ginger introduced her, "Good morning, ghosts. I'm Ginger S and a proud member of Ghostwriters Anonymous. Today's speaker is living proof that working the steps can lead us to accept our anonymity and find serenity."

Good. I felt more than a tad less than serene this morning. Not to mention unaccepting and insecure. Barbara gave us all a beatific smile.

"I'm Barbara B and I'm anonymous. The steps are my salvation. I'm delighted to share with you how I accepted both my anonymity and that my life had become unmanageable. Working the first and second steps on a daily basis has restored me to sanity . . . well, most of the time."

Several heads nodded. They identified. So did I . . . sort of. I loved the support of my fellow ghosts, but dreaded climbing those damn steps.

Barbara B went on, "The first half of step one comes easy for me. No one believed I was an author, anyway. Why should they? No book lover ever heard of me, so

I had no trouble admitting my powerlessness over anonymity. Oh, our close friends know we're ghosts, but if we're good ghosts, they don't know what we've written. If we're lucky we may have one or two articles a year published under our own names, but basically we're ghosts for hire—invisible to the people who count—book buyers."

A few ghosts applauded, I looked around the circle. Why did so many talented writers practice this masochistic profession? Being a ghost is a hell of a way to earn a living.

· · · · ·

When Barbara finished sharing, we took a coffee break. Ginger caught my eye and waved me over to the doorway. "Hi, Jake," she gave me a warm hug. "You look great; that shirt matches your eyes. The color of fresh celery stalks." Ginger liked to compare people to food and believed they should feel complimented. She was always saying he's a kumquat or she's a poached pear. I accepted celery stalks as high praise.

"Thanks, I'm going on a possible."

"Finished with Wagner?"

"Almost, just stuck on the setting for the stabbing."

"Murder's like real estate, Jake. Location, location, location."

"Yeah, but it's my Achilles heel; I never know where to kill them."

"You'll find a place, somewhere, you always do." Ginger motioned me out into the hall. We stood at the top of the winding staircase. "Listen Jake, I'm worried about Emmie." Ginger tapped her perfectly groomed, French-manicured fingernails on the mahogany banister.

"Why? What's wrong? She was a no-show at Mom's soiree last night. Where were you, by the way?"

"On chapter eight. I had a real breakthrough with the Palm Beach Puff Potatoes recipe. Princess Pain-In-The-Ass wanted me to use a dollop of curry. I remixed, I rebaked, I rewrote." I knew Ginger hated her current assignment, even though it had included all-expense-paid trips to Florida for research this past snow- and ice-filled winter.

"Anyway, I got this strange message on my machine. I'd only left the house to walk Napoleon and when I got back, Emmie had left this weird . . ."

"What did she say?"

"Oh something like—'I'm in deep trouble now. Curiosity kills truth seekers.'—Cryptic. She was way out there."

"Drinking?" I knew that Ginger was concerned about Emmie's drinking.

"I don't think so. It was about five . . . Em's early bird cocktail hour, but she sounded sober, Jake, just not sane. And she wanted me to call her right back. She absolutely had to talk to me, immediately."

"And?"

"So I called and got her machine. I left a message. And I kept calling, off and on, between baking and stuffing and writing—all evening—the entire curry batter went into the garbage . . ."

"What about Emmie? What did she say to you?"

"That's what I'm telling you." Ginger shrugged her elegant shoulders. "I didn't speak to her. She never returned my calls. But I'm going over there after the meeting. Can you come with me?"

"No. Sorry. My appointment's at one, and I can't be late, but call me. Mom doesn't trust that Hungarian, Igor."

"Not Igor. Ivan."

"Right. As in the terrible."

The ghosts were getting restless. We returned to the circle, and Ginger reconvened the meeting. Everyone had a chance to share. Most took advantage.

At the end of our meeting, all the ghosts joined hands and said the Serenity Prayer. Barbara B walked down the stairs with me. "Congratulations, Barbara, you sounded great. I envy your serenity."

"Don't, Jake. Like a good hair day, it comes and goes. It's not enough that I'm worried sick about Em; she called last night sounding frantic and told me an unbelievable story. If true, it's devastating! But you know how dramatic Emmie can be; she can't have her facts right. We're going to check them out, today. Expect a call from her. She wants to tell you, herself."

"There's something else, isn't there?" We were all used to Em's wild ideas.

"Just that last night I was scared stiff." Her gray eyes clouded.

"What's wrong, Barbara?"

"Let's just say I accepted an offer that I should have refused."

"For a new book deal?"

"No, for the one that's coming out this week. Avarice and pride colored my judgment."

"What is it—a book about the seven deadly sins?"

Barbara ignored my weak attempt at humor. She tucked her dark hair behind her Holly Golightly glasses. "Jake, I need to talk to you."

"I'm on my way down to Bloomie's for a haircut, before heading then over to Sutton Place."

"I'll walk with you," Barbara adjusted her long-legged stride to my gait. And fell silent.

"Well?" I finally asked.

"Jake, I'm really frightened."

"Of what?"

"Last night I got a call from a business associate of the father of the woman I'm ghosting for. He said her father was very unhappy with our project."

"Has he read the manuscript? Doesn't he like the way you wrote it?"

"It's not the way I wrote, it's what I wrote. And he's royally pissed at his darling daughter, too, for spilling the family's dirty laundry. It's a high-concept book, she's going on *Oprah* and CNBC this week, and that's just for starters. This book's going to be big."

"Who? What? Where?" I sounded like the lead in a newspaper article. Barbara pointed a shaky finger at me.

"Swear you won't reveal any of this to a living soul."

"For God's sake, Barbara, we've just left a Ghostwriters Anonymous meeting. If not me, who can you trust? I wouldn't break my own or any ghost's anonymity."

Barbara gulped, as if coming up for air after being knocked bowlegged by a wave, "Angela Scotti."

"The gangster? You ghosted *The Don's Daughter*, Jimmy Scotti's daughter's book?"

"LOWER YOUR VOICE," Barbara screamed.

"He's in jail. He can't hear us."

"This is serious, Jake. He's not at all pleased that Angela's peddling the family secrets."

"Is it hot stuff?"

"Oh, God, boiling."

"How did Scotti find out?"

"I don't understand. This deal was even more hush-hush than usual."

"Shit. Barbara, how did you get mixed up with the Mafia in the first place?"

"My literary attorney introduced me to Angela. He represents both of us. I think you know him. Dennis Kim."

Three

Was this an early Halloween party? Or were the costumes my luncheon companions wore their usual garb for a Saturday in June? Modesty would have a ball with this bunch. There did seem to be a theme: Come as your favorite character in literature.

Jonathan Arthur had chosen the Scarlet Pimpernel. He'd answered the door, breathless, dressed in black spandex tights, a deep red tunic, a matching ruby earring, and brandishing a sword. "Sorry, Ms. O'Hara, I've just finished my fencing lesson." Every bit as dashing as Leslie Howard. Jonathan returned his weapon to its sleeve, raised his face mask, and ushered me inside.

Chatting away, he led me through the foyer, an English manor house hallway, condensed to fit into the Georgian architecture of the Sutton Place townhouse, to a room he called the Conservatory. You could hear the capital "C" in his voice. If the exterior of the mansion had impressed me—red brick, lacquered black shutters, and a spectacular view of the 59th Street Bridge—the Conservatory took my breath away. White and blue. Delft figurines on the mantle. Floor-to-ceiling French doors leading to a tiny jewel of a garden. The table set for six with Wedgewood and Waterford gave Tiffany's second floor display department some stiff competition. I couldn't wait to describe it to Mom. The room commanded good cheer. I smiled on cue.

"Kate will be down directly," Jonathan said. "May I offer you a cocktail?" I opted for a Perrier and a better look at the gardens and the East River, walking over to the French doors. A Cecil Beaton set design. I should have come as Eliza Doolittle.

A cockney voice broke into my reverie. "Gin and bitters for me, Jonathan, and don't be stingy with the Gordon's. Me 'ead is pounding." As if I'd conjured her, a grunge-clad, thoroughly modern Eliza appeared on the scene.

"Ah," Jonathan said, as he handed me my drink, "Ms. O'Hara, may I present Caroline Evans, Kate's daughter."

"The 'orrid stepdaughter," the girl said. I stared at her.

She pouted. "Don't you like my new look?" Whatever the old look had been, it had my vote.

"Audacious," I said. Caroline grinned—my response seemed to please her—and extended milky white fingers ending in multicolored three-inch claws. It took some delicate maneuvering to avoid injury as we shook hands.

Caroline's black hip-hugger skirt was as short as her black hair was long. They met at, and barely covered, the bottom of her behind. Mickey Mouse shoelaces, loosely tied at her bosom, closed her studded leather vest. Any movement jiggled the two rings dangling from her belly button. Her ears and nose were pierced and bejeweled as well. Consistency. A true virtue. Barefoot—her toenails were painted to match her fingernails but, fortunately, were cut much shorter.

I couldn't take my eyes off her. Her makeup was early Madonna, she swallowed her drink in one gulp, and her big boobs danced as she spoke, "Gawd, make me another drink, Jonathan, and make it stronger . . . Oh, never mind, I'll do it meself." Caroline bounced to the bar. "So, you're the new 'elper. Kate's run through some 'apless 'elpers. You blokes ought to 'ave a union, Ms. . . ."

"Call me Jake." I thought she's only a kid, maybe eighteen, tops. Somehow I felt protective. God knows, I never considered myself motherly. "And you're right, Caroline. There are certain professions that cry for a union or a guild."

Caroline beamed. "See, Jonathan, contrary to popular belief around here, I do 'ave a brain in me 'ead." Jonathan looked doubtful, but before he could reply the doorbell rang.

"Please excuse me, ladies, that will be our other guest."

As soon as he was gone, Caroline whispered, "Things are seldom as they seem."

"Gilbert and Sullivan?" I asked. She nodded. "I can't remember the rest of it." Caroline opened her baby doll lips as if to tell me, when we heard voices and Jonathan returned.

"Jake, this is Patrick Hemmings." Jonathan allowed the man to precede him into the Conservatory.

My first thought was: Jonathan must have decided if Caroline could call me by my first name, so could he. As the other guest strode in, compact jeans covering the sexiest butt I'd seen in Manhattan, my second thought was: Patrick Hemmings had come as the Marlboro Man. Not literary, but certainly banned billboard pulp fiction. I wondered where he'd tethered his horse on Sutton Place. A suntan that no doubt glowed all year. Yards of gray hair. His blueberry eyes—Ginger wasn't the only ghost who could use food as physical description—locked into mine. God, just how desperate had I become? Patrick was the second man today who'd made me squirmy. And it wasn't yet two in the afternoon. Kate Lloyd Connors should have sent him instead of Jonathan as her messenger. I'd have followed Patrick straight to hell. No questions asked.

Caroline leapt into Patrick's arms, squealing, "Luv, it's good to see you." He bestowed a chaste kiss on her wan cheek and extended a hand to me.

Jonathan, the perfect host, filled drink orders and announced, "Our little group is almost complete." My attention shifted from Caroline to Patrick. Motherly interest forgotten. His direct gaze warmed and chilled me in rapid, sequential waves. Could this be early menopause?

"I understand that you're a writer, and Kate tells me you're one of the finest editors in New York as well."

"Thank you." Aha! Kate must pass her ghosts off as editors.

"It's wonderful meeting you, and I may need a referral. Do you know a good self-help editor?"

Pleased to be getting so much mileage out of my newly whitened teeth, I smiled. It's a tradition in Ghostwriters Anonymous to help a fellow ghost—lots of us did freelance editing—and, in doing so, I'd have a reason to talk to Patrick again. "I'm sure I can round up a few names and numbers for you. I'll call you Monday."

He tugged a card out of his jeans pocket. I'd become quite the business card collector these last two days. Patrick's was plain, yet attractive—like the man. Just the facts. Name, phone, address and occupation: Certified Hypnotherapist. Well, well, if I'd been playing *What's My Line?*, I'd never have guessed his.

"I'll wait to hear from you." His gaze held me spell-bound. Was I as flushed as I felt?

Our hostess swept into the room. Kate Lloyd Connors came as her own chic creation: Suzy Q. A black Chanel suit, trimmed with white braid, matching spectacles, her heavy silver hair drawn away from her face, held with a black bow. A woman of a certain age, looking ageless. "Darlings, I'm so sorry I'm late. You all must be fam-ished." She linked her arm through mine. "Jake, my dear, come sit next to me. We have much to talk about."

We all sat at the set-better-than Tiffany's table. Kate rang a little silver bell. Mrs. Danvers must have been hovering in the hall. She rolled in a huge cart, filled with what looked like takeout from the Russian Tearoom. And, although the sixth place remained empty, luncheon was served.

Her name, of course, wasn't Mrs. Danvers. But Vera Madison could have fooled me. The 'come-as-your-favorite-fictional-character theme' must have been easy for Vera—better for the role than Dame Judith Anderson or Dame Diana Rigg. Danvers seemed to possess Vera. And I ought to know. Mrs. Danvers had been scaring me for years.

Mom kept a long list of her favorite book titles and, as I became age appropriate, we'd cross them off. Her list never ended; as I started one book, she'd add another title. I read *Rebecca* on my fifteenth birthday, saw the movie in a revival house the same week and, forever more, identified with its heroine, Max de Winter's bride—who had no name. A ghost story. What else? All of this may, or may not, have something to do with why I've chosen a no-name-recognition profession.

After Vera served the blintzes, sour cream and fruit, she joined us at the table. Her dour presence filled the sixth seat. Kate Lloyd Connors, obviously a noblesse oblige–type employer, raised her glass and smiled, radiantly, at each of us. "May the wind always be at your back . . ."

"Up your Irish arse," Caroline's nasal vowels interrupted.

"Caroline, that's enough, excuse yourself." Jonathan sounded perturbed.

"You must forgive our Caroline, Jake." Kate rested her gold-bangle-bedecked wrist on my forearm. "She's just home from hospital and not quite herself."

Caroline jumped up. "I'm going to my room. The sour cream's laced with cyanide. Don't eat any, Jake." I looked from Caroline to the bowl of sour cream, speechless.

"If you don't believe me, ask Em . . ."

Unflappable, Kate turned to Vera, "Please escort Caroline upstairs and see that she takes her medication. Everyone, please try to put this unpleasantness out of your minds, and prepare your palates for charlotte russe." I thought if the cyanide doesn't kill us, the cholesterol will. Vera Madison took a firm hold on Caroline's thin wrist and propelled her away from the table.

Patrick asked Jonathan to pass the sour cream. Jesus, was he a psychic as well as a hypnotist? How could Patrick be sure about the cyanide or lack of? I planned to eat my blintz topless. And how did Emmie fit into all this? Could Mom be annoyingly right as usual? What did Caroline mean by "Ask Em?" My mother's best friend and tarot card reader, Gypsy Rose Liebowitz, often said, "All will be revealed." I hoped so.

We limped through lunch. Vera returned in time for dessert. As she poured Kate's coffee, I heard her say, "I gave her a sedative." Considering Caroline's concern about the poisoned sour cream, I was amazed that she'd taken a sedative administered by Vera. You couldn't get me to accept an aspirin from that woman if my head were in a vise.

Kate used her white linen napkin to pat her lips with a finality that signaled our meal was over. "Excellent, as always, Vera. Thank you." I was next up on Kate's agenda. "Are you ready, my dear? I thought we might have our little chat in the library."

"Fine, Miss Connors," I said, wondering just how many rooms were in this mansion.

．　．　．　．　．

All the library needed was Russell Baker and we'd be on the set of *Masterpiece Theatre*. I perched on the edge of an overstuffed chair in my convent schoolgirl pose, both feet flat on the floor, and waited. Kate Lloyd Connors seemed in no hurry to get down to business. Her slim hand jangled as she waved in the general direction of the fireplace. "This room comforts me, Jake. It's an old friend, holding memories of books read and words spoken. Do you believe that a room can be alive? That a room can take on its own persona? That a room can be your best friend?"

Kate saved me from giving the wrong response by answering her own questions. "Of course you do. You're such a sensitive, spiritual person. That's why I want to work with you. You're the type of writer who'd listen when a room speaks."

Could this be early Alzheimzer's? Was that why Kate needed a ghost? I tried to appear inscrutable; did I fool Kate? Probably not. I never could bluff my mother and Gypsy Rose when we played poker. Then again, Gypsy Rose might have been reading the cards, not my facial expressions. But Kate understood my silence as assent. "This room will reveal much to you, my dear. All you

will need to know, should you accept this assignment."
Kate pushed her Chippendale chair away from its
matching desk and walked to the bookcase lining the
west wall. She picked up a fat folder, holding what
looked like manuscript pages, from the bottom shelf.

"This is a labor of love," she said, running her fingers
across the top of the folder as if caressing a child's head.
"Read it, Jake; you're officially on the clock as a
consultant. I'll be back in twenty minutes to see if I can
sign my new co-author to a contract." She hesitated.
then said, "There's been something on my mind all
afternoon. You reminded me of someone. Now I know.
Jake, you look just like Annie Hall." She placed the
folder in my lap, and left, pulling the heavy oak double
doors shut. Was I locked inside?

Annie Hall? Had I dressed, without realizing it, as one
of *my* favorite fictional characters? Maybe everyday was
Halloween for some of us and we just don't know it. I
did know that the room may have spoken volumes to
Kate, but I hadn't uttered a single word.

. . . . .

The synopsis read well. *A Killing in Katmandu*
found Suzy Q in a sexless romance with an old friend,
the American Ambassador, whose about-to-be-ex-wife
has been brutally murdered. Suzy Q's suitor becomes
the prime suspect. I liked it. A few chapters and the
denouement were outlined. I guess the ghost would be
expected to fill in the blanks. Did Kate write all her
books this way? Twenty pages of plotting, then turning
it over to a nameless ghost? How had she gotten away
with it for so long? She'd had over fifteen best-sellers.
Won an Edgar. Where were her old ghosts? Did I know
any of them? The image of Emmie's heart-shaped face
and big brown eyes filled my head. Sometimes all this

anonymity drove me crazy. You never knew what your best friends were up to.

I put the synopsis down and stood up. Stretching, I realized how tired I felt. All that heavy food and wine. And now I had a decision to make. Did I want to ghost *A Killing in Katmandu*? Or did I want to walk away from this house full of loony tunes and write my own murder mystery? My heart cried for the latter. My credit cards cried louder. If the price was right, Kate and Suzy Q had bought themselves a new ghost.

. . . . .

The sunshine had been replaced with a summer squall. The skies were dark and brooding. I hurried over to Third Avenue to grab an uptown bus, clutching the contract to my bosom. In my most professional tone, I'd told Kate that I'd have to review the contract with my attorney. She'd seemed surprised. The advance was staggering—I should be able to take a year off to write my own book when I'd finished Kate's work-in-progress—and the deadline reasonable. The confidentiality clause, the strictest I'd ever seen, did have legal ramifications galore and raised anonymity to a secret status that I bet the CIA couldn't top. But what the hell? I'd use the third step and turn the problems over to a Power higher than myself. I'd been working on lack-of-identity issues for two years. I could handle this. But I understood now why no one ever suspected Connors used ghosts. Never in book publishing history had invisibility been so well covered.

Kate allowed that I could have Sam Kelley, our family attorney, review the contract provided that he, too, signed a ''never tell in his lifetime'' clause. ''However,'' she said, ''I don't think your Mr. Kelley will sweat the details. My attorney, Mr. Kim, has fine-tuned them through the years.''

As I left the library, I'd spied Patrick and Vera, deep in conversation, ascending the center hall staircase. Patrick held a tape recorder in one hand. Vera balanced a tray filled with medicine bottles. Neither noticed me.

. . . . .

I arrived at our house on 92nd Street, soaked, hair clinging to my cheeks in wet swirls, rain inside my shirt and shoes. Any chance that the contract had stayed dry seemed remote. The apartment door flew open before I could put my key in the lock. My mother must have been watching for me at a front window. She stood somber in the doorway. Gypsy Rose, by her side, crying.

"Oh Jake," my mother said, "one of the ghosts is dead."

"Emmie! I just knew something had happened to her." I dropped my briefcase as tears mixed with raindrops dripped down my face.

"No, darling. No one can find Emmie. Ginger's scoured the Upper East Side, looking for her."

"Then who's dead, Mom?"

"It's Barbara, dear. And God help us, she's been murdered. A Detective Rubin just called. He's on his way over. Jake, it seems you were the last one to see her alive."

Four

A hot shower and dry martini were not in the cards but, while Gypsy Rose made me a nice cup of tea, I changed into jeans and a T-shirt. My mother, between bouts of crying, nose blowing and laying the wet contract out to dry, eulogized Barbara. "She was so bright, Jake. If I've read any of her books, I know I must have loved them. It's just not fair to die while you're still a ghost and no one's had a chance to recognize your talent. Darling, let this be a lesson, you must write your own book, now."

"Mom, how did Barbara die?"

"Detective Rubin didn't say, and I was so shocked, I didn't think to ask."

Gypsy Rose brought the tea tray into the bedroom as I towel-dried my damp hair. "Drink this, Jake, and eat the bagel. You need energy. God knows how long the interrogation will be."

"Don't be so dramatic, Gypsy Rose—or are you receiving bad vibes? You don't think the police suspect Jake, do you?" My mother's voice cracked.

"Maura, I just don't want Jake to face the police on

an empty stomach, and I don't think she should answer any questions without an attorney.''

"Jake, maybe Gypsy Rose is right. Should I call Sam Kelley?''

I looked from one loving, anxious face to the other, thinking Sam had trouble wading through a book proposal, how would he manage to muddle through murder? "Ladies, ladies, stop worrying. Let's wait and see what the detective has to say." I took a sip of the hot tea, grateful as its warmth spread through my chills and, while I'd never been less inclined to eat, I took a small bite of the perfectly toasted bagel. It was easier to swallow than Gypsy Rose's haranguing would be.

Gypsy Rose and Mom had been best buddies since we'd moved to Carnegie Hill. Widowed in her early thirties—exactly like Jackie Kennedy, my mother always said—Gypsy Rose had used the late Louie Liebowitz's insurance money to open a tiny tearoom just off Madison on 93rd Street. Gifted with more than the ordinary woman's intuition and a crackerjack card player, Gypsy Rose combined those assets with a course in parapsychology at the 92nd Street Y to become Carnegie Hill's resident fortune-teller. Her tea shop was second only to the famed Sara Beth's in neighborhood popularity. And at Sara Beth's, a customer could eat the best muffins in Manhattan, but she couldn't have her future predicted. An avid bibliophile, Gypsy Rose often hosted an author's tea to help a neighbor launch his/her new book. The Hill housed writers galore and Gypsy Rose promoted them all, especially the alternate lifestylers. My mother said Gypsy Rose had been New Age before the movement had a name and swore that she'd had a previous-life love affair with Edgar Cayce. Gypsy Rose's Sunday Salon—literary readings mixed with tea-leaf readings—quickly became a New York "in" thing.

Authors from all over the city traveled uptown to discuss out-of-body experiences or polyamorous past lives as their rapt audiences sipped Twinings English Breakfast Tea from dainty china cups.

By the early eighties, Gypsy Rose had leased the adjacent store and began to sell upscale self-help books along with her spiritual growth tea-leaf readings. Mom left her job at the Corner Bookstore to manage the new section, while Gypsy Rose and two part-time sorceresses provided the tea and sympathy.

My bedroom was crowded with twenty-five years' worth of Gypsy Rose's Christmas past presents—giraffes, tigers, lions and other huge, stuffed animals from F.A.O. Schwarz. I loved Gypsy Rose, but when she and Mom ganged up on me, I could cheerfully have killed them.

Hell! What was I thinking? Of course, I didn't mean that, literally. However, my mind was full of murder. Who'd want to kill Barbara Bernside? All the ghosts admired her warmth and wisdom. She'd been a model of spirited but serene anonymity. Yet, our last conversation troubled me as it flash danced through my mind. Had Barbara been murdered by the mob? I shuddered as Gypsy Rose refilled my teacup and the downstairs doorbell rang. While Mom went to buzz in Detective Rubin, I fluffed my hair and, at Gypsy Rose's "You look like death warmed over," reapplied lipstick and blush.

With my favorite fortune-teller at my heels—maybe a lawyer would have been a better choice—I walked into the living room. I heard him before I saw him. A booming baritone. The voice matched the man. Detective Rubin filled our doorway. At least six-two, with wide shoulders, dark hair and firm jaw, he could have come to Kate Lloyd Connors' luncheon as Antonio Banderas.

My mother, in her lady-of-the-manor mode, introduced herself, invited him in and showed him to the Eames chair. He glanced around the room and caught my eye. I checked my watch. Six-thirty. And this was the third man, today, to tweak my sneaks.

"Ben Rubin." He managed to flip his ID open with one large hand as he extended the other for me to shake.

"Hi, I'm Jake O'Hara and this," I waved Gypsy Lee forward, "is our close family friend, Mrs. Liebowitz." Rubin smiled. A big, broad, sincere grin, revealing appealing dimples. People smiled when they met Gypsy Rose, and most everyone liked her. Her aura was perfect for a local family fortune-teller: warm concern and cool competence. The tough NYPD detective seemed as enchanted as all of her clients were. Gypsy Rose's wild, thick red hair clashed with her Versace hot pink silk suit, but on her, the offbeat combination worked. She was curvy, with creamy skin, bright blue eyes, and great legs. A siren at sixty. Gypsy put an arm around my waist and led me to the couch, where she sat next to me, arms crossed, chin thrust forward, ready to protect and defend me from the enemy. My mother stationed herself in the Casablanca chair where Jonathan had perched. God, was that only last night?

Detective Rubin, flanked by my mother to his right and Gypsy Rose to his left, decided to forge straight ahead and deal directly with me. I, after all, had been the last person to see Barbara alive. That thought stuck in my throat.

"Ms. O'Hara, I know this must be difficult for you, but I need to ask you a few questions." I nodded. I couldn't speak. I couldn't even swallow.

"This morning did you and the deceased attend a meeting at the Jan Hus Lutheran church?" Phrased in the form of a question, I knew he'd really made a simple declarative statement. I nodded again, then glanced at my mother.

"Jake never misses her weekly support group." My mother stole Detective Rubin's attention away from me. All too briefly.

"Mrs. O'Hara, I may have some questions for you later, but for now, I'd like Ms. O'Hara to answer those I'm asking her." My mother fussed with her bangs. I knew Rubin made her nervous.

He looked at me. "Had you known Barbara Bernside a long time?" I hated hearing him talk about Barbara in the past tense. I nodded for the third time.

"How long, Ms. O'Hara?" This was it. A question I couldn't answer with a nod. Please, God, let me speak. Give me back my voice. I opened my mouth. Nothing.

My mother began, "About two..." A glare from Rubin closed her mouth.

I tried again. "Two years," squeaked out. An answered prayer. "We were both founding members of Ghostwriters Anonymous." Now that the faucet had been turned on, I babbled.

"Ten of us ghosts formed a support group. You know—to deal with our anonymity issues."

Rubin stared at me, wrote something in his little black book, then said, "Go on."

"We meet every Saturday, we try to follow the principles of our twelve-step program in all our affairs." What did he want to know?

"And today, Ms. O'Hara, did anything unusual happen at this morning's meeting?"

"Well, Em wasn't there."

"Em?"

"Yes, Emmie Rogers. I figured she must have been the ghost who was killed." Rubin scribbled furiously. Now that I could talk again, I couldn't seem to shut up.

"She didn't come to my mother's cocktail party Friday night. And Ginger couldn't reach her. Barbara said Em had told her something potentially devastating. Then Em wasn't at the meeting. She's not like that."

"Not like what?"

"Like someone who'd go missing without letting any of us know. We ghosts are family."

Rubin shook his head. "Let's get back to Barbara Bernside. Reverend Hogland told me that he saw you and the deceased heading downtown, together, after the meeting ended. Is that correct?"

"Yes, Barbara walked me to Bloomie's. Well, most of the way. I had an eleven-thirty appointment for a haircut."

"Where did Ms. Bernside go when she left you?"

"Home, I guess." Once again, Rubin jotted in his notebook.

"And what did you two talk about on that walk from 71st and First to almost 59th and Third?"

"Well, actually—er—Barbara seemed upset." Would I break our group tradition of complete confidentiality if I told Detective Rubin that Barbara's Angela Scotti book could have been a motive for her murder? Did a ghost's anonymity follow her to the grave?

"About what, Ms. O'Hara?"

"What?" I sounded as flustered as I felt.

"Why was Barbara Bernside upset?" Rubin spoke deliberately, as if to a child.

"The mob," I mumbled.

"Did you say the mob?"

"Yes, Barbara told me she'd been threatened by the Mafia." Gypsy sat wide-eyed. My mother gasped and blew her nose. Rubin stared at his hands. No one spoke for a long moment.

Then Detective Rubin said, "Let's start at the top, Ms. O'Hara."

I told him all I knew. If I betrayed a step or violated a tradition, I did it to help a fellow ghost. Someone had killed Barbara. I wanted that someone found. I ended my tell-all with a question of my own. "Do you think it could have been the Mafia, Detective Rubin?"

He stood. "I'm sure I'll have lots more questions for you. Will you be home tomorrow?"

"Sunday. Yes, I think so. Detective Rubin, how was Barbara killed?"

"A blow to the base of the neck."

"The weapon?" I'd been writing death scenes for over a decade. I wanted to know.

Rubin shrugged. "Someone leaked that bit of evidence. It'll be in Sunday's *Post*. So, no harm telling you, now. Her neck was broken with a signed copy of *The Godfather*."

"Seems a little heavy-handed for the mob," my mother said. Rubin shrugged.

"Is it possible to kill someone with a book?" I was amazed.

"Well, it's not easy, but if you know exactly where to hit, and you strike with great force, using the spine, a book can be a deadly weapon."

"God help us!" I closed my eyes, thought a second, then asked, "The time of death?"

"Sometime after she'd left you, just before eleven-thirty, and when the building superintendent discovered the body at two. Narrows it down."

"You don't think it was the mob, do you, Detective Rubin?"

"I don't know, Ms. O'Hara. I do think, based on the information the deceased shared with you, that her murderer also might have known—a—Barbara had written the Scotti book, and—b—the Don was angry at her for spilling the family business. Maybe that's why *The Godfather* strikes me as an odd red herring.''

"Or else," Gypsy Rose said, "maybe a member of the mob has a madcap sense of irony."

"Death isn't a Frank Capra movie," My mother said.

Detective Rubin left. I had the distinct impression that he was glad to get out of here.

I settled on the couch, grumbling. Gypsy Rose rubbed my aching back while my mother put the kettle on and made us sandwiches. ''You do realize that I'm on the short list of candidates who Barbara might have told about her conversation with the mob? It's a damn good thing I have Mr. Pierre as an alibi from 11:30 to 12:30 and the Kate Lloyd Connors crazies from 1:00 to 2:00. My window of opportunity is mighty slim.''

My mother placed the tray on the coffee table. ''Jake, you can't believe that Detective Rubin considers you as a possible suspect!'' She handed me two extra-strength Tylenol.

I held her shaky hand. ''No, but only because he knows I'd have to be Mercury to dash from Bloomingdale's to 63rd and Madison and back over to Sutton Place between 12:30 and 1:00 P.M.''

Gypsy Rose selected a sandwich. ''What were you doing at Kate Lloyd Connors? I saw her home in *Town & Country* last month. Looked like a bit of jolly old England, transplanted to the East Side, with river view.''

Oh, hell. Had I become the biggest blabbermouth in Manhattan? What kind of a ghost would behave so cavalierly? As dear as I held Gypsy, only Mom and my attorney ever knew anything about my employers. ''She's a member of Sisters In Crime," I said. True enough if not the whole truth.

''Oh, are you doing an article on her?'' Gypsy Rose

knew I sometimes volunteered to write public relations pieces for the SIC's newsletter.

"Wouldn't that be wonderful? You must be psychic, Gypsy Rose. And, yes, her house was grand. I'll tell you all about it when I feel better." Again, I'd managed to tell nothing but the truth.

"Jake, why don't you just eat something and go to bed?" My mother passed me the tray of sandwiches. Real turkey breast on sourdough bread. Russian dressing. Suddenly hungry, I grabbed one. My mother smiled. "I have Jell-O, too."

"All my favorite comfort food."

"That's what mothers are for," mine said.

While we ate, my mother filled me in on Ginger's phone call. "Ginger spent most of the day visiting or calling all of Em's haunts. That turnip—Ginger's description, not mine—Ivan the Terrible claimed he hadn't seen or heard from Emmie since noon Friday. Ginger was stumped. She's left messages all over town and will call us in the morning to report any progress."

"Did Ginger say anything about Barbara's funeral arrangements?"

"She spoke with Barbara's brother in Pittsburgh. Bill, I think she said. He's flying in tomorrow, but he can't make any plans till the autopsy is done. The family's aiming for a viewing and service at Campbell's on Wednesday."

My eyes filled. "Poor Ginger's had a lousy day. Mine hasn't been the greatest, either. I'm taking a hot bath and your advice, Mom. I'm going to bed. This has been the longest goddamn day of my life."

At ten o'clock, comfy in my rag bag nightshirt and socks, I flipped on my computer. I hadn't checked my e-mail since yesterday afternoon before Mom's cocktail party. The first message read: Jake, I can't make the party. Meet me at eight at Elaine's. You must have the phone turned off while you're finishing the book. It's urgent that we talk. Alone!—'Skim milk masquerades as cream.' The e-mail had been sent at five on Friday; it was signed 'Emmie.'

Five

I called Emmie . . . and got the answering machine. What's a friend to do? Twenty-five hours late for Emmie's requested meeting, I dressed again, and hailed a cab to Elaine's. I figured Emmie wouldn't still be seated at the bar, but if she'd shown up last night, maybe the bartender or one of the regulars had chatted with her and could shed some neon on where she might be. Reliable ghosts don't disappear. Emmie had a lucrative assignment going. I now suspected that she'd been working for Kate Lloyd Connors. Had she quit, unexpectedly, on Friday? Was that why Jonathan had recruited me?

One of our Ghostwriters Anonymous program's traditions suggest that there are no coincidences. I concurred. It would have to be more than coincidence that Emmie's e-mail quote—"Skim milk masquerades as cream"—was the second line of the Gilbert and Sullivan couplet that Caroline Evans had whispered to me—"Things are seldom as they seem." I'd remembered as soon as I read Em's message.

Elaine's on Second Avenue, was just a block from the

Claridge House on Third Avenue, between 87th and 88th streets, where Emmie lived. A saloon, its atmosphere aged and stale, its food mediocre, and its bar area usually so jammed, you couldn't get a stool, Elaine's had attracted writers and sundry other celebrities for decades, even before it moved to the Upper East Side from its original Greenwich Village location. Our crowd, the working writers, felt at home here. Some of Elaine's customers were best-selling authors. Some were ghosts.

Tonight the joint was jumping. Joe Wynn, the James Bond of bartenders, worked his post, serving two drinks at once, while taking an order for three more. I squeezed past Dick Cavett and nodded to other regulars. There were no stools, but I positioned myself between a professional type—tweeds in June—to my west and a young model—I recognized her cover-girl face, but didn't know her name—to my east.

When I caught Joe's attention, I ordered a Perrier with lots of lime, afraid if I had any alcohol in my sleep-deprived state I'd pass out standing up. "Joe, if you get a minute, or take a break. I'd really like to talk to you."

"Talk, Jake, while you have me. It's catch as catch can." Joe decorated a Singapore Sling with an umbrella as he spoke. Jeez, who'd drink that pink mess?

"Was Emmie Rogers here last night around eight?"

"Yeah, you stood her up."

"I didn't mean to. I just got her invitation when I checked my e-mail an hour ago."

"Well, Emmie was pretty upset."

"Oh God, did she say anything, anything at all about what was bothering her? Or why she wanted to talk to me?" I felt guilty as hell.

Joe whisked the Martini & Rossi bottle over a shaker filled with Absolut vodka, allowing only a dollop of vermouth to make contact. After shaking gently, he poured the cocktail into a chilled glass, added two olives, and placed his work of art in front of the professor on my right. Someone at the front end of the bar called for a whiskey sour. "Just a minute, Jake, that sour's seated in my station."

Gus Henley, a fixture at Elaine's, covered the far end of the bar, closer to the dining room. He smiled at me as he plucked an orange slice from the fruit section. "Gus, did you see Emmie here last night?"

"My grandaughter's high school graduation, Jake," he called over his shoulder, walking toward the rear of the bar. "I had the night off."

"Congratulations!" I shouted at his back.

Joe worked his way back toward me, mopping up a spill, offering a drink, telling a joke. The noisy chatter gave me a headache, but Joe kept smiling. When the orders slowed down, he finally came over to me, wiping his hands on his apron. "Where were we? Oh, right, Emmie. Well, at first I thought it might be boyfriend trouble. Never did like that Igor."

"Ivan."

"Whatever. Anyway, I think it was more. Seemed real nervous. She downed two straight shots of Jack Daniels and tore up three coasters in ten minutes."

"But what did she say?"

Joe frowned. "I remember that she said something about thinking how you know a person and that person turns out to be someone you don't know at all."

A hand landed on my left shoulder. Startled, I turned my head and looked into the gold-flecked eyes of Dennis Kim.

"Buy you a drink, Jake?"

Suddenly, I needed one. "Yes, Dennis, you can. A glass of Dom Perignon, please." Since he was the most successful entertainment lawyer in Manhattan, I figured he could afford the best.

Joe went off to fill the order as the surge of the after-theater crowd swept in, shoving Dennis into me. We couldn't have been any closer if we were having sex. I squirmed to my right, almost knocking the professor off his stool.

Dennis grinned. "It's okay . . . I won't bite."

I had to laugh.

"Listen," he said, "I have a reserved table waiting. You want to join me for a late supper?"

I glanced at my watch. Eleven-thirty. In Spain, this would be the start of an evening. And I did have a few questions for Dennis Kim. I smiled. "Rigatoni Bolognese?"

"You got it." Dennis placed a hundred on the bar, picked up my champagne glass, asked Joe to send the bottle over to us, and led me through the crowd to a table next to Woody Allen's.

He brought up Barbara before I had a chance. "Can't believe Barbara's dead."

"How did you find out?"

"Your mother told my father while she squeezed a cantaloupe. Barbara was a brilliant writer, Jake."

"And a client of yours."

"Yes, for several years now. I've hooked her up with some great employers."

"Apparently, some not so great. I had a talk with Barbara this morning, right before . . ." My eyes filled with tears and my nose started to run. I'd dashed out of the house with only my keys and money in my blazer pocket. Embarrassed, I reached for a napkin. Dennis handed me his monogrammed handkerchief.

"It's a lousy deal, Jake. I'll miss her, too."

I blew my nose and tucked his handkerchief in my

pocket. "I'll return it, washed and ironed."

He patted my hand. Undeterred, I plunged. "Barbara told me how scared she was of Jimmy Scotti. She'd received a not-so-veiled threat on Friday."

Dennis's eyes went cold. "Really, I didn't know. My God, could that be why she was killed?"

I took a big gulp of champagne. "Do you represent many mobsters?"

"What are you thinking? Why would you ask that?" Dennis rubbed his forehead as if in pain.

"Well, you handled Barbara's contract with Angela Scotti, didn't you?"

"Yes, Angela, like dozens of my other clients, was a literary, not a mob referral. I don't do business with the Mafia, Jake."

"Then I guess you won't mind answering the police's questions. A Detective Rubin interviewed me tonight. I told him all I knew about Barbara and the boys, including the Dennis Kim connection."

"Look here, Jake, I just explained my connection, and I'll have no trouble discussing it with Homicide. What's wrong with you? For God's sake, you've known me for twenty-five years."

The waiter appeared with our order. "Here's our rigatoni. Let's not discuss this now. I want to enjoy my dinner. I guess I'm just tired." That's what I said. What I thought was: Gilbert and Sullivan and Emmie were right. How well do we know anyone?

· · · · ·

Over spumoni and espresso—I'd get no sleep tonight—I raised the table stakes and played the Kate Lloyd Connors card. "Dennis, you're all around this town like horse manure."

"Now, now, Jake, what happened to our well-bred

convent school graduate? What kind of dinner table conversation is that? The Madames of the Sacred Heart would be shocked to hear one of their young ladies sounding so vulgar.''

"Dennis, I had a D in deportment senior year. Was ranked incorrigible by the nun who taught Etiquette. Mom had to do some fast talking to Mother Superior or I wouldn't have graduated. And please don't try to distract me. Your clients seem to cover the entire East Side.''

"That's better.'' He poured a second cup from the double espresso pot the waiter had left on the table.

"I had lunch in Kate Lloyd Connors upscale Sutton Place loony bin.''

"Little girl, you've had a busy day.''

"Full of surprises. I never knew you were the attorney for the Queen of Murder-Most-Cozy.''

"Right. And I've never known either who you've ghosted for or who represents you.''

"Well, you'll soon be privy to that information. It looks like I'm Kate's ghost-elect, and you'll be dealing with my attorney, Sam Kelley.'' I detected a slight wrinkling of Dennis's nose when he heard Sam's name.

"It will be a pleasure doing business with you, my dear. Salut!'' Dennis raised his demitasse and clicked it against mine. "To my favorite ghost.''

"I bet you say that to all Kate's spooks.''

"Jake, you know former ghosts are best forgotten and that their employer's attorney would be the last person alive to admit they ever existed.''

"That's the spirit, Dennis. Now, please take me home. I have to get some sleep.''

I saved Emmie for the ride home. I'd never been in Dennis's cream-colored Rolls Royce convertible, though I often saw it parked, illegally, in front of his father's store. After the lawyer-client-ghost-confidentiality-as-a-religious-experience crap that Dennis had fed me along with the spumoni, I knew he'd never discuss whether Em had ghosted for Kate, but I wanted to see how he'd react to her disappearance. Dennis had known Emmie for years, from Elaine's and from Mom's cocktail parties, where he occasionally graced us with his presence. And we all knew Emmie was Mr. Kim's favorite ghost. But did Dennis also know her as Kate's ghostwriter?

"Missing? Just because she's not seen for a day doesn't mean Em's missing. Maybe she's gone off with that creep Igor."

"Ivan. No, he told Ginger that he doesn't know where she is, either," I laid my head back against the leather seat. It smelled rich. "I'm worried."

"Tomorrow's Sunday. Go to Mass with your mother, do the *Times* crossword puzzle, have tea with Gypsy Rose. Forget murder, mayhem and mysterious disappearance. Give yourself a day of rest."

"I just need a night of rest. I'll take two Tylenol and be fine in the morning." Dennis walked me to the door and kissed the tip of my nose. My toes curled. "Thanks for dinner." I kissed his left cheek. Then wondered why.

Six

By eleven o'clock Sunday morning, I'd finally killed Wagner, had an English muffin in the toaster oven, and was getting dressed for church. Using Mom's suggestion, I'd set the death scene, not in our bland, colorless kitchen, but in Ginger's country French–style kitchen/sitting room, complete with chic, state-of-the-art culinary appliances and overstuffed armchairs. I wanted all that requisite blood and gore to contrast with cozy gingham. And Ginger's roomy apartment, a block north of ours, had the cheeriest goddamn kitchen in Manhattan, possibly in the world.

My mother, delighted that "her heathen daughter" had decided to accompany her to 12:15 Mass at St. Thomas More's, followed me around, chatting, as I blew-dry my hair and gulped a cup of tea. "So, tell me more about Dennis and your dinner. Do you think his marriage to that Wu woman can be annulled?"

"We shared some rigatoni, Mom. We aren't announcing our engagement."

"Well, it takes months to get an annulment. More than enough time for a proper courtship."

"One more word and you go to church alone."

My mother knew when to retreat. She went to find her rosary beads and, no doubt, a new plan of attack. I went back to fighting my cowlick.

Ginger's nine-thirty call had awakened me from an angst-filled dream. We arranged to have brunch at her apartment after last Mass. Ginger hadn't found Emmie yesterday, but she had a hunch about Ivan. She'd spoken again to Bill Bernside and would give us an update on the funeral arrangements.

Now that Wagner was out of the way—I'd written the last chapter a week ago but had struggled with my on-going scene-of-the-crime phobia—I called Sam Kelley and made an appointment for him to review the Kate Lloyd Connors contract on Monday morning. Ghosts are fickle. Finish one death, blithely onto the next. Dennis was right; I deserved a day of rest. I'd thank God and the entire communion of saints if Detective Rubin didn't call before I left for Mass. I wanted to talk to Ginger before I dealt with him.

As we strolled down Madison Avenue to 89th Street in the bright midday sunshine, I thought how smart my mother looked: all beige and taupe, her short hair a shade darker than her linen jumpsuit, her figure slimmer than mine. Maybe I should join the gym at the 92nd Street Y.

"You're the one who should get married." Even joking, this was dangerous ground to tread. When my mother had been a divorcee, she'd dated a lot, but once she became a "widow," she announced there could never be anyone to take my father's place. I wondered if Jack O'Hara, wherever his spirit currently resided, knew that here on earth Mom had remained faithful to her ex-husband's ghost. I could almost hear him laughing.

My mother changed the subject. "After brunch, I'd like to run down to Bloomingdale's to find an outfit for Barbara's funeral. You need a black dress, too, Jake."

"Why?"

"Because you can't mourn properly in living color." Faced with logic like this, I agreed to go shopping. I did mourn Barbara, deeply.

I'd met Barbara when Ginger brought her to our first ever Ghostwriters Anonymous meeting. We weren't organized yet, just a bunch of ghosts nobody knew. Most of us didn't even know each other. Barbara's laid-back elegance and assurance impressed me. A natural leader. I'd liked her from page one, and the other anonymity sufferers seemed to feel the same way. That day, we ghosts made a decision to surrender our anonymity and to deal with our nonidentities.

. . . . .

Barbara had been the most prolific of the ghosts— except for Modesty's hundreds of ghosted romances and her 1,000 pages and counting, unpublished gothic horror—and made the most money. She came from money, too. Old money. Philadelphia's Main Line. Harvard. Oxford. I'd never seen her wear nail polish, and most of her wardrobe looked as if it had been purchased from an outdated Talbot's catalogue. Her vast townhouse apartment between Fifth and Madison on 63rd Street had to have been trust-funded. It reeked of DAR . . . like tea roses two days after they've been delivered. Faded chintz, tables cluttered with books, walls covered with an odd mix of Old Masters and cheaply framed posters from the Metropolitan Museum of Art. Barbara lived her life like the educated gentlewoman she was, surrounded by the things she loved. Her common sense, openness, and nonjudgmental attitude had the ghosts squabbling over whom she'd sponsor. Everyone wanted a piece of what Barbara had. Even miserable Modesty. Which is why I knew how upset Barbara had been by that call from the Don's henchman. Her unflappability was legend among us ghosts.

· · · · ·

After Mass, I lit a candle for Barbara's soul, wondering where card-carrying members of the Ethical Cultural Society went when they died. Wondering where I'd go. What the hell had the church done with purgatory? Was it still available? I'd have to check with Mom on current dogma. My mother loved the drama of Catholicism. She'd just lighted enough candles to burn down the borough of Manhattan. She stood in front of them, transfixed. A practicing pyromaniac.

"Mom, let's get out of here before someone calls the fire department." She sniffed. Inhaling holy smoke or showing disdain for me?

"I can only hope when I'm gone, you'll remember to light a candle for me each week. Did you light one for your father?"

Guilty, I shoved another dollar in the slot and scouted around for a fresh candle. All the ones in front of Mom's kneeler were ablaze.

Father Newell stood in the vestibule, expansively greeting everyone, shaking hands, and addressing most parishioners by name. My mother received a chaste kiss on the cheek—as well she should—and a warm, "Hello, Maura." I figured Mom had just dropped at least thirty bucks in the vigil light slots. I hoped her prayers would pay off.

· · · · ·

We arrived at Ginger's a little after one-thirty. Though grieving over Barbara and worrying about Emmie, Ginger remained the perfect hostess. Some people eat when they're stressed. Some people drink. Ginger cooked. And cleaned. Not that her dollhouse ever looked less than immaculate. Her home and hearth never seemed to lose their luster. Neither did Ginger. She was radiant this afternoon, her hair sleek in a French twist, dressed in a color she called Revere-Ware copper, her sandals matching her flowing silk slacks and shirt. If I'd as much as turned on the toaster oven, wearing that outfit, I'd go up in a bigger blaze than Mom's bonfire of candles. Ginger's skin glowed, her cheeks a deep pink—presumably from the heat of passionate preparations.

She served a pitcher of mimosas, along with wonderful crabmeat canapés, as she struggled to be her relentlessly cheery self, smiling through teary eyes, when she spoke about Emmie. "I didn't find a living soul who'd seen her since late Friday afternoon."

"Emmie was at Elaine's Friday night." I gave a full report on last night's investigation and the e-mail message that had precipitated it.

Ginger frowned. "I stopped at Elaine's earlier on Saturday, about three. Had a Bloody Mary. Too much cayenne as usual. Of course, the day shift was still on duty and no one had seen Emmie. I should have gone back."

"Doesn't matter," I said. "But now we know she was okay at 9:30 Friday night." I'd almost said still alive. I put that dreaded thought on hold.

"I wonder where she went when she left Elaine's," Ginger said.

"And why?" My mother looked puzzled. "Emmie really needed to see Jake. Why didn't she call or come by our house when Jake didn't show up?"

"You're right, Mom. Something or someone may have stopped her." I shivered.

"I think we need to speak to Ivan again." Ginger passed the canapés. "He said Emmie was really upset but claims that he doesn't know why. I don't believe him."

"If Em's problem was ghost-related, she'd never share it with Ivan." I took another crabmeat canapé and a sip of mimosa. "And she may have been thinking of ending their affair; she said sleeping with someone who looked like Dracula's kid brother but talked like Zsa Zsa Gabor was disconcerting."

My mother said, "You should question that crazy Hungarian, Jake. He may have answers he doesn't even know he has."

"Ginger, do you have any idea who Em was currently ghosting for?" I asked.

"No, I think the job came with one of those confidentiality clauses that you sign in blood."

The Kate Lloyd Connors contract crossed my mind, but I said nothing, and Ginger moved on to the main course. Dover sole. Poached to perfection, served with new potatoes and endive salad.

"The bread's from Zabar's; I'm sorry I didn't have time to bake."

"Ginger, why don't you just get up at four instead of five? That way you could stick the bread in the oven before you leave for the fish market." I said it with a smile. I was used to Ginger's penchant for perfection.

She'd been driving me crazy for years. We'd met when we co-ghosted *Cooked To Death* for an eccentric old chef who'd started a new career as a mystery writer. Each clue was a recipe. Ginger pronounced his white cream sauce too thick; I called his plot too thin. While whipping his potboiler into haute cuisine, we became good friends. And the book sold 50,000 copies, proving people will buy and try anything.

Along with the chocolate mousse, Ginger brought out the *Post*'s early edition. Barbara Bernside made the headline—bold, black and two inches high: GODFATHER WHACKS WRITER. There was a quarter-page photo of her below. The opposite quarter-page featured a shot of Jimmy Scotti. The caption beneath the two pictures read: Book, not bullet, kills Mafia's daughter's ghost. Detective Rubin said there had been a leak about the cause of death, but how did the *Post* know that Barbara had ghosted Angela's book? Was it from the same source?

I gave Ginger the nutshell versions of Barbara's threat from the mob, how I'd been the last one to see her before the murder, and Detective Rubin's Saturday evening visit.

"He doesn't suspect you, does he?" Ginger almost choked on her chocolate mousse.

"Of course not!" My mother and I answered in unison.

"Thank God." Ginger smiled. "Bill Bernside asked if you and I and Modesty would say a few words at Barbara's funeral. Not quite a eulogy, more like a farewell from her friends and fellow ghosts."

"That's lovely," my mother said. "You girls were all such good friends." She started to clear the table. "Help me, Jake. We've got to get to Bloomingdale's. If you're going to be standing at the lectern in Campbell's, you need to be wearing Donna Karan."

Every ghost in town had left a message on my answering machine when we arrived home from shopping. Sandwiched among the condolences and questions regarding Barbara's death was a message from

Detective Rubin, suggesting that I call him as soon as possible. Mom and I had to be at Gypsy Rose's tearoom/bookstore by seven. The two part-time sorceresses had this Sunday evening off, so Mom and I were hostesses du soir. I sighed but decided to wait to return my messages. I took off my Sunday-go-to-meeting clothes, put on a T-shirt and jeans, stashed my new widow's weeds in the closet, and dashed around the corner.

There was a good-size crowd gathered as Mom and I manned our station, behind a table holding a coffeemaker, cream, sugar, cups and a tray of cookies. "Who's the big draw, Mom?"

"Some hypnotist who studied under Brian Weiss."

I glanced over at the makeshift stage. A poster on a tripod read: "Hypnotize Yourself to Health." Standing to its right, Patrick Hemmings winked at me. I waved. Mom poured coffee as I put on another pot. Patrick was a hit.

"Hi, Maura. Hello, Jake." I turned. Dennis Kim was all smiles as he accepted a cup of coffee from my mother.

"Oh, Dennis, it's so good to see you," my mother gushed. "Jake told me what a grand eve . . ." My foot met my mother's shin with a quick kick, interrupting her probable engagement announcement, just as Detective Ben Rubin, looking grave, strode through the door and toward our table.

Seven

If someone became too pushy for my mother's sensibilities or insisted on an unwelcome intrusion into her professional or personal life, the guilty party would be castigated: "What unmitigated gall." If an event, experience or situation disappointed her—hey, sometimes life sucks, even for my mother—she'd say, "What a revoltin' development this has turned out to be." If Gypsy Rose were present, she'd say, "Chester A. Riley," then they would giggle like the school girls they'd been when William Bendix, starring in the '50s television series, *The Life of Riley,* found himself in weekly revolting developments. I'd say Patrick to my right, Dennis to my left, and Detective Rubin dead ahead qualified as a prime-time revolting development.

"Detective Rubin, how nice to see you. This is Dennis Kim and you know my mother." I bubbled as I walked around the buffet table and stood between them. George Sand at her Paris salon could not have been more charming.

Rubin grunted, "I know Mr. Kim." They both nodded. Coolly. As if each believed that shaking the other's hand might be a fatal touch.

"You two have met?" I asked.

Dennis put his arm around me and gave me a squeeze. Why was he acting so cozy?

"Detective Rubin dropped by to see me this morning. About Barbara Bernside. As you know, I represented her." Dennis sounded sincere and saddened by the horror of it all. He cast his eyes downward and applied more pressure to my none-too-firm bicep. I jerked away from his grip, rubbing my upper arm.

"Barbara told me that yesterday morning," I reminded him, "just before someone killed her."

Rubin spoke before Dennis could reply. "Ms. O'Hara, I left two messages, but you didn't return my calls. I stopped by your house, ran into a Mrs. McMahon in the lobby; she sent me over here. Is there somewhere we can talk privately?"

"I guess we can use Gypsy Rose's office. It's on the third floor. Up that stairway to our left."

"Let's go," Rubin said.

"Give me a minute. I need to find someone to pour the coffee," my mother said, looking around for a candidate. "Dennis, would you be a dear and keep an eye on the tab . . ."

"Mrs. O'Hara, I want to speak to Ms. O'Hara, alone. Why don't you stay here and mind the store? We won't be long."

"I'm a great coffee maker, Mrs. O. Please allow me be your second in command." Dennis beamed those golden eyes at my mother.

I led the way up the old circular staircase, gripping the oak banister, not sure if I was more nervous about my talk with Rubin or about leaving Dennis alone with my mother. Would I wind up the evening arrested for murder or engaged to be married?

The red brick building, serving as bookstore, tearoom and Gypsy Rose's home, dated back to the early 1900s, when Andrew Carnegie had moved into his mansion on Fifth Avenue and the fashionable folk followed him uptown, creating a new neighborhood, Carnegie Hill. Now, Detective Rubin followed me as we climbed the Persian-carpeted steps to Gypsy Rose's office. The door was closed but not locked. I switched on the chandelier, and the lovely little room glowed. I chose the burgundy leather chair behind the Mission period desk; Rubin sat on one of the gray tweed love seats, facing me.

"There's no easy way to tell you this, Ms. O'Hara . . ."

"What? Tell me what?" I knew this wasn't going to be good news.

"Emmie Rogers is dead."

"Oh, Jesus . . . oh, God . . . no." I needed air. My heart had landed in my mouth and was choking me. Emmie's mother and father must be . . . I couldn't find a word. How would I tell Mom? Rubin poured a glass of water from the pitcher on Gypsy Rose's desk and handed it to me.

"I'm sorry, Ms. O'Hara. Eerie, isn't it? Yesterday, you thought Emmie was the victim. Today, she is. Although she'd been murdered before Barbara."

Sorrow gagged me. I gulped the water. A few drops spilled onto the walnut desk. Ben Rubin used his handkerchief as a blotter. "How? When?" I asked.

"The Medical Examiner places time of death as somewhere between ten P.M. Friday night and three or four Saturday morning."

Soon after she'd left Elaine's. "Where?"

"In her apartment at the Claridge. Her parents reported her missing this morning. I recognized Emmie's name from our conversation last night and had the super let us in. Odd that her parents didn't have a key.''

Odd, indeed. My mother would have a key to my apartment if she had to sleep with the concierge to get it. Why didn't Linda Rogers have one? Poor Emmie hadn't gone missing at all. She'd been home alone, murdered. I told Rubin how dreadful I'd felt about not reading Em's e-mail until Saturday. Then asked, ''Detective Rubin? How was Emmie killed?''

''A sharp blow to the head with *Crime and Punishment.*''

God! A literary serial killer? Murdering the ghosts? Could that be possible? What book would he use to bash in my head? Maybe Webster's dictionary—my constant companion—I'm the writing world's worst speller. I rubbed my temple, then looked at my fingers, almost expecting to see blood.

''Look, Ms. O'Hara, it's getting late. You're missing how to hypnotize yourself to health, and I'm missing sleep. Please drop by the station in the morning. I want to go over a few details with you.''

''I have an appointment with my attorney in the morning.''

Rubin smiled wickedly.

''No. No. It's to review a book contract. I'm starting a new job tomorrow. I could see you after I'm finished with him, around eleven.''

''Good. And did you happen to save that e-mail from Emmie?''

· · · · ·

I stopped in the second-floor bathroom on my way downstairs. Even in its soft pink lighting, my skin was ashen; I felt as sick as I looked. A bolt of bile shot up from my stomach, and I spit into the john, then waited to see if vomit would follow. The sound of laughter wafted up the stairs. Patrick must be an amusing speaker. New Agers are dead serious. A tough audience. When my insides calmed down, I splashed cold water on my face, pulled my lipstick out of my jeans pocket, and rubbed Clinique's Bronze Buff on my lips, then on my cheeks, using my index and middle fingers as a blush brush, then finger-combed my hair, shrugging at my reflection. It would have to do; I just didn't want to frighten my mother and Gypsy Rose.

Patrick fended a question-and-answer session as I returned to the coffee and cookie station. A lady in red asked about her asthma during a previous life in ancient Babylon. Patrick explained how stress-related ailments can follow us through all our incarnations. God, would poor Emmie carry her PMS to her future lives? What if she came back as a guy? I decided not to tell Mom that Emmie's current incarnation had ended. That sad news could wait till we got home.

Dennis stood, sipping coffee, seeming to savor every word Patrick said. As a kid, I'd lost enough card games to Dennis to know he had a poker face. Just how well were he and Patrick Hemmings acquainted? After all, they both provided professional services to Kate Lloyd Connors. Their paths must have crossed in her Sutton Place mansion. And why was Dennis here tonight?

"Everything okay, Jake?" Dennis whispered.

"Fine." I busied myself rearranging the cookies. There were hardly any left; New Agers tend to gobble up free food. "Where's my mother?" Dennis gestured to the rear. Mom and Gypsy Rose sat in the last row, apparently spellbound by Patrick. It must have been a hell of a talk. Maybe Jane D could make some real money if she ghosted his book. I'd give her a call in the

morning. My stomach lurched again as I realized none
of the ghosts knew Emmie was dead. I didn't plan on
being the one to tell them. I had to get out of here. Now.

"Dennis, can you cover the table till Mom gets
back?"

"Sure. What's wrong? You look like hell."

"I'm okay. Just whipped. Tell Mom I'll see her at
home. Thanks." I was gone before he could ask any
more questions.

. . . . .

I almost made it home, but crossing 92nd and
Madison, I spotted Ivan pacing from Mr. Kim's fruit
stand to my apartment house door and back again. There
was no way to avoid him.

"Hey, darlink! Jake, I vant talk to you."

"Ivan, I . . . I'm not feeling well."

"Not vell. You are not vell. Vell, Emmie is dead. I
call her for two days. I try to go in her apartment.
Building manager is KGB. I am vorried. Vere is she? I
call her Mama. Emmie's parents like me not, still I tell
them. Tonight, policeman—Rubin—answer phone. Vere
she is . . . is dead. Jake, do you know zis?"

"Yes. Detective Rubin just told me." I started to cry.
Ivan patted me awkwardly on the shoulder. He wore
black from head to toe, his jeans too tight, his T-shirt
cropped, and his flowery cologne overpowered me. How
had Emmie ever slept with this guy?

"Darlink, vat do ve do? I love her. I lose her. Now
this Rubin policeman vants to see me in the morning.
Vat are you thinkink about zat?"

"I think Rubin's going to have a busy morning. I'm
sorry, Ivan, but can we talk tomorrow?"

"Jake, ve talk now. I have somethink for you. Emmie
give it to me for safe keep. You understand?"

"Yes. What Ivan, what did Emmie give you?"

"Envelope. She laugh. Say, hold for me. Don't lose. Give to Jake, if you no hear from me. I think she is joking. No joke, Jake."

"When did Emmie give you the envelope, Ivan?"

"Friday, ve have lunch at Budapest East. Goulash. Emmie says she is planning to meet you that night. I am thinkink, darlink, you don't meet Emmie, so you no receive information she vanted to give you. Zat is correct?"

"Correct." I could barely stand.

Ivan reached into his back pocket and, with some difficulty, pulled out a twice-folded, slightly soiled white envelope. I grabbed it. "Thanks, Ivan. I'll talk to you tomorrow. I promise."

"Vill you find out vhy our Emmie is killed? Vill you, Jake?"

"I'll try, Ivan. I'll try."

Mrs. McMahon lurked in the lobby, waiting for the elevator. I dodged her, took the stairs, and cried all the way to the apartment.

Collapsed on the couch, for the second night in a row, I opened the envelope. My fingers shook. Inside was a photocopy of an old newspaper clipping. The date—February 15, 1957. The paper—the *Honey Bucket Record*. The state—Michigan.

LOCAL FISHERMAN DROWNS IN
FREEZING LAKE SUPERIOR

John Hansen, fifty-eight, died under mysterious circumstances, yesterday, February 14, while ice fishing in Lake Superior. The Honey Bucket police are investigating the possibility of foul play, calling the death suspicious. Sources close to the investigation say the homicide team is asking: Did Hansen fall in? Or was he pushed? Police Chief Carl Rutland said, "Sarah Anne Hansen, 17, the deceased's only child apparently left town, late yesterday." A detective with the Honey Bucket Police Department added, "We would like to question the missing girl." Hansen, a widower, had been employed as a logger at Swenson's Timber, for over twenty years. Sarah Anne is a senior at Honey Bucket High School.

Who the hell was Sarah Anne Hansen? How could a town be named Honey Bucket? And why did Emmie Rogers have this clipping?

Eight

The desk sergeant at the Nineteenth Precinct reminded me of Dennis Franz with Lady Bird's '60s bouffant. I told her I had an appointment with Detective Rubin and she growled, "Have a seat." Eleven o'clock, but I'd had a full morning and was grateful to just sit and wait.

Mom reacted to the news of Emmie's murder about as I'd expected. Bad. She'd arrived home last night, flustered. "Why did you leave Gypsy Rose's without a word? Where are your manners, Jake?" Her fluster turned to fright when I told her about Emmie. "Jesus, Mary and Joseph! Could someone be killing the ghosts? Poor Em. Oh, Jake, I don't know what I'd do if anything happened to you. God, I must call Linda Rogers." While Mom made her condolence call, I packed my briefcase for my morning rounds. The contract for Sam Kelley to review. The notes I'd made on Kate Lloyd Connors' *A Killing in Katmandu*. And Emmie's envelope containing a newspaper clipping, going back over forty years, for Detective Rubin. Were all these items somehow connected? How?

When I awoke this morning at seven, Mom was still on the phone. Only the fact that she now wore a bathrobe indicated that she'd ever gotten off. She was talking to Gypsy. They were making plans to visit the Rogers in their Jackson Heights apartment. I poured Mom a cup of tea, then gave her my itinerary for the day. "Mom, while you're helping Linda and Mike arrange the wake, could you ask a few questions?" My mother nodded, buttering a piece of rye toast.

"Try to find out who Emmie'd been ghosting for, then ask the Rogers if they know—or ever heard Emmie mention—a Sarah Anne Hansen." I showed my mother the clipping.

Her eyes brightened. I knew that as sad as she felt, my mother loved a mystery and that she'd jump at the chance to play a Manhattan Miss Marple. Younger and more chic, of course. As I was leaving, Mom said, "Please be careful, Jake." I've heard those same words for over a quarter of a century as I exited this same front door. Today, I listened.

My appointment with Sam Kelley also went as expected. He took a long drag on his cigar, blowing smoke all over me, as he expressed delight with the big advance. Then he puffed, sputtered and stubbed out the stogie. The nasty smell filled my nostrils. "No royalties," he groused.

"Well . . ."

"A shame, but Jake," he tented his tobacco-stained fingers, peering at me over them, "Take the money and write." I knew he'd already calculated his percentage and planned his next trip to Belmont's $500 Win window, without changing even one word in the contract drafted by Dennis Kim. No wonder Dennis snickered whenever Sam's name came up.

. . . . .

I'd waited about ten minutes when Ben Rubin
appeared, full of apologies, contrition and smiles. We
walked from the civil-service-green waiting room, down
a dreary hall, into his office. Here the color proved
harder to call. Maybe mud-clay. His desk was metal and
messy. However, the muddy walls were covered with
posters from the Metropolitan Museum of Art's
exhibits—mostly Matisse and Monet—and scattered
among the legal folders and law books spilling over his
bookcases were novels: Fitzgerald, Hemingway,
Dickens. Ben Rubin was more than just a pretty face. I
picked up *The Sun Also Rises*. A favorite of mine.

"You look like Lady Brett," he said. "Er, that is like
I'd always pictured she'd look."

I laughed, "Minus money, title and wardrobe, but
thanks." I brushed my hair out of my eyes. Right now
I probably looked more like a sheepdog than
Hemingway's Brett. As usual my hair stylist had left my
bangs so long that I was half blind.

Rubin made an abrupt swing from bibliophile to
murder investigator. "Ms. O'Hara . . ."

"Why don't you call me Jake? I have a feeling we're
going to be spending a lot of time together."

He got busy, rearranging the piles on his desk,
completely avoiding eye contact, appearing flushed.
"Okay, and I'm Ben." For a split second, I felt as if we
were teenagers who'd just experienced a spark, but then
Ben blew the moment. "So, Jake, tell me again. Where
were you between ten Friday night and three o'clock
Saturday morning?"

I recapped. Then offered my unasked-for opinions,
along with a copy of Emmie's e-mail and the clipping
Ivan had delivered. Regarding my theory that the ghosts'

deaths must have been connected to what Em had told
Barbara, and that I believed the murders were job related
. . . ghostwriting somehow had gotten them killed, Rubin
assured me that he'd be talking to their former
employers. He didn't mention who they might be.
Regarding the newspaper article, Rubin told me Ivan
was due in five minutes.

"Maybe he knows something more about this
clipping, but I don't think so."

"Thanks for coming in, Jake. I'll be in touch." I was
dismissed.

· · · · ·

After a lunch of bagel, banana and coffee at the
Third Avenue deli, I arrived at Kate Lloyd Connors'
house at one o'clock. Mrs. Madison—still as dour as
Mrs. Danvers—opened the door. "Miss Connors is on
an international conference call. There's coffee in the
Conservatory, you can wait for her there." She motioned
me down the hall, then retreated upstairs. I poured a cup
of coffee I didn't need and walked over to the French
doors with their great view of the river. Caroline waved
to me from the garden, a basket of fresh-cut roses in one
hand, a pair of shears in the other. I opened the door
and she bounced in. Caroline wore black shorts, cut off
to show lots of cheek, a black leather bra and high-top
black sneakers. Her raven hair was hidden under a black
baseball cap, but she sported full war paint. She gave
me a warm smile. "Welcome to our 'appy little family."

"Thanks. Want some coffee?" I wanted to talk to
Caroline, believing that she would be the most likely of
the loony tunes to confirm Emmie's employment at
Kate's ghost as well as to ask about any problems Em
might have encountered on the job. "Lovely roses,

Caroline, do you enjoy gardening?" I handed her a cup of coffee.

"I like being out of this 'ouse, even if it's only in the garden."

"How long have you lived here?"

"Since me foster mum plucked me out of a London orphanage five years ago. Annie had Daddy Warbucks. Didn't she? I've got Mummy Connors."

"How did Kate find you?"

"She was writing *Larceny in London,* it had to do with baby brokering, and she'd visited our orphanage for her research. As the oldest girl in the 'ome, I presented the famous lady with a bouquet." Caroline placed the roses in a Waterford vase on the Chippendale table near the French doors. "Roses, in fact."

"I guess you've seen lots of Kate's editorial assistants come and go."

Caroline giggled. "Vanish right into thin air, don't they?" She smelled like Coppertone. I guess she didn't want to lose that vampire pallor.

"Did Emmie Rogers work for Kate?"

The door from the foyer flew open and Kate Lloyd Connors swept in, wearing a flowing white caftan that matched both her hair and her snow-capped teeth, bared in a wide smile. "Jake, hello and welcome!" She extended her hand and took hold of my arm, steering me toward the door, bubbling. "We'll go straight to the library. I can't wait to get to work." As we exited, she called back to Caroline, "Tea in the drawing room at four-thirty, darling. Plan on joining us." Caroline shrugged her bare shoulders and said nothing.

Kate and I spent the next few hours discussing Suzy Q's style, voice and point of view. Caught up in *A Killing in Katmandu,* I almost forgot the Manhattan murders of my two dear friends.

Jonathan Arthur tapped at the door, "Tea time, ladies." And we all trooped down to the drawing room, where Mrs. Madison's spread must have outdone Buckingham Palace. I devoured three scones while Jonathan and Kate planned an upcoming book tour. Then the conversation shifted to the new book and never veered from it. Amazing. All the morning newspapers and television shows had carried the story of Emmie's death and the probable link to Barbara's murder. This household either was totally unaware that someone had killed the ghostwriters or, if they knew, it wasn't considered tea time talk. I put down my cup, agreed to report to work at nine the next morning and left. Caroline was a no-show.

Turned out that she was otherwise engaged. As I walked past the staircase to the front door, I glanced up. On the second-floor landing, Caroline was wrapped in Patrick Hemming's arms. Her hands, under his running shorts, gripped his ass. A T-shirt, sneakers and a towel draped around his neck completed his outfit. I had to admit he looked great. Suddenly, Patrick broke away from her and bounded down the stairs. Caroline's cockney whine turned into a loud screech, "You can't run away from the truth, 'Emmings." She picked up a Ming bowl from a small lacquered table on the landing and heaved it at him, barely missing her moving target's head. Patrick reached the first floor in seconds and stood, agape, when he spotted me.

"Oh, Jake, please don't be upset, Caroline's not herself today."

Figuring ghosts rush in where angels fear to tread, I asked, "What happened? She seemed fine earlier this afternoon."

Patrick looked embarrassed and sounded frantic, "It's her medicine. Needs adjusting."

I smiled. "What seems to need adjusting is your shorts. They're bordering on indecent exposure."

Caroline's laughter followed me out the door.

. . . . .

My mother had information to report. "Jake, your hunch was right. Emmie swore Linda to secrecy, but now that she's gone," my mother's voice cracked, "Linda thinks you should know. Not only did Emmie ghost for Kate Lloyd Connors, but Linda said Emmie was really upset when she spoke to her on the phone Friday afternoon."

"What did Emmie tell Linda? Anything about Sarah Anne Hansen?"

"No. Neither Linda nor Mike has ever heard of Sarah Anne. But, Emmie did tell her mother that she had to decide what to do with some very disturbing information she'd discovered at Kate's. Em planned on discussing whatever it was with you."

"And what did Linda think about that?"

"At first, Linda hadn't been too concerned; you know how Emmie can overreact. But Linda never heard from Emmie again. On Sunday morning, she called the police."

Emmie had tried to reach me. I didn't read her e-mail in time to meet her Friday night, and someone had bashed in her skull. Barbara's, too. All because I didn't show up at Elaine's. Goddamn, I felt responsible. I'd find out who murdered my two friends if it killed me.

Nine

I called an emergency meeting of Ghostwriters Anonymous. Ginger not only agreed to help round up the ghosts, but offered her home for the impromptu meeting. She'd just finished baking a batch of fresh-picked blueberry pies, experimenting with a new criss-cross crust recipe. Instead of freezing them, she'd serve them, still warm, to the ghosts. "Maybe with a little homemade vanilla ice cream. And, Jake, I have some wonderful, bold, French roast beans, I'll make espresso. We'll need to be wide awake, and it will give me a chance to use my new demitasse set from Williams-Sonoma." Even in my bleakest moments, Ginger could serve up a splash of sunshine.

Before leaving for Ginger's, Mom and I shared a sad little supper, toying with our scrambled eggs and English muffins, much too glum to eat. Both the eggs and the muffins were overcooked. Mom was no Ginger in the kitchen. But who, short of Julia Childs, was? I doused my eggs with catsup, then gave them another push around the plate. My mother said, "Linda and Mike would like to have the funeral at Saint Joan's on Saturday, which would mean a viewing on Friday. Do you think the Medical Examiner will have released the body by then?''

''I don't know, Mom. Have Mike talk to Detective Rubin. Maybe he can hustle things along.''

Saint Joan of Arc's in Jackson Heights was the church where Linda and Mike Rogers had been married and where, coincidentally, both Emmie and I had been christened. Now she would be buried from there.

''Two of our ghosts' funerals in one week. I can't believe it, Jake.''

I'd forgotten that Barbara's memorial service would be Wednesday. If this didn't qualify as the week from hell, I couldn't imagine what week would. I grabbed a quick shower, threw on my sweats and sneaks, kissed my mother good-bye, and arrived at Ginger's at eight-forty.

．　．　．　．　．

The ghosts, united in their grief, made a strong showing. Joined together in our sadness, we held what amounted to a private wake, for two of our own. However, combined with sorrow, fear and anger had made us ghosts edgy. We weren't there five minutes when Modesty got in Ginger's face as our hostess poured her French roast espresso. ''Well, why don't you have any decaf espresso?''

Ginger jumped all over her. ''A decaf espresso is an oxymoron. Just for tonight, try not to be such a miserable mango, Modesty.''

Then Jane's serenity was severely jolted when I blurted out that there might be a serial ghost killer loose in Manhattan. But she bravely suggested we turn that concern over to our Higher Power. Too Tall Tom, a how-to handyman ghost who moonlighted as a carpenter, where he doubled his writing salary, chided Jane: "God helps those who help themselves." Other ghosts flipped out, demanding to know what steps we should take to protect ourselves.

Seeing Jane so upset, Ginger relented, "Sorry, Modesty, why don't you brew some of that Irish Creme decaf? I know you like it." I then officially opened the meeting.

"My name is Jake O and I'm anonymous. I've called this special meeting of Ghostwriters Anonymous to discuss the brutal murders of our members and to share my guilt over their deaths with you. And to ask all of you to consider breaking our tradition of confidentiality and to share any information that might help solve Barbara's and Em's murders." A collective gasp filled the room. I then related all I knew regarding the events of the past weekend, concluding with why I held myself responsible for Emmie's and, probably, Barbara's death. In return, the ghosts showered their love and support on me.

Buoyed by the ghosts' acceptance of my controversial stand, I went on, "In Ghostwriters Anonymous we share our experience, strength and hope. Tonight, let's share all that we think, feel or know about Emmie and Barbara's recent activities. New York, New York's literary community is not unlike Smalltown, USA. Let's get to work and find out who killed our fellow ghosts."

With a sense of purpose, we devoured our pie, dropped some of our anonymity, and discussed our strategy. No one had ever heard of Sarah Anne Hansen, but everyone agreed that the clipping had to be connected to Emmie's death. Modesty had grown up in Michigan and had an aunt in the Upper Peninsula. She'd give her a call and see what Auntie remembered about the 1957 drowning. I asked if any of the ghosts had ever heard Em or Barbara mention any of the loony tunes who made up Kate Lloyd Connors's household.

Laura T, a celebrity ghost, whose White Diamond perfume competed with the aroma of the freshly baked pies, sat next to me. Her Ivana hairdo and Lagerfield pantsuit identified her as one of the rich . . . but not famous. Ghosting for the stars, Laura made tons of money, yet still suffered from the same anonymity as the rest of us ghosts. She told us that her current work-in-progress was an "autobiography" of a rock star who couldn't read. Laura's advance was over three hundred thousand dollars, but she claimed to spend it as fast as she wrote. Checking out her outfit, which included a Rolex with a price tag higher than most compact cars', I, for one, believed her.

Laura called for the group's attention. "Last week, I went with Gen-X to his hypnotherapist, Patrick Hemmings. We're including Gen-X's past lives in the book, and I sat in on a regression session, so I could meet some of the people he used to be. Anyway, according to Gen-X, this Patrick is quite the ladies' man. While we were in his office, Patrick took an important phone call from a woman named Kate. It sure sounded as if she were more than a client. Patrick kept saying, 'I'll be over later. Everything will be fine.' He seemed embarrassed that he'd taken the call in front of us. And guess who was in the waiting room when we came out?" Laura paused for dramatic effect. Her audience hung on her every word. "Emmie! Of course she recognized Gen-X and never said a word to me. I asked her later and she told me she'd been in regression therapy with Patrick for several months." The enraptured ghosts digested this information, and they all promised never to reveal the name of Laura's famous client.

Patrick got around. Modesty had met him at a New Age seminar, where he enjoyed a long conversation with Barbara. When Modesty had pressed Barbara about where she'd met him, Barbara only said, "Patrick's an old soul. It seems as if I've known him for an eternity."

Too Tall Tom said, "I saw Em and Igor . . ."

"Ivan," I said, by rote.

Too Tall Tom moved right along, "Anyway, they were having lunch on Friday at Budapest East. They appeared to be quarreling. I wouldn't count that crazy Hungarian out. Emmie did give him an envelope. I guess it held the Sarah Anne Hansen clipping, but then Emmie left in a huff, and Ivan screamed after her, 'You vill be sorry.' He almost knocked over my waitress on his way to the kitchen."

Charles K, a true-crime ghost, took lessons at the same fencing school as Jonathan Archer. Jonathan told Charles that he had a potential award-winning, true-crime exposé work-in-progress, and Charles had replied, "Haven't we all?" I wondered if Kate knew that she harbored a budding writer in her household.

Who'd have guessed what a fountain of information my fellow ghosts would turn out to be? I tried to take notes as fast as they talked. Jane thought Barbara might have been one of Kate's earlier ghosts; Barbara had once mentioned working for a best-selling mystery writer. But Ginger felt strongly that we shouldn't rule out the mob's involvement in Barbara's death. Ginger stressed that Barbara had been terrified at the Ghostwriters Anonymous meeting on Saturday morning and, while Barbara hadn't revealed her client's name to Ginger, she did indicate her upcoming book might have triggered a mob-related problem. My later conversation with Barbara confirmed that fear. Modesty seemed convinced Kate Lloyd Connors had to be guilty. "She's a real bitch, just like all my clients. I met her at Sleuth Fest last year; believe me the Queen-of-Murder-Most-Cozy is capable of killing the ghosts. Probably to make sure they never talked.''

Ginger glared at Modesty. ''Do you have baked beans for brains? Based on that one meeting, you've judged this woman to be a murderer?'' And we ghosts seemed to be back where we started.

. . . . .

I walked home, full of new and confusing notions, but without a theory, much less a strategy. Ginger and Modesty would pick up Barbara's brother at Kennedy, tomorrow morning. I had to work from nine to one and couldn't join them, but we'd all agreed to get together later in the day. Maybe a good night's sleep would make my head stop whirling. As I reached 92nd Street, I watched my mother exiting the Wales Hotel on Madison Avenue, between 92nd and 93rd streets. She was with two men. I waited on our corner, tapping my left foot, my arms folded, my expression stem. My mother noticed me, after pulling her eyes away from the older of the two men, as they all crossed the street. The object of my mother's attention looked like the patriarch in a Ralph Lauren ad. His gray hair was curly and thick; his stance was straight and tall. The younger man was Detective Ben Rubin. What the hell was going on?

''Oh hi, Jake,'' my mother bubbled. ''Say hello to Aaron Rubin, Detective Rubin's father.''

I uncrossed my arms and shook the elder Rubin's hand, giving my mother a disapproving glance. ''And just what have you three been doing?''

''Detective Rubin . . . Ben . . . happened to be in the neighborhood and dropped by with his father. Ben wanted to see you. They caught me at a bad moment;

I'd been talking to Linda about Emmie's funeral, and I was crying. Aaron suggested we all go to Sara Beth's for decaf cappuccinos and, afterward, I felt so much better that I showed them the Wales lobby and Pied Piper Salon.'' My mother flashed her Miss Rheingold second-place smile at Ben's father. ''Aaron's a retired Manhattan district attorney. Worked under Ed Koch. Jake, his insight into the ghosts' murders is wonderful. And Ben will try to have Emmie's body released in time for the wake on Friday.''

''Yeah, well, it's late and I have to go to work in the morning. What was it that you wanted to see me about, Detective Rubin?'' Ice wouldn't melt in my mouth.

Ben Rubin got the message. His reply was all business and his delivery as cold as mine had been. ''I spoke with the detective who'd covered the Hansen case. He's long retired, but he remembers rumors that Sarah Anne, who, incidentally, was never found, had been sexually abused by her father at the time of her disappearance. The Honey Bucket Police Department is sending us the case file. Just thought you might be interested, Ms. O'Hara.''

Conflicting emotions swept through my soul. Detective Rubin had gone out of his way to keep me informed. Why was I so bothered by his showing up at our house? And even more bothered by my mother's obvious interest in his father? I wondered what the late, now sainted, Jack O'Hara would think about all this. He'd think his daughter was a jerk, that's what.

''Look, I'm sorry if I sounded short. Overtired and cranky, I guess. I really do appreciate your keeping me posted and please let me know what the Michigan records reveal.''

Ben's sleepy-eyed smile warmed any lingering chill.

Ten

A pretty Hispanic maid, wearing a crisp uniform, answered the door at Kate's townhouse. "Good morning, Miss O'Hara, I'm Carla. Miss Kate said you'd be working in the library. I've put out coffee and sweet rolls for you."

"Thanks, Carla. Nice to meet you. Isn't Miss Connors at home?"

"They're all out. Miss Kate and Mr. Jonathan are at the publisher's and Mrs. Madison has taken Miss Caroline to see her therapist. I'm the only one here and, after I get you settled in, I have to run an errand, if that's okay with you."

I smiled—wow—what an opportunity. Where would I snoop first? "Of course it's okay, Carla, take as long as you like."

Once we were in the library, I asked, "Where is Mr. Arthur's office?"

"Why, it's in the room next to this one. Miss Kate does all her writing at her desk here in the library and she likes to have Mr. Jonathan nearby." Carla served me coffee, adding a dollop of cream, then started out the double doors. "Miss O'Hara, you see that door," she gestured to the far end of the library, "it leads into Mr. Jonathan's office, though his bedroom's on the fourth floor; he's always joking about the inconvenience."

"Is Caroline's room on the fourth floor as well?"

"No, her room's on the third floor, right across from Miss Connor's suite. Will there be anything else, Miss O'Hara?"

I smiled, "No, thank you, Carla, you've been most helpful."

Sipping my coffee, I waited until I heard Carla go out the front door. Then I crossed the the length of the library—not a short span—and tried the door to Jonathan's office. The square room, located in the back of the mansion, was larger than I expected. Its two windows faced north, overlooking a flagstone patio and a small backyard. The furniture all came from the Doyle Galleries, one of my favorite antique stores. If we had our druthers, Mom and I would have chosen Doyle's over Rooms-to-Go, but credit considerations had strongly influenced our decor. Jonathan's British Colonial motif was reinforced by his strategically placed accessories: a campaign chest; a full-length portrait of Queen Elizabeth and Prince Philip circa 1953; and the Union Jack, which stood in the corner behind his desk. All harking back to a time when the sun never set on the British Empire. Eerie.

Jonathan, no surprise, was a neat freak. His desktop held a phone, a computer, a mouse pad, a picture of him and Kate, both on horseback in formal riding attire, with several hounds in the foreground and an English manor house in the background. And nothing else. Not a piece of paper. Not a paper clip. Not a pen. Did someone really work here? Or was this a still from *Out of Africa*?

All the desk drawers were locked. The distressed file cabinets, also from Doyle's, and looking as if they were decades removed and continents away from modern-day Manhattan, were unlocked. But a cursory inspection indicated that the papers, primarily old business correspondence, seemed to be innocuous.

Wondering how much time I had before someone came home, I checked out his bookcase. We liked some of the same authors: Graham Greene, Evelyn Waugh and Beryl Markam. There were also several writing manuals, including one I considered to be the Bible: Strunk and White's *The Elements of Style,* as well as one titled *How to Write a True Crime Thriller.* What could the dear boy be working on?

"Is there something you're looking for, Miss O'Hara?"

Shaken, I spun around to face the formidable Mrs. Madison, straddling the open doorway between the library and Jonathan's office. She didn't look happy. Even though I felt every bit as intimidated as the second Mrs. de Winter had been made to feel by Mrs. Danvers, I decided on a strong offensive play. "Mrs. Madison, you startled me! Did you knock on the library door? If you did, I didn't hear you."

She seemed taken aback, but made a swift recovery. "I certainly did knock and, being concerned when you didn't answer, I entered only to discover you in Mr. Arthur's office." Mrs. Madison made it sound as if I'd just been tried and convicted of mass murder.

"It's not as sinister as you might think, Mrs. Madison. The door was ajar, and I must admit the furnishings caught my eye. I just stepped in to admire this charming room," I lied. Damn good thing she hadn't arrived in time to catch me trying to pry open Jonathan's locked desk drawers. Or had she?

"Well, it's most unusual for Mr. Arthur to leave this door open. I'll be sure to mention it to him." Mrs. Madison stood to one side, allowing me to precede her out of the room. She locked the door behind us. "Is there something you need, Miss O'Hara?" She paraphrased her original question.

"No, thank you, Mrs. Madison. As I told you, I wasn't looking for anything, just absorbing the atmosphere."

"Then I'll leave you to your work." She glanced over at my computer—its screen blank—and at my legal pad—its pages empty. Her gaunt face now expressionless, but her tone imperious.

"Miss Connors will not be returning until after you've finished for the day. Is there any message you wish me to give her?"

"Tell her to have a nice day. And please tell her I have to attend a funeral tomorrow; I'll see her on Thursday. Oh, and Mrs. Madison . . ."

"Yes, Miss O'Hara?"

"You have a nice day, too."

She pulled the double doors shut more forcefully than I considered necessary. Since my snooping had come to an ignominious end, I went to work.

．　．　．　．　．

I met my mother at Gypsy Rose's tearoom and the three of us had lunch together. "So, Mom, what about Aaron Rubin?" I asked.

"Why, Maura O'Hara, you're blushing," Gypsy Rose teased.

"Did my mother tell you she went out with two men last night behind her daughter's back?"

"For your information, Jake, I thought Aaron was charming, witty and smart. And good-looking, too.

That's why when he called this morning, I agreed to have dinner with him on Sunday . . . after this ghastly week is over."

"Fast worker." Was I referring to my mother or her new beau? I turned to Gypsy Rose, whose forkful of chicken was suspended in midair, her mouth agape, forming a perfect O. My mother did sound way out of character.

"Do you think we should be making a list for the bridal shower?"

"Right after I buy my matron of honor gown," Gypsy Rose giggled.

"You two are very funny," my mother said, her tone terse.

"Now you know how I feel when you're arranging my marriage to any and all available strangers." I smiled, but deep inside the recesses of my black soul, I had to confess that I felt a tad jealous of my mother.

I left Gypsy Rose and Mom to their wedding plans—better than the funeral arrangements they'd been obsessing over—saying I had an appointment. The truth was, I had no appointment, but I was going to pay an unscheduled visit to Patrick Hemmings, hypnotherapist and rumored womanizer.

· · · · ·

I stopped at home and called Ben Rubin. In my pique last night, I'd forgotten to mention that Laura T, the celebrity ghost, had spotted Emmie in Hemmings's waiting room, and Modesty believed that Patrick had more than a passing acquaintance with Barbara. Rubin was not at his desk. I left a lengthy message, using up all the tape available and still not finishing. I washed my face and carefully applied makeup while the curling iron heated. Then I changed into a cream silk shirt, matching trousers with flattering front pleats, and bone-colored kid stacked-heeled sandals, telling myself I wouldn't have time to change before my meeting with Barbara's brother and the ghosts, but asking myself if I preened for Patrick.

The Lexington Avenue bus dropped me two blocks from Patrick's Murray Hill office. It was four o'clock; I'd better hustle if I wanted to be on time for cocktails at the Carlyle at five. Both his building, one of those post–World War II monstrosities—all square and no style—and the street, itself, though situated between Park and Lex, looked a little seedy. An area for people on their way up or on their way down. I felt confident that Patrick Hemmings was on his way uptown.

A few feet from Patrick's doorway, I started, as Dennis Kim emerged from the lobby and walked toward Park Avenue. His cream-colored Rolls awaited, illegally parked in front of an old brownstone a few buildings west of Patrick's. I ran after him. "Yo, Dennis!" It was his turn to be startled.

"Jake, what a pleasant surprise!"

He had been about to put the key in the car door, when my unladylike screech had interrupted him. He sauntered back to where I waited under the canopy in front of Patrick's building. "So, Dennis, been doing a little past life regression?"

"I have enough trouble in this lifetime. How about you?"

Thinking, this is one situation he's not going to sing his way out of, I said, "Or is Patrick Hemmings a client of yours?"

"Jake, haven't we established that I never discuss my clients? You, of all people, should grasp the concept of professional confidentiality." Those gold-flecked eyes glittered in the late afternoon sunlight.

A meter maid ticketed his Rolls, as I spat, "Dennis, I hope you spend all of your future lives in Hell, serving for eternity as F. Lee Bailey's second chair."

．．．．．

The receptionist's well-coifed gray hair matched the gray walls in Patrick's waiting room. Matronly, professional and warm, she graciously explained that Mr. Hemmings had someone with him, but then he had no appointments scheduled for the rest of the afternoon. "Please have a seat and as soon as he's free, I'll tell Mr. Hemmings you're here."

Now that I was here, I wondered why I'd come. Patrick would play the confidentiality card, too. Did I really think he'd tell me if Emmie and Barbara had been patients? Clients? Customers? What did nonmedical hypnotists call the people who paid for their services? I'd about decided to leave when the door from Patrick's office opened and Kate Lloyd Connors came out. I buried my head in Volume III of *The Journal of Hypnotism,* and Kate exited the waiting room, apparently not noticing me. Less than a minute later, the receptionist ushered me into the inner sanctum.

"Jake O'Hara, how nice to see you. What can I do for you?" Patrick managed to sound pleased but puzzled. A far more cordial greeting than I'd expected, based on our last meeting.

"I—er—was in the neighborhood and thought I'd take a chance that you were free."

"Well, good . . . good."

"Yes. I—er—found a self-help writer to assist you with your book-in-progress. Her name's Jane." I breathed easier, having come up with a reason for being there. Poor Jane.

"Great, I'll look forward to meeting her."

Screw this. Why should I care what this man thinks? I decided to go for the jugular. "Look, Patrick, I'm sorry if I seemed out of line, yesterday afternoon. Whatever's going on between you and Caroline is none of my business."

He flushed, then furiously fidgeted with the file on his desk. "Jake, Caroline and I have a professional relationship; that's all. I'm close to the family and consider Kate a good friend, but Caroline is my patient."

Now I knew the correct term. "Do your patients usually become so amorous?"

His blueberry eyes were darting all over the room. "I can't discuss my cases, I'm sure you understand that, Jake."

Case closed. Files sealed. Contracts confidential. Oh yes, I understood. I also understood that while I couldn't get any answers from Patrick, Ben Rubin sure as hell could.

· · · · ·

From a dirty phone booth on Madison and Thirty-sixth, I checked my phone messages. Ben Rubin's thanked me for the information, but Emmie's datebook indicated that she'd been a patient of Hemmings. Ben would be talking to Patrick later today and said he'd question him about Barbara, as well. Then, with a chuckle, Ben asked if I thought his father and my mother were an item.

I rode Madison Avenue bus up to the Carlyle. The bar was packed, wall-to-wall with smartly dressed people, paying ten dollars a pop for a martini. Maybe Barbara's brother would be buying.

Eleven

Campbell's, the funeral home that WASP families valued above all other Manhattan mortuaries, resounded with a string quartet playing Bach and the murmured condolences offered by the large gathering of mourners. By ten-thirty on Wednesday morning the crowd spilled out of Chapel A, into the hall, the foyer, and onto the sidewalk, necessitating the fussy funeral director to open the doors to Chapel B. His assistant undertakers, dressed like his clones in cutaways, striped pants and spats, scurried to seat the enormous somber crowd, as well as those still arriving.

Ginger, Modesty, Mom, Gypsy Rose and I served as greeters in the foyer, while Barbara's brother, Bill, and her Aunt Lucy and Uncle Henry Bernside, formed a mini receiving line in Chapel A, the designated viewing room. We ladies lined up, just inside the front entrance, shaking hands, hugging, kissing cheeks and often crying, as the mourners walked in from the blazing hot June sunshine to a blast of Campbell's arctic air-conditioning. Those paying their respects were an eclectic group. Among the first to arrive were Detective Ben Rubin and his father, Aaron. My mother fluttered her lashes as Aaron Rubin pecked her right cheek; then she offered her left cheek to Ben. I resented my mother flirting at a funeral with both Rubins. I might be interested in Ben Rubin, and he might be interested in me, if he wasn't more interested in what I knew. But why did my mother's attraction to his father still annoy me?

The ghosts came out in full force, most arriving early enough to sit en masse, filling the rows behind the family in Chapel A. They seemed to be the most grief-stricken. The Ethical Culture Society members and Barbara's small family were much more self-contained, reserved and formal. Angela Scotti arrived early, too, swathed, like an elderly Italian widow, in basic black. Only Angela's mourning ensemble was Versace. Her two bodyguards sported $1,000 Armani suits and bent noses. Other, less well-dressed Mafia types trailed behind them. But, by far, the largest clique of mourners were the morbidly curious, multicultural necrophiles of varying ages and attire, who shared a passion: attending the funerals of the rich, the famous or the sensationalized dead. The press and television coverage of Barbara's and Emmie's deaths had been more than sensational enough to draw ghouls from the five boroughs as well as far distant states. And Barbara's brother had made a big mistake in not limiting the memorial to invitation only. The media circus, with their cameras and microphones, were behind barricades. However, I suspected many more of them were in the chapels, passing as real people. There were several cops posing as people, too.

Modesty's funeral attire went beyond bizarre. Anne Rice's vampire morphed with Mary Shelley's monster. Barbara's Aunt Lucy had gasped out loud, then tried but failed to turn that gasp into an embarrassed cough when she'd met Modesty earlier this morning. Ginger and I were worried about Modesty's eulogy. Last night, over cocktails with Bill, which, thank God, had turned out to be an early evening, Ginger and I shared the gist of our short eulogies. Modesty had remained mute, claiming she was still working on the final draft. Barbara had been the only woman Modesty ever liked and, as her sponsor, Barbara had kept Modesty in check; now God only knew what miserable Modesty might say.

I peered around a weeping Mrs. McMahon—who never missed any wake held within three square miles of Carnegie Hill—and through the open doors, at the long stream of mourners. I watched as Dennis Kim circled the block for the second time, then pulled into a no parking zone to the right of the funeral parlor. Mr. Kim was with him. They took their places at the end of the line as a limousine stopped directly in front of the door, and Caroline Evans emerged.

Caroline's retro, skintight, black satin catsuit and hip-high patent leather boots—worn despite the heat—when combined with her *Night of the Living Dead* makeup, had to win the prize for the most outrageous funeral attire ever to cross Campbell's threshold. "Who is that?" my mother asked in horror.

"Kate Lloyd Connors's adopted daughter. Now can you admit how comparatively well I've turned out?"

Caroline got in line behind Dennis and snuggled up to him, spoon style, her arms circling him. The mourners at the front of the line buzzed and, reluctantly, I turned away from Caroline's antics to see who had so intrigued the crowd. The chauffeur held the limo door open and Kate—agile and lithe as a girl—had stepped out. So she had known Barbara. And well enough to drag Caroline along to her memorial. Kate's black hat, like the one Audrey Hepburn had worn in *Breakfast at Tiffany's,* and a black linen summer Chanel drew all eyes to her. Big, square-shaped sunglasses and the huge hat covered most of Kate's famous face; but her crowd of admirers had no trouble recognizing the reigning Queen-of-Murder Mysteries. Jonathan exited last, took Kate's arm, and they cut right through the line and into the foyer.

Gypsy Rose hustled a weeping Jane D along, "Wipe your eyes, darling, and do hurry on in, so you can sit with the rest of the ghosts in the A chapel." Then Gypsy Rose turned to me, literary stars shining in her eyes, "Jake, you must introduce me to Kate Lloyd Connors."

Kate kissed me on the cheek and simultaneously held Modesty's hand, saying, "We've met—at a writer's conference, wasn't it? I'm only sorry we're meeting again under such sad circumstances." For once Modesty was speechless, as surprised as I that Kate remembered her. I introduced Kate to my awed mother and a gushing-at-length Gypsy Rose. Where had Ginger disappeared to? Someone had to move this line along. Jonathan half bowed to me and Mom, then half pushed Kate out of Gypsy Rose's clutches, aiming, at my suggestion, for Chapel A. Who'd ever have expected such a crowd? The Connors contingent might have to sit in the bleachers.

The funeral director appeared at my side and discreetly suggested that our little receiving line move into Chapel A. The Campbell staff would seat latecomers for five more minutes; then the service would begin and no one else would be admitted. That was okay with me. Dealing with my fellow mourners, my own grief and my pinched toes in the designer pumps Mom had insisted that I buy, I felt exhausted and cranky, despite having fallen into bed at ten last night. Mom, Gypsy Rose, Modesty and I took our assigned places in the second row behind Barbara's family. Where the hell had Ginger gone? I put a program on the chair next to me. Both chapels were packed and stragglers weren't shy about grabbing any empty spot. What ever happened to WASP decorum? Or were all these pushy people from Staten Island?

Glancing around, I noticed that Dennis and Mr. Kim were scrounging for seats in the last row. They had a lot of company. Ginger dashed in, just as the staff pulled the doors shut, and the string quartet began playing "Clair de Lune." "What's wrong?" I asked her.

She shook her head. "Nothing. I've been tossing my bran muffin. And I tried a new recipe, too." Ginger managed a brave smile. I patted her hand, thinking that even perky Ginger had succumbed to today's horror.

Just then, the door reopened, and Patrick Hemming entered, with the very displeased funeral director on his heels. Patrick strode across the chapel and kissed Barbara's Aunt Lucy, shaking hands with her Uncle Henry and hugging her brother Bill. He then sat in the front-row seat they'd been saving. Who'd have ever imagined that Patrick would be the one to fill it?

"That's the hypnotist!" I whispered to Ginger, while pointing to Patrick. She looked too sick to care.

But my mother, seated on my left, nudged me, "The plot thickens." For once, I had to agree with her.

The string quartet's rendition of "Claire de Lune" drew to a close and the memorial service began. Bill Bernside stood at the podium, surrounded by mounds of white flowers. Baskets of lilies, wreaths of roses, vases of tulips. Their scent suddenly seemed sickening in the silence before Bill spoke. Barbara had loved white flowers in simple arrangements and often sent baskets of them to her friends. Her signature. Now her friends had sent them to her . . . for the last time. Tears spilled from my eyes. My mother wiped hers, as Gypsy Rose took her hand. Ginger, usually posture perfect, slumped in her seat, her chin almost on her chest. Modesty, who sat in an aisle seat next to Gypsy Rose, groaned. I prayed we'd all get through this.

There was no casket. Barbara's ashes were in an urn, perched somewhat precariously, in my mother's opinion, on a narrow table to the right of the podium. An 11" by 14" portrait of her—taken in the hope that one day it would appear on a book jacket—had been placed next to the urn. One lonely lighted candle flickered on the other side of the urn. I contrasted the Ethical Culture Society's memorial service with the Roman Catholic Requiem Mass send-off and decided no contest. This humanistic atmosphere's cold comfort could have used a little old-time religion: the smell of incense, a splash of holy water, a few familiar prayers, gold and white vestments draped on a sympathetic priest, and an organ filling the aisles with "Amazing Grace" and "Ave Maria." Not to mention the mourners receiving Jesus Christ's body in the sacrament of Holy Communion, then offering it up for the dearly departed's soul. Practically a passport to heaven.

Bill's tribute to his sister celebrated her life and suggested that she would live forever through her books. Except for the ghosts, none of the mourners seemed to grasp that ghostwriters don't have any more credit piled on them after they're dead than they'd received when they were alive.

When Bill finished, the quartet played the Beatles' "Eleanor Rigby" as I mulled over possible murderers and motives. What were Kate, Caroline and Jonathan doing here? Barbara must have ghosted for Kate at one time, unless the Connors knew the Bernside family socially. I'd never heard Barbara talk about Kate and company and, as far as I knew, she'd never mentioned the Connors to any of the ghosts. When . . . if . . . Barbara worked for Kate, had she stumbled on dangerous knowledge? Or was Barbara murdered, for the reason I'd originally suspected, because Emmie had confided in her and the killer had somehow found out? But what could that secret be? The Sarah Anne Hansen case? Visions of plot points danced in my head. Could Jonathan's writing project compromise Kate? Could Emmie or Barbara have threatened to expose him? Caroline did carry on like a sex-crazed Lolita. But was she as loony as she looked? Or, as I believed, too smart for her own good? Was the teenager kept on a tight chain and, maybe, given drugs or hypnotized, so she couldn't talk, or if she did, wouldn't be credible? Then what about Kate and all her ghosts? Wouldn't she be ripe for blackmail? I'd no doubt Vera Madison would murder to protect Kate. From what?

And other than the Connors's household? Well, Ivan was a dark horse's ass. Ginger liked the Mafia. But if Barbara's death was a hit, who killed Emmie? A mob doubleheader? Why Em? Could Dennis Kim, the boy I'd bitten with such fervor and the man I'd so cavalierly kissed the other night, be involved? He had introduced Angela Scotti to Barbara, and he did seem to be crawling all over these crimes like a omnipresent cockroach. I was convinced that he knew a hell of a lot more than he admitted. Riding high on my list of suspects was the Marlboro Man poster boy, Patrick Hemmings, hypnotherapist to the stars, alleged womanizer and obviously a close family friend of the bereaved Bernsides.

My mother interrupted my next plot twist. "Jake, Bill called you to the podium. You're on."

Jesus, I'd completely forgotten I had to deliver a eulogy. We'd decided that I'd go first, then Ginger, with Modesty as the closing act. In a service with no prayers—except silent ones—no hymns and no talk of an afterlife, the eulogies set the tone. Mine wished Barbara Godspeed on her final journey and, speaking for myself, said I thought we'd meet again. My mother winked at me. Then I read "The Funeral of Youth," Rupert Brooke's poem, that Barbara, the humanist, had loved. Ginger followed me, seeming to have recovered both her poise and physical well-being, delivering an elegant eulogy on the writing life—its sorrows and its joys. Neither of our talks replaced the stirring emotions of the 23rd Psalm, but the mourners were moved to tears. Finally, Modesty clutched the podium and began to moan. This was one wordy woman. She'd told me last night that her gothic romance had reached 1,200 pages, with no denouement in sight.

Fearing the worst, my hands grew clammy. I turned to my mother. "Do you have a tissue?" The best ladies' room in Manhattan could be found at the Waldorf Astoria. Private rooms in lieu of stalls, with your own sink, flattering lighting, beauty supplies and tissues. Unending tissues. My mother managed to carry a Waldorf mini-john in her purse.

"How could you come to a funeral without a tissue, Jake?" My mother stuffed several—white, unscented Kleenex—in my lap. I wiped my hands, dried my eyes, and placed the extras in my tiny, new mock croc purse that my mother assured me went perfectly with my DKNY black crepe and the drastically reduced Ferragamo shoes that were killing me.

I listened to Modesty and felt her pain. Barbara, her one friend in all the world, was gone. "Murdered . . ." Modesty raised her voice and repeated, "Murdered. Is her killer among us this morning? Is he or she sitting to your right or left?"

Her audience squirmed, stealing furtive glances at their neighbors. My emotions were mixed. On one hand,

Modesty had voiced what I'd been thinking but wouldn't dare speak aloud. On the other hand, the shock value seemed tasteless and out of place at Barbara's funeral, as her family and friends mourned her loss. Bill half rose from his chair. God, would he remove Modesty from the podium? But she removed herself, closing with, "My friend's death will be avenged." The quartet broke the deadly silence, closing with Chopin.

Then Bill Bernside made his second big mistake in memorial planning. He invited all the mourners to a reception at the Harvard Club.

Twelve

In the cab downtown to West 44th Street, Gypsy Rose managed to repair her makeup while having a psychic experience. I'd never seen her in black before and suspected that the last time she'd worn black had been at the late Louie Liebowitz's funeral. A colorful woman, Gypsy liked bright outfits to match her bright outlook. However, her St. John's knit suit and cloche were flattering and, with that red hair and those coral lips, Gypsy Rose could never look drab. She returned her eyeliner brush to her cosmetic case, "It still has me shaking. God knows how I lined my eyes without a smudge."

"What?" I asked.

"The same evil aura that overwhelmed me at the service just grabbed me again."

"Evil?" My mother shuddered.

"Yes. When Modesty said the murderer might be sitting among us, I knew she was right. Barbara's killer attended the memorial service. The presence of evil I felt in that room leaves no room for doubt."

"Could you put a face on this feeling?" It wasn't that I didn't believe Gypsy Rose. Her hunches, readings and predictions had too often been right on, even convincing a skeptic like me. But I wanted more details. As Gypsy Rose frequently said, the devil is in the details.

"No; but the presence of evil can be well covered. The murderer could be anyone, seemingly as innocent as you or I or Maura. I only know he—or—she was there."

"Things are seldom as they seem." I quoted.

"Exactly." Gypsy Rose passed her cosmetic case to me. "You could use a little blush, Jake."

. . . . .

The Harvard Club, along with several other private clubs, was on 44th Street, between Fifth and Sixth avenues, its location a few yards east of the Algonquin Hotel. Grand Central Station rose out of the ground to the east and Broadway beckoned to the west. I'd never been inside the club, although I'd passed its austere facade countless times on my way to the Algonquin, where the 1920s literati lunch bunch had met at the Round Table and where today's writers still gathered to swap stories in its old-fashioned lobby. Unless you wanted to be trendy, then you drank, where Tina Brown used to hang out across the street at the Euro-trash-trendy Royalton.

"Maybe, if this day ever ends, we can stop at the Algonquin for drinks," my mother said, paying the driver. Gypsy Rose and I agreed that was a splendid idea.

. . . . .

Most of those who'd been in attendance at the service—who'd miss a freebie at the Harvard Club?—now crowded round the buffet table and two open bars. Bill, Aunt Lucy and Uncle Henry gamely walked among the throng, introducing themselves and inquiring of their guests: How did you know Barbara? The problem was that the majority of these people hadn't known or cared about Barbara, much less her family.

Gypsy Rose gestured grandly over the masses. "All this Park Slope polyester and Staten Island mall hair could ruin the Main Liners' appetites."

"Probably just proves to them that the Philadelphians' jaundiced view of all New Yorkers is correct." I smiled as a woman dressed in sneakers and a lavender jogging suit snapped pictures of the buffet table.

My mother recoiled as a reporter shoved a mike in her face, while a hand-held camcorder closed in. "Please, go away," she said.

"Get lost." I said, leading Gypsy Rose and my mother away from the manic media. How did American News Network get in?

Dennis Kim, holding what looked like a stiff scotch, joined us. "Anything I can do for you ladies? May I bring you something to eat?"

A waiter, carrying a tray of drinks, breezed by. "No thanks," I said. "But how about three white wines?"

"Be right back." Dennis trailed behind the waiter, attacking from the rear, then backtracked, victorious, with the waiter and wine in tow.

"To Barbara, may her spirit soar," my mother raised her glass. We all raised ours, clicked them together, and drank.

"What will the family do with Barbara's ashes?" Gypsy Rose asked.

Dennis said, "They're taking them home to be buried in . . ."

And my mother interrupted, laughing, "All things considered, I'd rather be in Philadelphia."

"Is Kate Lloyd Connors here?" Gypsy Rose asked

Dennis, just as a boy about twelve, dressed in long, loose shorts and a baseball cap, worn backward, slid down the banister, as his mother screamed, "Bruce, you'll hurt yourself!"

Dennis grinned, "No, she said they'd pass."

"Smart move," I said, as the kid landed on my aching feet.

"Let's pay our respects to the Bernsides and get out of here," my mother said. "I'll treat you and Gypsy Rose to lunch at the Algonquin."

"Cool." I looked around, but brother Bill and Barbara's aunt and uncle had been swallowed up by the maddening crowd. "I'll find them. Stay right here." I pointed to a window facing the street. "And never fear, I shall return."

Dennis moved with me into the fray. Too Tall Tom's head, like a beacon, drew me to the dessert table. "Hi, Jake, looking for someone?" It helped, at moments like these to be acquainted with the tallest person in the room. Too Tall Tom zeroed in on Bill in seconds. Barbara's brother was in deep conversation with Patrick Hemmings. I decided to skip the good-byes to the family, but, to my surprise, Dennis decided to join Patrick and Bill. On my way back to collect my mother and Gypsy Rose, I ran into Ben Rubin. "This place is a zoo," he said. "I've been looking for you, Jake. It's all arranged; I've just left the morgue. Emmie's body will be released in time for a viewing on Friday."

"Thanks, the Rogers will be so grateful." I smiled. "And so am I."

He stared at the floor. "Jake?"

"Yes, Ben?"

"I shouldn't be telling you this, but there's something else, I think you ought to know. The results of the post mortem conclude that Emmie was three months pregnant."

Thirteen

Impulsively, I asked Ben to join us for lunch at the Algonquin, figuring, if my mother could have dinner with Rubin père, she could pick up the lunch tab for his son. Of course, Mom was delighted with this unexpected opportunity to brainwash Ben with all my best attributes. Dennis may have been her first choice, but having been a runner-up, herself, my mother respected and carefully considered all contenders.

"Oak Room?" Gypsy Rose asked, as the four of us stood in the lobby. I disliked its recent redecoration, which aped the shabby original, but totally lost its wonderfully, frayed old-world charm. Matilda, the longtime Algonquin cat, had died about the same time as the lobby; her replacement brushed against Ben's leg. I smiled as Ben knelt to stroke her ears.

"Oh, let's sit at the faux Round Table"—I gestured to its new location—"I can still pretend I'm Dorothy Parker."

Ben asked, "Can I be Robert Benchley?" I smiled, again.

"Certainly," my mother said, getting in the spirit of

times past. "And I'll be Lynn Fontanne. You can be Tallulah, Gypsy Rose."

"Type casting, darlings," Gypsy Rose drawled. Then, still using a husky, southern accent, she asked the maitre d', "Please bring us a bottle of Mouton Cadet, just as quickly as you can, darling."

We talked of Kaufman and Hart's *The Man Who Came to Dinner,* of Woollcott's wit and of whether or not Mrs. Parker had ever slept with Mr. Benchley. When the wine arrived, we toasted Barbara, and Mom, Gypsy Rose and I shared our favorite Barbara stories with Ben. That launched a discussion of the ghosts' double murders, where Gypsy Rose, Mom and I spewed forth opinions and hypothesized on motives and opportunities. Ben talked in generalities about his previous murder cases with zest but offered no information or specifics in this investigation. As a big fan of true crime—I'd once flown to New England to attend an au pair murder trial—I reveled in the company of a man who thrived on homicide both as a professional and an armchair detective.

Ben and I considered *In Cold Blood* to be the finest piece of nonfiction, providing insight into the minds of two murderers. And, in the genre of detective novels, we agreed on Arthur Conan Doyle and Agatha Christe but disagreed on P. D. James. Ben found her too talky. In the middle of our heated conversation, I glanced over at my mother and Gypsy Rose, whose smug, satisfied smiles stopped me cold. "More wine, ladies?" I asked, ready to pour it over their heads. Ben ordered Irish coffees, the conversation veered back to Barbara, and by three o'clock that afternoon, when Ben asked for the check, over Mom's feeble protests, we were all a tad tipsy. Our Algonquin luncheon had turned into a mini wake. And I felt better for it.

My mother and Gypsy Rose went downstairs to the ladies' room, but I had a few questions for Ben. "How did your meeting with Patrick go? What did he say about Emmie?"

"That she'd been one of Kate's editors and, while he regretted violating Kate's confidentiality regarding her employees, he assumed I knew that, anyway. And I did. In addition to what Mrs. Rogers had told your mother, I found a contract proving Emmie had ghosted for Kate."

"Did Patrick say anything about his personal or professional relationship with Emmie? Remember, I told you that Laura, one of the ghosts, spotted Emmie in his office."

"Denied the former. Admitted to the latter. Said Emmie had been his patient. They'd been doing regression therapy—having chats with her younger selves." Rubin shook his head. "Smooth as silk, that Patrick is."

"He knew you'd be privy to that information. He had to tell you."

"You're on target. I did know Emmie had been seeing him professionally; her check stubs confirmed it."

"But do you believe he was romantically involved her? Patrick's quite the Don Juan."

Rubin grinned. "Do you think so?"

Already warm from the Irish coffee, I felt a full flush spread across my face. "That opinion is based on what I've been told and what I've observed, Detective. Not from personal experience."

"Well, Patrick told me that he never allows his patients to become emotionally attached to him."

"Not true. I've watched Caroline with him. Emotionally attached? She's hot as hell for him."

"Jake, I'm not dropping this, especially now that we know Emmie was pregnant."

I pulled out one of my mother's tissues, wiped my eyes, and blew my nose, "Jesus, could Patrick be the father? That would explain why Emmie and Ivan quarreled during lunch at Budapest East on Friday. Oh my God, Ben, maybe Ivan did kill her!"

"He can just take his place in line with all the other possible suspects."

"Am I among them? You're sharing a lot of information with me, Ben. Why?

"I think you know why." This time his cheeks turned ruddy. "And you're not a suspect. No opportunity in Barbara's case and, if you had a motive for either murder, it's eluded me. But you're playing Nancy Drew. A dangerous avocation. Someone's killing the ghosts; you're one ghost I want to keep alive. If you believe I've followed up on your suggestions, maybe you'll allow Homicide to solve these murders. All I ask is that you don't repeat what's been said to anyone. That goes for your mother and Gypsy Rose."

"You have my word. As a member of Ghostwriters Anonymous, I know how to keep my mouth shut." I said, thinking, I've been spilling every bit of information I'd gathered to all the ghosts. No more. Ben was right. I didn't want to put them or Mom and Gypsy Rose in jeopardy. In the future I'd work alone, but I saw no reason to have Ben worry about that. "Now, have you talked to Kate Lloyd Connors?"

"Indeed. Monday evening, at her Sutton Place manor, after you'd left for the day. Quite the grande dame, isn't she?"

"And?"

"Kate told me she'd adored Emmie, what a fine editor Emmie had been, and how she'd cried all morning after hearing about the murder."

"Well, she'd pulled herself together by time I arrived.

No one in that house even mentioned Emmie. I tried to question Caroline, but Kate barged in.''

"Of course, Kate couldn't shed any light on Emmie's death. Jonathan was there, too. He had even less to say. The stepdaughter wasn't home."

"I'll bet Kate saw to that. Without question, Caroline holds the key to the secrets in that house."

Ben reached around my empty wineglass and took my hand. "I'll talk to Caroline."

"Thanks. Oh, what about Barbara? Did Kate admit to knowing her?"

"Only casually. Kate claims she met Barbara through Patrick, when they all participated in some New Age seminar. And I've found no evidence linking Barbara to Kate as either a ghost or a friend."

"Yet, she shows up at Barbara's memorial with her stepdaughter and Jonathan in tow."

"I was as surprised as you were." Ben squeezed my hand.

"If only we could find out why Emmie had the Sarah Anne Hansen clipping."

"The file should be here tomorrow or the next day. I'd like to get into Emmie's computer, but our computer nerds can't crack the pass code. Did she ever give it to you?"

"Emmie rotated her pass code as often as most people wash their hair. She loved the soaps. Can you believe she actually wrote while they were on? I never understood how she did that. She was into *Another World* last week. Try that or try Rachel. Emmie really identified with Rachel."

Ben jotted down the soap and its heroine in his little black book, then took my hand again and brought it to his lips. "Okay. Now promise me you'll stop playing detective, Jake."

My mother and Gypsy Rose returned to the table, and I never answered him. I couldn't wait to get to Kate's tomorrow morning.

. . . . .

Ben went back to Homicide at the Nineteenth Precinct, and Gypsy Rose insisted we grab a taxi home. The longtime doorman, who knew all three of us "girls" to be Algonquin regulars, hustled us into the next hotel arrival's vacant cab, no doubt annoying the other harried hailers. Although well ahead of official rush hour, the thick traffic on Madison Avenue slowed our driver to a crawl. Gypsy Rose dozed while Mom, wound up, chatted. "Kate Lloyd Connors is very attractive, Jake, and she seems so nice."

There's that "seems" again.

"Caroline looks like a Mia Farrow reject," my mother continued. "Kate must have known that girl would be nothing but trouble when she adopted her and brought her here from England."

"Actually, Mom, there's something sweet about Caroline, or that's how it *seems* to me." God, would I ever take anything or anyone at face value again? Should we accept each other as we are or is as we are only what we want to "seem"?

My mother, less philosophical and far more pragmatic than I, said, "Just be on guard while you're in Kate's castle, Jake. One of that bunch may have murdered our ghosts. I wish you'd quit."

"Oh, Mom, I'm probably safer in that house than in our home. Remember both Emmie and Barbara were killed in their own apartments."

My mother brushed my bangs out of my eyes. "That's because neither one of them lived with her mother."

I laughed, but I did promise to watch my back . . . especially, the back of my head . . . for any heavy book aimed my way.

Mom switched gears. "Ben's a charmer and so bright. He's an attorney, you know, but prefers solving murders to practicing law. That decision doesn't thrill his father."

"I'll bet. No, I didn't know. You're full of Rubin family facts. Did you play 'Twenty Questions' with father and son the night before last?"

"Don't I always?"

"So, what else did you learn?"

Gypsy Rose to my mother's right snored lightly. The cabbie lurched left into an opening in the traffic; we all slid across the back seat, throwing me into the left passenger door, Gypsy Rose's head landed in my mother's lap, while her handbag flew off her own lap and landed on my aching feet. Did she carry gold bricks in her Fendi?

My mother sighed. "We'll probably be killed in this taxi . . . and all my worrying will have been wasted."

"I've been telling you that for years. Why worry? You can't change the outcome."

"Well, in case we do survive this ride from hell, you should know that Ben's an only child and lives with his father. He's a good son."

Ironic, two bright thirty-somethings, each living with a parent, develop a strong mutual attraction, just as each respective parent discovers the other. Freud would have a field day.

"Where's Momma?"

"In Mount Lebanon Cemetery—for two years."

"You like Aaron, don't you, Mom?"

"Yes. I think I do. You like Ben, don't you, Jake?"

"Yes. I think I do."

Our laughter woke up Sleeping Beauty.

. . . . .

We dropped Gypsy Rose at her tearoom. She had to relieve the two part-time sorceresses, and Mom and I stopped at Mr. Kim's to pick up some fresh fruit and veggies. He'd enjoyed the memorial and regretted he hadn't been able to attend the Harvard Club reception. "Did you see Dennis there?"

"Yes, he plowed through the masses and brought us wine," I said.

"Dennis works too hard, plays too little. Like you, Jake. You two should go to the Hamptons after Emmie's funeral. Live a little. Have some fun."

I kissed Mr. Kim on the cheek. "We'll see." Mom and he made some vague plans to ride to Emmie's funeral mass together and we headed home.

My mother, mulling over my romantic options, said, "To think on Friday, you had no gentlemen callers, now three men are interested."

Wondering who lurked behind door #3, I asked, "What are you talking about?"

"Patrick Hemmings, of course. Didn't you notice how he kept turning around and staring at you all through the service? You've hypnotized the hypnotist, Jake."

Fourteen

"Kim Novak is no Grace Kelly," my mother said. We were watching *Vertigo*. I'd gone up to our local video store on Madison and 95th Street and opted for Hitchcock. Somehow the master of movie suspense soothed my mother's nerves and I'd inherited her propensity for using psychological mind games, terror and murder as tranquilizers.

"Hitchcock swept Kim's blonde hair into a sleek French twist and dressed her in a classic gray suit, but you can't turn a siren into a lady. After Grace married Prince Rainier, Hitch searched in vain for another cool goddess. Eva Marie Saint, Tippi Hedren, even Doris Day, for heaven's sake, but ..."

"Mom," I interrupted her running, critical commentary, "if you'd quit being Siskel and Ebert, I could judge for myself." What a novel idea! I should have brought home *Rear Window* or *To Catch a Thief*. Either one would have shut her up.

The phone rang. "I'll put the stop button on," my mother said, oblivious to the oxymoron.

"Don't bother, the story's so convoluted and, besides,

I've seen this flick ten or twelve times. If I miss a plot point, it's no big deal. I'll get the phone.'' I popped another slice of Mr. Kim's perfect peach into my mouth and took the call on my bedroom extension.

Modesty sounded excited. "My Auntie Charity knew Sarah Anne Hansen.''

"No way!''

"Yeah, they were cheerleaders at rival high schools in the mid-'50s. Met at football games and a soda fountain fraternized by both teams.''

I tried to picture Modesty's Auntie Charity as a cheerleader. I'd never met the woman, but I imagined what Modesty might be like as a little old lady. Cranky and testy. Visualizing either Modesty or Auntie Charity as a perky teenager required real effort.

"Auntie says this Sarah Anne was a real beauty. Great shape. Long, thick, black hair and big blue eyes. But Sarah Anne never went on a date. She had no boy-friends—nor girlfriends, for that matter. Her father tracked her like a hound dog. Daddy showed up at every game, never took his eyes off Sarah Anne. He was her biggest fan. If a boy even spoke to Sarah Anne, and Daddy got wind of it, she'd be grounded.''

"What did Aunt Charity recall about the drowning and disappearance?''

"Folks said John Hansen's possessiveness toward Sarah Anne was unnatural and it accelerated when Mrs. Hansen died in an accident, when Sarah Anne had been ten or eleven. People in Honey Bucket figured that Sarah Anne couldn't take any more of her daddy's unwanted attention and shoved him into that freezing water, or if he fell in, stood by and let him drown. Either way she was out of there before the cops could question her.''

"How did your aunt call it?''

"Said John Hansen was an angry loner, whose two

reasons for living seemed to be his hobby, ice fishing, and his daughter. Maybe she was a hobby, too. My auntie hoped Sarah Anne killed the bastard.''

We talked a bit about Barbara's funeral and the reception at the Harvard Club. Modesty said Bill would be in town till Sunday night; he planned to attend Emmie's mass and hoped we could all get together before he left. ''Jake, are you aware that Patrick Hemmings is an old friend of Bill's? I guess that's why Barbara claimed she'd known him forever.''

''Well, either that or they'd been acquainted in previous incarnations.'' I sounded flip and almost as testy as Modesty. ''Actually, I only found out today that Patrick and the Bernsides summered together as kids.''

''And are you also aware that Bill Bernside dates Jonathan Arthur?''

''WHAT?''

''I gather I can take that piercing scream as a no.''

''How the hell did you discover that tidbit?''

''Too Tall Tom ran into them late last night, dancing at a gay club in Tribeca.''

I asked Modesty to arrange a meeting with Bill Bernside tomorrow or Friday and let me know where and when. Then I hung up, my head reeling. How could Barbara's brother go dancing on the night before her funeral? I'd felt guilty about ghosting this week but justified my decision with my detective work. I went back to *Vertigo*; I could use a tranquilizer.

· · · · ·

Before and after Modesty's phone calls, I tried to reach Ivan the terrible. I wanted to see him up close and personal to ask him what he and Emmie had quarreled about on the day that she was murdered. The headwaiter at Budapest East told me Ivan had taken the day off for a funeral. I'd glimpsed him at Campbell's but hadn't seen him at the Harvard Club. That didn't mean he hadn't attended the reception; the place was such a zoo, he could have been swallowed up by the crowd.

I called Ivan's apartment and left two messages, prompted by his answering machine: "If you vant to speak, you vill begin ven music stops." After several bars of "The Blue Danube" came one long beep, then a chance to record a very brief message. God, he was weird, but was he a killer?

While the *Vertigo* tape rewound, Mom startled me. She held a tray piled with the residue of our light supper of salad and fruit, as I wiped off the coffee table with paper towels. "Jake, did you notice Angela Scotti when we left Campbells?"

"No. Why?"

"She went tete-à-tete with Patrick Hemmings. As if she were scolding him. At one point, she wagged a finger under his nose. I think you and Gypsy Rose were hailing a cab about then."

"So it seemed as if they knew each other?"

"Oh, no question. They not only knew each other, their body language shouted intimacy. I wanted to tell you earlier, but I forgot."

"But you said Patrick only had eyes for me. Should I be crushed?"

"He looked at you with lust or longing, or at least intrigue. He looked at Angela with murder in his eyes."

"And this you forget?"

"It's been a long day, my darling daughter."

I couldn't argue with that. "And I, for one, am going to bed."

.   .   .   .   .

"You give money to a bum and it encourages him to loaf," Mrs. McMahon said, as I exited our front door at seven o'clock on Thursday morning on my way to the Reservoir for my power walk. Bob, a Vietnam vet, was Carnegie Hill's longest homeless resident. He had a salt-and-pepper beard to the middle of his chest, hair caught in a ponytail, wore army fatigues, and lived, most of the time, on 92nd Street. On summer nights, he slept on a bench abutting Central Park and during the long, cold winters he slept in doorways, rotating them to keep ahead of the cops. But his daylight hours were spent walking the streets, and for some reason he'd cottoned to our block. Perhaps because Mr. Kim often fed him and people like me slipped him an occasional buck.

I gave Mrs. McMahon a nasty look, hoping Bob hadn't heard her. If he had, he might not have understood; some days he was really out of touch. He tucked the dollar in one of his deep pants pockets, then buttoned it, and flashed me an almost toothless smile but said nothing. I wondered if Bob had always been a quiet man. He ambled toward Park Avenue, where he'd circle the blocks from 91st to 93rd Street, between Park and Fifth, all day. Bob had been covering the same ground on a daily basis for twenty years.

"Quite a wingding, that party at the Harvard Club. I didn't think much of the service at Campbell's, though. Did you know that Barbara Barnside, the dead girl? I read in the *Post* that she was a writer."

"Bernside. Yes, Mrs. McMahon, I only attend the funerals of people I know." Wasn't I being a bitch? However, Mrs. McMahon either chose to ignore my snide remark or didn't consider it to be offensive.

She rattled on. "I've seen her with Dennis Kim. And doesn't he carry on like a hotshot attorney? Pretty cozy, they were, riding around in that Rolls Royce of his. I myself don't approve of interracial romances.''

I literally bit my tongue. Mrs. McMahon's bigotry drove me crazy, but I also experienced a ripple of jealously as I thought about Dennis being cozy with Barbara. That feeling was followed by a tidal wave of suspicion. Jesus, what was wrong with me? Why was I reacting to gossip and innuendo, based on one old witch's prejudiced opinion? My suspicion ebbed. The jealousy clung to me like grainy sand on a sun-tan-oiled body.

I'd worked up a sweat and, when I checked my watch, was surprised to see it was eight o'clock. Time to get these buns home and into the shower.

Mr. Kim waved; I stopped and bought an Evian, gulping it as he and I exchanged good mornings and recapped yesterday. Then, like a jilted schoolgirl confronting a cheating boyfriend's father, I questioned the unsuspecting Mr. Kim. "How well did you know Barbara?''

"Dennis represented her. I met her two or three times, once at one of your mother's parties. I really liked her.''

"Had you been in her company recently?''

"Yes, as a matter of fact, Dennis and she had brunch about a week ago at Sara Beth's. They stopped by to say hello.''

"Did you think—er—did something seem to trouble her? A problem . . . ?''

"I heard Barbara talking to Dennis about a gold digger who was chasing after her brother. You know the Bernsides come from old money, Jake. Piles and piles of it. Barbara seemed very upset about Bill's new relationship.''

Jonathan Arthur, I presume.

Mr. Kim continued, "Then there was that business with the mob. Barbara wrote Scotti's daughter's book.''

"How do you know that???"

"Why, Barbara told me."

And I'd believed that Barbara had only confided in me. How many people knew the mob was mad at her? Had one of them used *The Godfather* as a herring? Then again, just how strongly had Barbara objected to her brother's new gold-digging boyfriend, Jonathan Arthur?

Fifteen

On the Second Avenue bus downtown, I planned my offense. Caroline was the weakest link in the Connors's camp, and I still wanted to talk to her first. After Modesty's revelation regarding Jonathan Arthur's love life, he'd gone up a notch or two on my hit parade of suspects. Now, he had mixed motives. Theory A—Either Emmie or Barbara had found out—then confided in her fellow ghost—that he'd written some sort of tell-all about Kate Lloyd Connors, and Jonathan had killed them both to keep his moneymaking story a secret. Or—Theory B—he killed Barbara so she couldn't break up his potentially much bigger moneymaking romance with brother Bill. In Theory B, I hadn't figured out why he'd killed Emmie. But my favorite—Theory C—combined the two motives, turning Barbara's death into a bonus for Jonathan: free reign to pursue Bill. If Jonathan had killed the ghosts, I needed to check out his work-in-progress to prove it. Since Mrs. Madison had caught me snooping, this presented a challenge.

Engrossed, I rode a block past my stop and would have gone all the way to the Bowery if the man in the next seat hadn't offended my sense of smell when he unwrapped a salami and provolone hero. I maneuvered past his bulk, disturbing his breakfast, and scrambled through the standees to the rear exit. Most of my life I've run ten minutes behind. Today proved to be no exception.

Carla was vacuuming the foyer and Mrs. Madison, carrying a tray filled with goodies, was climbing the stairs when Caroline opened the front door, wearing a string bikini—black. I'd like to buy this kid a coat of many colors.

" 'Ow are you, Jake?''

"Hi, Caroline. . . .''

"Is that you, Jake? Come right upstairs, darling, I'm ready to go to work.'' Kate stood on the second-floor landing, ushering Mrs. Madison and her tray to the library.

Before I could reply, Kate scolded Caroline, "Put something over that bikini, now!''

Caroline scooped up a long, black cotton T-shirt from the small love seat near the Conservatory, put it on, and yelled up to Kate, "Don't get your knickers in a twist.''

Carla smiled, then moved the vacuum so I could go to work.

Kate was all business; we drank our coffee and ate our cream cheese and bagels as we line-edited *A Killing in Katmandu*'s first chapter. Whatever thoughts Kate may have harbored about Barbara and yesterday's memorial remained private. At eleven o'clock, she stood, stretched, started across the room, and said, "I have to leave for an appointment. Luncheon will be at one o'clock. You can enter the changes and start chapter two. I should be back before you leave. Have a grand and productive day.'' Kate knocked on Jonathan's door. He opened it at once and said, "Good morning,

Jake.'' Then he asked Kate, ''Can you just give me a moment to go through my mail before we leave?'' Although, as always, Jonathan was impeccably turned out, in a blue linen blazer, crisp chinos, and school tie, he appeared harried and his eyes were puffy as if he hadn't gotten enough sleep.

''We're going now or else we'll be late. You can open your mail when we return.''

''But . . . !''

''No buts about it. We're leaving. This very minute. Move it, Jonathan!''

Jonathan retrieved his briefcase from his desk and locked his office door behind him. Kate grabbed her Gucci carryall and her coral silk jacket; then they were off. And I was alone.

From the library's bay window facing the front of the house, I watched Kate and Jonathan get into a waiting limo, wondering where they were going. Carla had reached the second floor and I could hear the constant noise as she ran the vacuum across the Oriental rugs and dark oak floors. So the library door into Jonathan's office was locked; I hadn't expected otherwise. I went back to my computer.

By twelve-thirty, Carla had moved up to the third floor and I'd ventured out of the library for a quick look about. Only the now distant hum of the vacuum indicated anyone else was in the house. I tried the hall door into Jonathan's office. Locked. One door down, I discovered a bathroom and decided to use the facilities. The vastness overwhelmed me. This john was bigger than many of my friends' Manhattan studios. Its gleaming, ultramodern plumbing included a Jacuzzi, a bathtub big enough to hold the entire Connors household—that conjured up an interesting picture—and two separate johns, each enclosed and equipped with its own bidet, sink, and dressing table. Its futuristic design contrasted sharply with the English manor theme that prevailed in the rest of the house.

The salon section of the bathroom had two doors. The one on the left opened into a guest room. And, the one on the right, though locked, had to open into Jonathan's office. The lock looked uncomplicated. I returned to the library, grabbed my VISA GOLD credit card, ran it between the door frame and the lock and, voila, the door opened. I was glad for the opportunity to use my VISA card; I certainly couldn't charge on it.

Inside Jonathan's office, the drawers to his desk were still locked; however, I scanned the room, even tidier than Mom's kitchen, searching—in vain—for a hiding place for a key. His desktop was in perfect order, except for the scattered pile of unopened mail. I rifled through it. There were about a dozen envelopes and assorted magazines and catalogues for Kate. Jonathan's personal mail included bills from Brooks Brothers and Burberry's, a postcard from his Park Avenue dentist reminding him of a July 1 appointment, and a letter from the *National Enquirer*. Did Jonathan always open his and Kate's mail? Who picked up the mail from the outside box and brought it into the house? Hadn't it occurred to Jonathan that a letter from the *National Enquirer* might pique somebody's curiosity? It sure as hell piqued mine.

I took the letter into the bathroom and, with all three of its doors locked, turned the Jacuzzi on hot and high, and steamed it open. The *National Enquirer* confirmed the tabloid's offer of 500,000 dollars for Jonathan's three-part exposé of the Queen-of-Murder-Most-Cozy's multiple ghosts. Final acceptance of the project, as had been previously discussed, required the newspaper's attorneys' review of supporting documents: contracts, correspondence between Kate and her ghosts for hire, and tape recordings. Wow! Jonathan's work-in-progress would be sensationally serialized in America's leading tabloid. And his story appeared to be more true confession than true crime. What a snake!

The last paragraph puzzled me. *We could be interested in the other angle in your proposal. However, before we can either make an offer or even consider publication regarding the identity issue, you would need to present positive proof. Our legal department advises that what you've submitted is inadequate. If you can prove your allegations beyond any doubt, we can reopen negotiations.*

Identity issue? What the hell was that all about?

I returned to the library, made a copy, stuffed it in my bag, located some glue in my desk's bottom drawer, resealed the envelope, scooted through the bathroom into Jonathan's office, replaced the letter exactly where I'd found it on his desktop, then, again via the bathroom, started back to the library. But as I opened the door from the john into the hall, I ran into Mrs. Madison. Her puss was sourer than ever.

"Luncheon is served, Miss O'Hara. I see you've already washed your hands."

. . . . .

Caroline sat in the Conservatory at the table set for two. She'd changed into black jeans and a T-shirt and piled her hair into a washerwoman's topknot; with no makeup, she looked pretty, but paler than death.

"Hi," I said. "Just the two of us?"

"Righto. Kate and Jonathan popped over to Dennis Kim's. 'E's 'er solicitor. Do you know 'im?"

"Yes. We grew up on the same block."

"It's a small world after all . . ." Caroline sang the Disney attraction's theme song very well.

"You have a great voice."

"A regular Spice Girl, aren't I?"

Mrs. Madison marched in with a serving cart holding plates filled with chicken salad, a basket of hot rolls and a pitcher of ice tea. I realized that I was starving. Playing Nancy Drew worked up an appetite. Vera served the meal in silence and left. I guess she only ate with the family when Kate was in residence.

"So, would you like to be a singer?"

"Not bloody likely."

"Why?"

"No one in this 'ouse even believes I'm capable of going out alone. 'Ow can a crazy woman 'ave a career as a singer?"

"Caroline, you're not crazy." I buttered my roll, thinking, well, no crazier than the rest of the Connors loonies. Now that I finally had Caroline all to myself, I didn't know where to start. With her adoption? With Emmie's employment and what she might have uncovered? With Patrick's unprofessional relationship with Caroline and possibly Emmie? Perhaps I'd start with her remark, that first day, about the sour cream being poisoned.

"Listen, Caroline, I've wondered why you believed that there was cyanide in the sour cream. Who did you think put it there?"

"Why, Jake," she said, swallowing half a roll in one gulp, "Kate put the poison in the sour cream, didn't she?" Caroline sounded surprised that I wasn't privy to this information. "Who else would it be? Kate's in love with Patrick, but everyone knows 'e's in love with me. Don't you see? She's trying to kill me."

Jesus, maybe she was crazier than the rest of them.

Sixteen

When my mother had said that even Mia Farrow wouldn't adopt this kid, I figured she was only being her snobby self. Caroline was grunge incarnate. Mom and Gypsy Rose, dearly as I loved them, were two of the most judgmental women I knew. Maybe, it was generational. They'd grown up reading all those Emily Post columns, while wearing white gloves, pretty dresses and hats. Their notions of proper behavior were archaic. I don't believe either one of them was aware that she could be considered snooty and, if she were, might construe it as a compliment. Anyway, my lunch with Caroline left me with both indigestion and the distinct impression that this time my mother's call had been right on.

After we'd finished eating, I'd gone back to my desk, but not back to work on Kate's *A Killing in Katmandu*'s chapter two. Instead, I pulled my legal pad from my briefcase and recorded as best I could the conversation that had transpired between Caroline and me.

. . . . .

I almost choked on a piece of chicken when Caroline had stated so cavalierly that Kate was trying to kill her. I'd taken a swig of my ice tea, wishing it were a martini, and decided to keep my questions coming. Caroline had been delighted to answer them all.

"Caroline, why did you say—'If you don't believe me, ask Em'—in reference to the poison in the sour cream? Was Emmie aware of your—er—your mother's jealousy over your relationship with Patrick?"

"Not Emmie. I wasn't talking about Emmie. I'd started to say, 'Emmings'—Patrick—'e knows Kate's trying to kill me, but the wicked witch, Mrs. Madison, dragged me out of the room before I could finish."

All this time, I'd thought Caroline believed Emmie had knowledge of a possible poisoning. "Things are seldom as they seem." Not Emmie, but Hemmings. Caroline's cockney accent dropped haitches all over the place. And wasn't it interesting that Patrick, who'd supposedly believed there was cyanide in the sour cream, had been the first one to dive into it? Could Caroline's cyanide concern be a figment of her imagination? Or could it be that she suffered from hallucinations because she was on drugs?

"Have you and Patrick actually discussed the possibility of Kate's killing you?"

Caroline took umbrage. "And 'aven't I been telling you that? Patrick says Kate's the one who should die. Then I'll inherit most of 'er money."

Could any of this be true? Or was Caroline certifiable?

I changed tack. "Tell me about your adoption. How did Kate come to chose you? She must have loved you then, don't you think?"

"Gawky and plain as plum pudding, I was. My fourteenth birthday less than a month away. But Kate seemed bound and determined to 'ave me. God knows why. She's a strange one, isn't she?''

Strange couldn't begin to describe any of the Connors clan, but I kept that opinion to myself.

Caroline continued, ''Before I knew what 'ad 'appened, I was adopted and on a plane for New York.''

''I notice you never refer to Kate as mother.''

''She said we were more like mates than mother and daughter. I even kept my own surname. Evans.''

''Did you know your birth mother, Caroline?''

''No. Both my parents were killed in a car accident. They'd been drinking. Flew right over the White Cliffs of Dover, didn't they? I was two months old, left behind at the flat with a baby sitter. Neither my mum nor my dad 'ad any family. Off I went to the 'ome.''

''And you have no information about them? No clue as to who they were?''

''Only their certificate of marriage and a copy of my birth record. All in the correct order. I'm not a bastard.''

I grinned. ''I never thought you were.''

Caroline laughed. ''My mum was an American.''

''Really?''

''That's right. You know where it says place of birth on a wedding certificate . . .''

''Yes . . . ?''

''Well, my mum was born in Detroit. My dad come from Liverpool. But the authorities couldn't locate any living family on either side of the Atlantic. When the police in Detroit checked out my mum's background, they said she'd lived in foster 'omes and 'ad no known relatives. Her mother 'ad given 'er away—straight from 'ospital. At least my parents 'adn't dropped me on the orphanage doorstep. They died. I was a proper orphan, wasn't I?''

''What was your mother's maiden name?''

" 'ansen. Lily 'ansen."

Then, as my mouth hung open, Mrs. Madison had wheeled in the apple pie and ice cream, and my heartburn kicked in.

I knew writing Kate's fiction would be impossible this afternoon; her real-life mystery had become so much more intriguing. And Caroline had proved to be an enigma. On one hand, relating the story of her adoption, she'd seemed more than credible, but the love triangle and the tale of poison, with Kate as her daughter's potential killer, sounded inane as well as insane.

Or did it?

This case had gotten out of control. The suspects running amok all over the board like pieces in an erratic checker game. Kate Lloyd Connors had just jumped over all the other checkered players and been crowned most-likely-killer.

Sarah Anne Hansen? Lily Hansen? Coincidence? I didn't think so. Our Ghostwriters Anonymous program tells us there are no coincidences. Caroline's mother, Lily Hansen, had been born in Detroit, Michigan, in July 1957, then raised in foster homes. Eighteen-year-old Sarah Anne Hansen had fled Honey Bucket, Michigan, on Valentine's Day, 1957, after her father had been pushed—or fallen—through the ice and drowned. Kate Lloyd Connors and Sarah Anne Hansen would be about the same age. Were they the same person? I'd always thought of Kate as a native New Yorker—things are seldom as they seem—she could be from Upper Michigan, have a wretched past and, maybe, no one knew it. Not her publisher, not her readers, not Dennis Kim, certainly not Caroline. And not her ghosts—until Emmie stumbled on Kate's sordid secret and shared it with her sponsor, Barbara. If Kate had killed John

Hansen and changed her identity, wouldn't she kill again to keep Emmie and Barbara quiet?

I needed to dig for proof. Evidence that Kate and Sarah Anne were one and the same. Evidence that Kate knew Emmie had not only unearthed her past but had also told Barbara. I'd find that proof, and I'd solve this case. For Emmie and for Barbara.

Kate may have been the current king, but she wasn't the only player remaining on my checkerboard.

Either Jonathan or Patrick was in position to jump over Kate and be crowned as king of suspects. And Ivan, Vera, Angela, Caroline—even Dennis—might be only a move or two behind.

Jonathan's dirty deal with the *National Enquirer* now took on a whole new dimension. Was the "identity issue" that the editor had referred to in his letter the Sarah Anne Hansen/Kate Lloyd Connors connection? Jonathan was getting 500,000 dollars for his ghost story. What could he command for exposing America's Queen-of-Murder-Most-Cozy's long-ago, real-life incest/ murder/baby abandonment story? A million dollar motive. Barbara might have told Kate's secret to her brother—God knows she'd told Mr. Kim and, for all I knew, the immediate world about her threat from the mob—and Bill might have slipped that information to Jonathan during pillow talk. If the ghosts had talked to the police, before his publication date, Jonathan's golden goose was cooked. Then, too, Jonathan was a greedy bastard and, with Barbara dead, Bill controlled the Bernside fortune.

Was Patrick really romancing both Kate and Caroline? How much control could a hypnotist exert over a patient? I called my good friend, Gypsy Rose Liebowitz—an expert in parapsychology, New Age soul-searching and those people, who for a price, healed other folks' spiritual woes.

She launched into an in-depth discussion of hypnotherapy, explaining regression and parts therapy. Regression brings a patient back in time, often to his past lives, in order to deal with current emotional, psychological or physical problems. The theory: Confront the past, enjoy the present. In parts therapy, a patient faces the negative and positive side of all her emotions.

"For example?" I asked.

"You see, in a person's heart—or soul—creativity may dwell side by side with fear and negativity. They're two parts of the same feeling, the latter stifling the former's chances to express itself. The patient's conservative side, afraid of rejection, prevents his wild side from the joy of creating. Get it?"

I sure as hell didn't, but I just said, "Go on."

"Sometimes, the patient will find his wild part in, say, his right foot. After successful treatment by a competent hypnotist, he'll know where he needs to channel his energy and what body part to concentrate on, when he needs to take a risk."

Well, that certainly cleared everything up. "Gypsy Rose, can a person be hypnotized to do something that she'd rather not do? Wouldn't, in fact, ever do under normal circumstances."

"No. Never. The power of the hypnotist's suggestions can be strong; however, an honest person would not, for instance, turn into a thief."

Or a murderer, I thought. But would Patrick himself kill if the reward was marrying into Kate's empire? My gut feeling was that he'd kill for a lot less.

What I really wanted to do was call another

emergency meeting of the ghosts, but hesitated, not wanting to share dangerous knowledge with them. I decided to get out of Dodge before Kate and Jonathan came home. I had places to go and people to see . . . and a killer to catch.

Seventeen

Washington Square Park and the wonderful nineteenth-century homes surrounding it evoked images of *The Heiress*. The handsome con man Morris banging and begging at the front door while the plain, spurned Catherine ignored his pleas for forgiveness.

I'd taken the subway to Astor Place, walked the few blocks downtown to West Fourth and paused near the park, eating up the atmosphere. No Ho—North of Houston—was a neighborhood as diversified as any in Manhattan. College kids from NYU shared benches with the homeless and the wealthy dowagers who lived in the elegant Washington Square houses. Young mothers pushed baby carriages as teenagers roller-bladed around them. Tower Records, three floors filled with music, from rap to Rachmaninov, was jumping. The flea market in the empty lot to its south swarmed with shoppers. The street vendors were hawking ethnic food grazings, ranging from Italian to Thai. I hadn't spotted one drug dealer or pimp. On this Thursday afternoon in June, Washington Square was alive with the sights, sounds and smells of the city I loved.

My destination, Christopher Street, epitomized Greenwich Village. Too Tall Tom, the handiest man in Manhattan, had crafted a Victorian gingerbread home in an old townhouse only nine feet wide. He'd told me, when I'd called to make sure he'd be there when I arrived, that he'd have the tea cart ready.

. . . . .

Before leaving Kate's, I'd made several calls. Ivan had answered, sounding annoyed, telling me that he'd left two messages on my machine. He'd been heading out the door to Budapest East for his evening shift. He'd finish at eleven. We agreed to meet at Elaine's for a drink. I'd be buying.

Patrick's polite, elderly receptionist told me his last patient would finish at seven. When Patrick picked up the phone, I was armed and ready to fire. "I'll be at your office at seven, when you're through for the day." Unless he canceled his last appointment or ordered his receptionist to banish me, I had—so to speak—a date with Patrick.

When I finally checked my messages, there was one from Modesty. She, Ginger and I were to have dinner with Bill Bernside at the Stanhope at eight. My dance card for the evening was full.

. . . . .

Too Tall Tom welcomed me with a bear hug, lifting me so high off his Persian carpet that I could have grabbed hold of the Venetian glass chandelier. As always, being around this great guy comforted me. Too Tall Tom eked out a wage, slightly more than minimum, as a how-to-ghost; however, as a jack of all trades and master carpenter who could transform Manhattan box-shaped apartments into Edwardian flats, he made some

real money. Selective in his customers—after all, he was
a writer who dabbled in handicraft, not the other way
around—he budgeted his time to turn out one ghost-
written project a year. Like the rest of the ghosts, he
hadn't succeeded in selling any of his own works-in-
progress. Too esoteric, he'd been told.

Sipping Earl Gray tea—not my favorite, I think it
smells like perfume—sitting on a red settee, with Too
Tall Tom perched on a high ladder-back oak chair, I
admired the tea sandwiches and cream puffs. "Did you
make all this?"

"Jake, why do you think God gave us delis and
French bakeries? Your phone call prompted a walk over
to Giattois. Now what's so important?"

"Tell me about running into Bill Bernside and
Jonathan Arthur on Tuesday night. They strike me as
the odd couple. Had you met either one of them before
the memorial service that morning?"

"No. Remember Bill's from Philadelphia . . . and I
guess Jonathan never made the Tribeca scene. I
recognized them from the funeral. Why, I'd had a long
chat with Bill at the Harvard Club, so I dashed right
over to say hello."

"And?"

"Well, neither of them seemed happy to see me.
Before I'd pushed through the crowd, they'd been
dancing cheek to cheek and had held hands on their way
back to the bar. Being so tall, I don't miss much. But
when I approached them, they seemed reserved. Stuffy."

"Jonathan is stuffy. Maybe the stuffiest stiff in New
York." I reached for another cream puff, hating myself,
and added, "If he seemed loose on the dance floor, that's
not his usual style."

Too Tall Tom thought for moment. "I didn't speak

to him at any length at the reception, but I agree with you, Jake, he struck me as a prig.''

''Yet he and Bill were openly romantic?''

''Oh, my dear, yes. As a long time observer of the mating game, I'd say in the throes of a passionate courtship.''

''In most love affairs, one person seems to be the pursuer, one seems to want the other more, to care more . . .''

Too Tall Tom banged his Royal Doulton teacup down on its saucer, ''You're right, and I always seem destined to be the one giving chase! In this romance, however, Bill was the most smitten. He had the look of love smeared all over his face while they were dancing.''

''Do you think any of the club regulars might know either Bill or Jonathan?''

''I don't know, Jake, I'll ask around. Of course Bill's an out-of-towner, but if Jonathan has ever stepped out of his closet and into any of the gay clubs, I'll know someone who knows him.''

Too Tall Tom promised to call me with any information, advised me to be careful and kissed me good-bye. I splurged on a cab home. I wanted to talk to Mom and change my clothes. Dinner at the Stanhope required mascara, high heels and a skirt. Or could it be the meeting with Patrick that required those items?

. . . . .

My mother had news. Linda Rogers had been told by the police that Emmie had been pregnant.

''What do you think of that?'' Mom asked.

''I don't know what to think, Mom.'' That was true enough.

''Ivan,'' my mother almost snarled. ''I told you he was no good. Maybe he murdered Emmie and Barbara, too, because somehow she'd found out. His aura's so strong that Gypsy surely could have picked it up at Campbell's.''

''I think you're confusing Ivan's aura with his odor.'' But it's amazing how my mother's bizarre thought processes so often made sense. ''Ivan certainly could be guilty.'' I decided not to tell her that I was meeting Ivan the Terrible later that evening. Maura O'Hara had elevated worry to an applied science. I did tell her that Ginger, Modesty and I were dining with Bill—not to wait up—and I had an appointment before that, so I'd better move my buns.

As I fished in my closet for Stanhope-appropriate dinner attire, I checked my messages. The warmth that flash-flooded through my body when I heard Ben's voice, surprised me.

''Jake, it's Ben, I need to talk to you.'' But he was neither at the police station nor at home. Frustrated, I left messages both places, telling him I probably wouldn't be back till midnight. And decided as soon as I received my advance from Kate, I was buying a cellular phone.

I kissed my mother good-bye; she advised me to be on my guard and that she approved of my dress. As I hailed my second taxi of the day—I was turning into Gypsy Rose Liebowitz, whose idea of the great outdoors was the space between the hotel lobby and the taxi—I pondered my mother's parting query. ''What are you wearing to Emmie's viewing tomorrow night?'' When Armargeddon strikes, I know my mother will have just the right outfit.

• • • • •

Reversing my modus operandi, I actually arrived at Patrick's twenty minutes early. The receptionist exited

Patrick's office, calling, "Good night," over her shoulder as I entered the waiting room. It appeared as if I'd startled her.

"Oh . . . yes, Miss O'Hara, isn't it? I was just leaving." Her handbag dangled from one arm; a perky straw hat topped her stylish gray hair. Ready to go. I figured she'd planned on locking the waiting room door, leaving me stranded in the hall. Maybe arriving early has its merits.

Flustered, she looked from Patrick's door to me to the hallway . . . knowing I'd heard her say, "good night," and she had no reason to go back into his office to warn him that the enemy had landed. Mumbling, "Goodbye," she left, probably wondering if she'd have a job in the morning.

In her confusion, she'd not noticed that the door leading into Patrick's office hadn't clicked shut. It appeared closed but, in fact, had remained infinitesimally open. I inched in as close as I could get to the tiny crack and eavesdropped.

Patrick's last patient of the day was Kate Lloyd Connors. It sounded as if they were having a spat. About me!

"How can you be so certain?" Kate asked Patrick. "Vera says she's caught Jake spying in Jonathan's office on two separate occasions. Once this very afternoon. God knows I don't think she'd find anything there, Jonathan's office is an autoclave. But if she starts going through my . . ."

"You don't keep any important papers in the library, do you?"

"Of course not. Too damn many ghosts have been in that room. I just think Jake's too smart for her own good. If she's digging she'll find dirt. Maybe I should fire her."

"Don't overreact, dearest lady, you don't want to make her suspicious. Your past belongs only to you. Wait a while."

Dearest lady. Indeed! Maybe Patrick did practice hands-on therapy with both mother and daughter. I wanted to throw up.

"Then there's Caroline," Kate said, as if reading my mind. "I scolded Vera for leaving her and Jake alone during lunch. One can only imagine what Caroline had to say to her. Vera wants to tape their conversations from now on. I wish she'd started today."

Jesus! Damn good thing she hadn't or I'd be out of Chez Connors in a Manhattan millisecond.

"Let me stop by later tonight. We'll work on tension. I promise you'll feel better when I'm finished." Patrick's voice soothed. "But now, you'd better go before Jake arrives."

"I thought your receptionist locked the outside door."

"Yes, but you don't want to run into Jake in the hall."

I panicked. What should I do? Crouch behind the couch? Make a dash for the hallway? Brazen it out? Before I could decide, Kate pulled the door open, strode into the reception room, then stopped dead when she saw me. Patrick was right behind her. Seeing the expressions on their faces seemed worth the price of admission—whatever that might be.

"Hi, Kate, I guess you're Patrick's last patient for the day; my visit's a social call." I'd call that bold if not brazen. Kate regained control almost immediately, her face falling back into neutral.

"Jake, how nice to see you. Well, good night, Patrick. I look forward to tomorrow's work session, Jake."

I watched her walk out with great style. Whatever else I felt about the lady, she had class.

Patrick, too, had made a fast recovery. "Jake, please come into my office. What can I do for you?"

I followed him into his office, but I remained standing. "Is Caroline on drugs?"

"Why do you ask?"

"Is she under a psychiatrist's care?"

"Yes, she is. I thought you knew that."

"And does he have her on drug therapy?"

"Jake, I've told you I can't discuss my patients."

"Who's her doctor? Does he know how much she's taking? I'd bet not."

"I tell you what, Jake. I'll voice your concerns to Caroline's doctor. Is there anything else?"

He stood, crossed in front of me, gesturing toward the door. "If not," he added, "it's been a long day."

I should have left then, but I had to have the last word. "Just one more thing. Are you the father of Emmie Roger's baby?"

His response surprised me. "Maybe you should consider seeing Caroline's psychiatrist. It sounds as if you could use one."

I walked to the hallway door, paused, and swung around to face him. "Then I guess you'd have no objection to taking a paternity test." I stomped out—if not with as much style as Kate—with a definite flare. Of anger.

My date with Patrick over early, I rode the Madison Avenue bus uptown for dinner at eight at the Stanhope.

· · · · ·

The solicitous waiters, the serene atmosphere, and the sophisticated conversation while we dined, almost made me forget that one murder had brought the four of us together tonight and that a second would reunite us at tomorrow evening's viewing.

Over a peach brandy soufflé, almost too sinful to swallow, I brought up Jonathan. "One of the ghosts tells me that you're a good friend of Jonathan Arthur's, Bill."

Bill blushed. Honest to God . . . scarlet. Ginger raised a perfectly plucked brow. Her eyebrows always reminded me of Candice Bergen's. Modesty gave me a filthy look. I realized that she thought the ghost I'd referred to was her.

"Yes," I went on, "Too Tall Tom and I had tea together this afternoon, and he mentioned running into you and Jonathan on Tuesday night."

Modesty relaxed her shoulders.

"Jake, I do know Jonathan. Patrick Hemmings, an old friend of mine, introduced us on one of my visits to Barbara. I met Jonathan's employer, the famous mystery writer, Kate Lloyd Connors, as well." Bill worked hard to make his remarks seem easy—and, oh so casual. Then he excused himself and went to the john.

Modesty demanded, "Why are you cross-examining Bill?"

"Jonathan Arthur's a dangerous man. I bet Bill has no idea what a money-grabbing turncoat caught his fancy."

The waiter interrupted me. "More decaf, ladies?"

When Bill returned, he asked for the check, then excused himself, saying he was exhausted and would see us at the viewing. Modesty, Ginger and I stayed for another cup of coffee, then shared a cab. I dropped them off and asked the driver to take me to Elaine's.

. . . . .

For the second time in the same evening, I arrived early for an appointment. Today had proved memorable in more ways than one. And I found an empty bar stool.

"Sit down, it has your name on it, Jake." Joe smiled. "Haven't seen you since the night after you stood Emmie up."

"Jesus, Joe!"

"Well—er—I just meant who'da thought she turn up dead? That, in fact, she'd already been murdered?" With those comforting words, he mixed a Bloody Mary for the man to my right.

I guess Joe felt guilty for upsetting me. When he served my white wine spritzer, he said, "It's on the house."

Ivan caught me unaware. "Jake, vat is it you vant to talk about?" He stood so close, smelling not like garlic, but goulash.

With Ivan, I could be direct. "Why did you and Emmie quarrel last Friday at Budapest East?"

"Vat do you mean?"

I was tired, cranky and fresh out of charm. "Several people heard you scream at Emmie. What about?"

"Igor, what are you drinking?" Joe asked.

"Ivan," Ivan and I said in unison.

I smiled at Joe, nodding to Ivan. "My treat." I said.

Ivan ordered Louis XIII Cognac. And a Coke! What a creep. Did I have enough money on me? No way. I hoped my OPTIMA card worked.

"So?" I said, as Joe went to fetch Ivan's one-hundred-thirty-five-dollar after-dinner drink.

"So vat? Nothink. I loved Emmie. That's vat."

"And were you the father of her child?"

Ivan's answer like Patrick's took me by surprise.

"I would have married her, Jake, but I can't be any baby's father. The mumps. Two years ago. I'm sterile."

Eighteen

The phone rang as I entered my bedroom at 11:40 P.M. I was tempted not to answer, but it might be Ben. Caroline's loud, agitated voice hurt my ear.

"Jake, I've run away from 'ome. Can I pop over to your 'ouse for a while?"

"Caroline, I need my job with your stepmother. If she found out that you came here, I'd be fired. What's wrong?"

"Kate and I had an ugly scene over Patrick. Our 'andsome 'ypnotist left a little bit ago. They'd been closeted in 'er bedroom. You know 'e's mine."

"Where are you now?"

"I'm in a pub near Times Square. I'm afraid to go over to Patrick's, but I might."

"Go home, Caroline. I'll be at work at ten in the morning; we'll talk then. Promise me you'll go straight home."

She promised, but I didn't believe her.

Should I call Patrick in a half hour and see if she'd arrived? Or should I leave Eliza and the Marlboro Man to their own devices. Should I tell Ben? Should I mind my own business? Caroline might be crazy, but so were several of my acquaintances. I didn't try to control them, and I couldn't control Caroline.

The gurgling of the Water Pik muffled the sound, but no question, I had another phone call. This time, it was Ben, offering to drive me to Emmie's viewing. Getting to Queens on a Friday evening in June, fighting the exodus to Long Island, could be a royal pain in the butt. I accepted.

Ben had spent the afternoon and much of the evening discussing "opportunity" with the various members of Connors and company.

"Do tell."

"Okay, let's start with Emmie's murder. We know it happened sometime between late Friday night and quite early Saturday morning. Kate Lloyd Connors claims she was in bed with a good book. Read till midnight. Then fell asleep."

"The book wasn't *Crime and Punishment,* was it?"

Ignoring me, Ben continued. "Mrs. Vera Madison, now there's a charmer, said she went to bed at nine P.M. She had a glass of warm milk, and awoke, as she always does, at five A.M."

"What about Jonathan? He's a hot prospect." I never mentioned today's snooping.

"Jonathan attended a movie, near Lincoln Center, from nine to eleven-thirty. Alone. Never spoke to anyone. Walked all the way home. Everyone was asleep, he says. He went directly to his room."

"That's a hell of a long walk. Did he cut through the Park—alone—at that hour?"

"So he says."

"Next, I spoke to Caroline Evans. What a nut! Says she had a late therapy session at Patrick's. Arrived home at ten o'clock. Caroline assumed Kate and Mrs. Madison

were in their rooms. Carla let her in and she went—
'straight away'—to her room. But who's to say she
stayed home? Early-to-bedders, aren't they all?''

"Yeah, right. What about Patrick?"

"Patrick spent the rest of the night alone after putting
Caroline in a taxi, reading the most recent issue of the
Journal of Hypnotism."

My frustration grew with Ben's every word; I was
convinced that some of these people were liars. Barbara's death had occurred sometime after I'd left her at
eleven-thirty Saturday morning and before the super had
discovered her body at two that afternoon. I'd arrived at
Kate's at one. Caroline and Jonathan were there to greet
me. I asked Ben where they'd been before that, especially from eleven to twelve-thirty.

"Caroline jogged on the F.D.R. Drive Saturday, till
twelve-thirty, then came home, and dashed upstairs to
shower and get ready for lunch."

"As I recall, she looked pretty grubby when I met
her. Does she have anyone to vouch for her alibi?"

"Not a living soul. Neither does Jonathan, though
he's covered till noon. At his fencing lesson. His dueling
partner turned out to be one of your fellow ghosts. Anyway, he says he came straight home and stayed there."

"Ben, he was still dressed in his tights when he let
me in. If he went directly home after his lesson, why
hadn't he changed?"

"Does he have good legs? Maybe he wanted to show
them off."

"Or, maybe, he'd stopped at Barbara's on his way
home, killed her, and had just walked in?"

I remembered that Kate had made a grand entrance.
Late. Almost one-thirty. She told Ben that she'd been
swept away in a plotting tidal wave in the library from
ten to twelve-thirty, then scooted to her bedroom to dress

for lunch. And where had Mrs. Madison been, since rising at five? A little predawn cleaning, the shopping, then the cooking. And Vera had no idea what the rest of the household was up to: "The kitchen is so far removed from the other rooms." What really intrigued me was that not one of the suspects had seen any of the others on the morning in question.

Ben said, "Patrick had been at his health club from eight to ten, then was home, alone, till he left for Kate's luncheon. I'm showing all their pictures to the doormen and staff at Emmie's and Barbara's."

"When did you visit Patrick?"

"Why?"

"Just curious."

"Around six."

No wonder Patrick and Kate had been edgy when I'd arrived at his office. Not only me snooping, but the NYPD Homicide Department had been on their case.

So none of the Connors household or Patrick had airtight alibis for either murder. I thanked Ben for following up on his promise and felt guilty about not sharing my investigation results with him. But I'd played Nancy Drew despite his strong warning. He'd done exactly what I'd asked him to do; I'd done exactly what he'd asked me not to do.

I'd tell him when I had more hard evidence. Right now I had to go to bed.

Nineteen

We slept late. Mom scurried around the kitchen, packing food from the Madison Avenue deli, where I often would run into former Manhattan Borough President Andrew Stein; we both loved their chicken soup. I used to occasionally run into JFK, Jr., before he'd broken my mother's heart by getting married; she'd harbored some vague hope of becoming his mother-in-law. Gypsy Rose arrived to help Mom load the two wicker hampers, filling them with ham, baked macaroni, rolls, plus Gypsy Rose's contributions, an oven-baked turkey, string bean casserole, and two homemade pies—peach and chocolate cream.

Linda and Mike Rogers were holding a small wake after the viewing ended at nine o'clock. Mom and Gypsy Rose had enough food to feed the French Foreign Legion. Mr. Kim, who'd adored Emmie, provided all the fruit, veggies and salads, while Dennis had the wine and booze covered. With tonight's Queens crowd and all the ghosts, that would be the biggest expense.

"And Dennis is sending a limo here at ten o'clock

this morning to transport all this stuff to Jackson Heights,'' my mother said.

''Are you girls staying out there?'' I asked.

My mother pointed at Gypsy Rose, dressed in slacks and a blazer, then gestured to her own cotton jumpsuit, and looked at me as if I were crazy. ''No, of course not. The viewing's at seven; we'll come back home to change.''

Silly me!

''Dennis will pick up his father and us at six. In the Rolls.'' My mother, the Machiavelli of the matchmakers, grinned, ''Want to ride with us?''

''Thanks, but I already have a ride.''

''Oh?''

I left her pondering whose chariot I'd be riding in and went to shower.

* * * * *

Applying the conditioner, I decided: One of the few perks of being a ghostwriter is you get to make your own hours. Choose the days you want to work. Labor twelve hours on a Sunday; fly to Fresno on a Monday . . . or whatever. As long as you meet your deadline, you can pretty much call the shots. At least that had been my experience up to now. Kate Lloyd Connors, a control freak, liked her ghosts in house. Usually I wrote in bed or at our kitchen table, my first draft always done in longhand—red pen and white legal pad—but, with this assignment, I'd be doing most of my writing on Kate's turf.

Today I'd work straight through from ten to two. Two luncheons in the Connors's Conservatory had given me more than enough food for thought. Maybe I could persuade Mom to provide me with a snack to eat at my desk.

Jane, Modesty, Ginger, Too Tall Tom and I were meeting at Sara Beth's at three for tea and empathy. Good friends hoisting a prewake cup of Orange Pekoe to our dearly departed ghost. Emmie loved Sara Beth's strawberry butter and homemade biscuits. I'd have a few for her.

Dashing for the door—yesterday afternoon's on-time mode seemed to have wound down this morning—I heard the phone ring. My mother yelled from the kitchen, "Jake. For you."

"I'm late, Mom. Who is it?"

My mother appeared in the foyer, waving the portable phone at me and whispering, "Angela Scotti."

I called Castle Connors, spoke to Carla, and asked her to tell Kate that I'd be an hour late. Then off I went, detouring over to Serendipity's to meet the Don's daughter for cappuccino and conversation.

· · · · ·

Angela looked radiant, if somewhat nervous. Her dark hair hung in a thick braid halfway down her back. And her wide, white pants and crisp navy and white striped shirt looked very Southampton, where she was headed for the weekend.

"The cottage's tucked among the dunes. Do you know the area?" Angela voice reflected years of diction lessons. Probably at some finishing school like Miss Porter's. It wasn't easy to lose a Queens accent. I'd tried.

"Yes. Beautiful beaches. My mother says the finest in the country."

I checked out the mothers and kids and well-heeled matrons—Bloomingdale's designer customers—stopping for a frothy libation, before foraying into the store for a day of serious shopping. Not a Mafia type among them.

Angela smiled at me. "I'm alone this morning. It was tricky, but I lost the bodyguards. For the time being, they'll catch up with me in the Hamptons. My poppa is so over protective."

"How is your father?" I asked, somewhat hesitantly, unsure of proper protocol. Should you inquire about someone's famous relative if her relative happened to be serving time in a federal prison?

"He's why I'm here."

Jesus! "Oh?" I managed.

"Yes, our family's concerned over rumors that Poppa had something to do with Barbara's death. I want to assure you that those rumors are completely unfounded."

Why was this woman telling me all this?

Angela continued, answering my unasked question. "Jake, last Saturday about eleven-forty-five in the morning, I called Barbara. She was most upset. She'd received a threatening call from someone who'd claimed to represent our family, saying my father was angry about the book. Barbara also said that she'd just told you the same story. So, you're well aware just how frightened she was."

"Do the police know you spoke to Barbara that morning? It had to be just before she was killed!"

"I called from a phone booth. And, no, I haven't discussed this with the police." Angela made talking to the police sound like a mortal sin. "But I want you to understand that what Barbara feared so much had no basis in fact."

"How's that?"

"My poppa loves the book. Thinks it makes him look like an Italian Robin Hood. Whoever called Barbara was not a member of our family. Barbara spoke of you often, Jake. She trusted you. Now I ask you to trust me. Someone lied to Barbara. Probably the same someone who killed her.''

''But who'd want to do that? And why?''

Angela shrugged.

''Does Dennis Kim know you're telling me all this?''

''He suggested it.''

. . . . .

As we climbed into her white Jag convertible, I stared at her profile. Very Sophia Loren. This was one sexy woman. Somehow that reminded me of Patrick and, before thinking it through, I blurted, ''How well do you know Patrick Hemmings?''

Angela sparkled. ''Oh, Barbara turned me on to him. Patrick's fantastic!'' Her words wrapped in multiple meanings.

''Yeah? How so?''

''He introduced me to the conflicting parts of my body and soul's emotions. True joy had been smothered in my lower rib cage. Patrick helped me set it free and allowed my unbound pleasure to soar to the apex of ecstasy.'' Angela's upper lip glistened with moisture as color flooded her cheeks. ''I highly recommend him for parts therapy Jake, but I warn you: all his women patients fall a little bit in love with him.''

''I'll bet.'' So much for Angela's ''murder'' that my mother had read in Patrick's eyes. Once again, are things seldom as they seem?

She dropped me at Kate's and kissed me on both cheeks, saying, ''Ciao.'' Then, as she put the car in gear, returned to the reason for our meeting, ''And killing Barbara with a copy of *The Godfather!* Really! Show biz. Just show biz. Jake, our family business would never have been handled so unprofessionally.''

Now, that was a comforting thought.

As Angela's Jag pulled away from the curb, heading for the F.D.R. Drive, through the Queens-Midtown Tunnel to the L.I.E., then on to the Southampton dunes, I headed for *A Killing in Katmandu.*

. . . . .

Ghostwriters Anonymous suggested that we keep our own and our employers' confidentiality under cover. In that spirit, I'd told the other ghosts that my Kate Lloyd Connors assignment was as an editor. While committing a venial sin of confidentiality breaking, I hadn't totally compromised my—or her—anonymity.

The occupational hazard of ghosting made me crazy: You had to write what the name-on-the-book-as-author told you to write. Kate had been particularly persnickety today. No comment about our brief encounter at Patrick's yesterday, but instead she bustled about, all business. My vision of Katmandu's killer-on-the-loose seemed hazy. My voice missed the magic that Kate's readers craved. My volume proved to be less than expected.

The Queen-of-Murder-Most-Cozy readily agreed that I should work straight through with no lunch. She actually said, ''Idle hands are the devil's workshop!'' No wonder Kate needed a ghost; the last time she had an original idea was probably the same year she watched her father drown. Then I felt like a jerk that I'd let the royal-pain-in-the-butt get to me.

Carla seemed to be the only other one at home; the rest of the crew were out and about. When I took my one break to go to the john, I saw Carla waxing the banister. ''Where's everyone today?''

"Mrs. Madison's gone to pick up Caroline. She stayed overnight at a friend's house."

Aha! Caroline had gone to Patrick's and, apparently, survived the visit. Who'd arranged for Vera to fetch her? Did Kate know whose bed her darling daughter had slept in? Or had Mrs. Madison protected her from that tidbit?

"And it's Mr. Jonathan's day off. He's spending it with a friend." Carla grinned.

I'd bet the co-op that friend was Bill Bernside. Caroline and Jonathan were quite the social butterflies, weren't they? "Carla, did Miss Connors send Mrs. Madison to bring Caroline home?"

Carla stared over my right shoulder, perplexed. I glanced behind me. Kate stood in the open French doors to the library. "Jake, if you any questions about either my daughter or my staff, why don't you ask me?"

I apologized—blaming the mystery writer in me— and promised that it wouldn't happen again. Kate Lloyd Connors didn't believe me, though she said she did, but surprisingly, I still had my job. For now.

. . . . .

I sat with my fellow ghostwriters, feeling fortunate to have four good friends who'd listen to my gripes. They empathized with an abridged version of my day and when the ghosts' reassurances had calmed me down, we all tea-toasted Emmie and Barbara, too.

Both Too Tall Tom and Jane had news. Jonathan and Bill had been regulars at a sedate little bistro on Prince Street. Too Tall Tom told us that his informant had said, "They'd been seen quarreling—then passionately making up. . . ."

"What were they fighting about?" Ginger asked.

"My friend says money. He overheard Bill telling Jonathan that he needed big bucks to buy out some computer company and that they weren't going to Cannes as planned. Jonathan had shouted, then left in a huff, with Bill right behind him, begging him to try and understand."

"I believe that Barbara had control over the family trust fund, but I don't know why," an angry-sounding Modesty said. "Was this lovers' spat before or after Barbara's death?"

"Before." Too Tall Tom patted Modesty's arm and, surprisingly, she didn't pull away.

Jane reported on her new assignment as Patrick's self-help book "editor." "He's really great," she said, as if challenging me to disagree.

But before I had the chance, Modesty snarled, "Has your seldom-used libido finally driven you to madness?"

I figured Jane would lash out at Modesty, but she said, "That's exactly right. I'd covered my natural lust for life with prudish behavior. Patrick unleashed that lust from where it had been hiding, deep in my left elbow. That's why I could never play tennis."

Ginger was the one who reacted, "Jane, you're a rotten Macintosh turned into applesauce by the snake-hypnotist from hell. I've always thought chastity was a choice you'd made to enhance your serenity. No men in one's life does tend to make it less complicated. But for once I agree with Modesty. Falling for Patrick's line of bull is a disgrace to womanhood and to Ghostwriters Anonymous!"

Too Tall Tom jumped in, pointing out that it was getting late. Wondering where my repressed emotions might be hiding, I said I still had to pick up a Mass card at St. Thomas More's rectory and press my dress. Then we all went home to get ready to visit our second dead ghost in as many days.

· · · · ·

I had one message from Ben. He'd be here at six.
And one unsigned e-mail. It read, ''Meddlers will be

Twenty

"**You're pale as** a ghost!" My mother whirled through the front door, blow-dried and looking great, direct from the talented hands of her longtime hair stylist. "What's wrong, darling? Why aren't you dressed? Aren't you feeling well? Can I do something?" Mom's questions were both rhetorical and on target. When I didn't answer, she added, "We don't want to be late for Emmie's wake."

"She's not going anywhere, Mom."

"Don't be cynical, Jake, it's tough enough."

"You're right." I gave her a kiss on the cheek. "And why aren't *you* ready, Maura O'Hara? Dennis Kim's probably outside by now tooting his own horn."

"God, what time is it?"

"Five-thirty-something."

"Let's get moving." My mother patted my head while fluffing a pillow, then bolted down the hallway to her bedroom.

What would she say if she knew that I had just received a death threat? By e-mail, yet. Her only daughter, her pride and joy—though she sometimes stashed those emotions, maybe Patrick could release them from her right kidney or some other more interesting body part. Would I live long enough to use this plot twist in a future cozy? I should be more frantic. Why wasn't I? Did true terror freeze the central nervous system? Ben's ETA was less than an half hour away. That seemed an eternity.

. . . . .

As I pressed the DKNY black linen, I decided I was getting my money's worth out of this dress. What would Ginger, Modesty and Jane wear to my funeral? Would they buy new outfits or just recycle their mourning threads from this week's funerals? God Almighty! I draped the dress over the dishwasher and poured myself a goblet-sized glass of my mother's Old Cave Tawny. I'll never understand why Mom and Gypsy Rose drink this stuff, but any port in a storm. I downed it in record time and considered pouring a second as my mind went into spin cycle and my body started to shake.

Now terror thundered through me. My speeding heart rate might soon prove fatal. A trembling finger landed on the hot iron. God, what next? I watched a red welt appear on the back of my right pinkie. While applying ice to the burn, my mood changed. Fear, still entrenched in my soul, moved over, allowing room for anger. Hot as the iron. I would not become the next victim of some serial killer who had it in for New York's ghosts. I'd out this murderer and use my fear and anger to help me do it. But first I had to pull myself together. On my way to get dressed, I knocked on my mother's bedroom door. "Mom, can I borrow your red lipstick and maybe those gold hoop earrings?"

. . . . .

I printed a hard copy of the terse threat. It originated at a Kinko's on 86th Street near Lexington Avenue at five-ten this afternoon with, of course, no clue as to the sender.

Does a person have to give his—or her—name and ID in order to use a computer's e-mail at a mailbox services' store? Probably the killer would have given false ID; Ben could check that out. Aloud, I addressed my subconscious: "Well, I guess we've decided to tell Ben."

"Tell Ben what?" My mother appeared in my doorway, holding a metal tray awash with cosmetics and gold.

"Oh, to warn his father that Maura O'Hara's both a busybody and a bossy broad."

"Well, forewarned is foreplay or something like that." My mother smiled. "Now, do you like these gold shells or the small hoops? And, hurry up, I just looked out the window. Both Dennis and Ben are double-parked, and Gypsy Rose and Mr. Kim are waiting in the Rolls."

"Go ahead on down, Mom. Tell Ben I'll be there in five minutes." I struggled as I pulled the sheath on and smoothed it over my hips, then pointed to the gold shells. "And which one of these lipsticks is that coral-color I like on you?"

My mother handed me a Revlon tube and the earrings. "Darling, I know you're sad. God, it's all so sad. But we'll get through this, Jake. You'll see. Life will go on."

Giving her a hug, I thought: From your mouth to God's ears.

. . . . .

God may not have gotten an earful, but during our ride to Queens, via the Triborough Bridge, Ben certainly did. Too tired and too frightened to edit creatively, I spilled my guts. Ben listened, asked the right questions, promised to put the heat on Jonathan, Patrick and Kate Lloyd Connors, and showed concern, while remaining calm. Stoic, almost. Somehow his attitude was contagious. My insides ceased churning and my heart rate slowed down.

"Now what?' I asked. We were exiting the bridge, approaching Queens Boulevard. The Friday evening traffic crawled.

"Now it's my turn at bat." Ben took his eyes off the road for a second and looked into mine. "You're retired. Close the book on Nancy Drew, Miss Marple and Jessica Fletcher. Your career as a detective is finished. And why can't you quit your job? I don't want you at Kate Lloyd Connors's madhouse."

I bristled. "No way! I can't give up the ghostwriting, but maybe I can work at home more often." Was that really a possibility? Or just a placebo for Ben's agitation?

He gripped the wheel and swerved to the right, easing an inch ahead of where we'd been stuck, only to become trapped in another lane. "If I can get an officer assigned to you, starting tonight, I will."

"Don't you dare! Use all your manpower to find the killer. We know my nosing around has made him nervous. Maybe he—or she—will try something else to scare me."

"That's what I'm afraid of, Jake. You could be scared to death."

A horn from behind us distracted Ben. Then he seized the small opening ahead of us to return to our original position in the left lane.

. . . . .

We arrived at Conway's Funeral Home on Northern Boulevard and 83rd Street in Jackson Heights at seven o'clock sharp. Totally amazing! Finding a parking spot would be another story. I'd forgotten that my driver was an NYPD detective. We parked at a fire hydrant.

Jackson Heights was five miles and light years away from Midtown Manhattan. Quintessential Queens. Once home to judges, doctors and movie stars—the old Astoria studios' location was only a short limo ride away—as well as sundry, lower-middle-class Irish, Italian and Jewish white- and blue-collar workers, living side-by-side with upper-middle-class, old-guard WASPS, Jackson Heights had undergone a cultural metamorphosis.

Famed as "A Garden in a City" from the twenties to the fifties, now it reigned as the most ethnically diverse neighborhood in America. A small town whose residents spoke forty different languages and came from seventy different countries, offering as many national dishes and cooking odors—an area regarded by its denizens as either a multicultural mecca or a third-world country. The young professionals snatching up its condos and two-family homes considered it the former, while the elderly WASPS who'd remained in their lovely Tudors and huge co-ops considered it the latter. Most of the Irish, Italians and Jews were long gone to the suburbs.

All seven continents were represented in the faces of its residents strolling along the tree-lined streets. Seventy-fourth Street, from Roosevelt Avenue to 35th Avenue, had become the sari center of the United States. The smell of curry and incense filling the air and the racks of clothes lining the sidewalks made me feel like a character in a Rumer Godden novel. The drug deals on Roosevelt Avenue contrasted with fine dining around

the corner. Argentina may boast a better steak house
than La Porteña, but Jackson Heights is only a twenty-
minute subway ride from Carnegie Hill. Mr. Kim and
Dennis frequent a Korean restaurant on 37 Avenue, and
they have cousins by the dozens in the neighborhood.

I found Jackson Heights exhilarating and exciting; my
mother found its crowded street scenes somewhat
disturbing and dangerous.

· · · · ·

The old Boulevard movie theater across the street
from Connolly's was now a pentecostal church, its
marquee advertising redemption in lieu of double
features. I pointed the landmark out to Ben. My mother
had spent every Saturday of her childhood at this theater,
devouring Bette Davis flicks and White Castle
hamburgers, and had told me, ''Of all the changes in
Jackson Heights, the death of my favorite movie house
upset me the most.''

As Ben and I scanned the crowd in Connolly's largest
viewing room, I spotted Kate, Caroline and Mrs.
Madison in the second row, right side. Dennis Kim
chatted with Bill Bernside and Jonathan Arthur in a far
corner on the far side of the room. Ivan knelt in front
of the closed casket, head down, weeping loudly enough
to be heard in Chicago. Ginger sat with Mom and Gypsy
Rose in the row in front of Kate. They were comforting
a sobbing Linda Rogers. Mike Rogers and Mr. Kim
stood in front of Emmie's picture. Tears swept down
Mr. Kim's face, and Mike put his big arm around the
slim shoulder of his daughter's old friend. Modesty had
distanced herself from the living, flitting from bouquet
to bouquet, reading the cards attached to the wreaths and
flower arrangements. Mrs. McMahon, who'd left her zip
code far behind to attend this wake, waved the largest

set of rosary beads west of the Vatican, jabbing the cross in Too Tall Tom's chest. They sat in the last row on the left, not far from Dennis Kim's little group. Patrick stood in the center of the room, almost backed into the wall by his admirers. Several ghosts, including Jane, were among them.

Now this was a Jackson Heights scene I did find somewhat disturbing and dangerous.

Twenty-one

The cachet of a murdered ghost's Manhattan memorial service at Campbell's apparently hadn't extended across the East River to another murdered ghost's Queens wake at Connolly's. No hordes from Flatbush or Staten Island danced attendance. The outer boroughs—other than the one we were in—were represented only by Emmie's twin cousins from the Bronx, Dale and Roy Rogers and their mother, Em's Aunt Veronica, widow of Mike Rogers's brother, and lover of singing Westerns. And no strangers had arrived uninvited from out of state.

I kissed Mom, Gypsy Rose and Linda, giving Emmie's mother an extra hug. Tonight, she looked as frail and frightened as I felt. Ginger gestured toward Jane, starstruck at Patrick's side. "Someone ought to expose that phony sweet potato. Why don't you go for parts therapy, Jake? You may discover all kinds of zesty emotions wasting away under your kneecaps."

Ben laughed but said, "Jake's keeping a low profile with Connors and company."

"I'm glad to hear you say that, Ben," my mother

said. "God knows she won't listen to me."

"Mom!" I began.

Mike Rogers's booming baritone drowned me out. "Father Doyle is here to lead us in the Rosary." On the last syllable, Mike's voice broke. The crowd grew quiet as people settled down. Ben and I found two seats in the last row.

Jim Doyle, pastor at St. Joan of Arc's, had officiated at Linda and Mike's marriage, baptized their only daughter, Emily Brontë Rogers, and would offer her Mass of Requiem, tomorrow. He spoke about the Rogers family—Emmie had three younger brothers—with love and admiration. At least half the assembly was in tears, including me. I knew I had tissues in my bag. Where had I stashed it? I thought I'd shoved it under my seat; now I couldn't find it.

Father Doyle had segued from his sob-evoking eulogy to the Sorrowful Mysteries. The Catholics knelt and recited the Hail Marys, Glory Bes and Our Fathers, along with him. The rest of the mourners bowed their heads, some joining in to say the Lord's Prayer that introduced each decade. I, however, was on my hands and knees, squirming under my chair.

"What are you looking for?" Ben asked.

"My bag. I need a tissue."

Ben reached into his pocket and passed his handkerchief down to me. Why have I always been dependent on the kindness of others to blow my goddamn nose? And where had my tote disappeared to? I'd had no time to change from my working writer's oversized tote to my chic, mock-croc clutch. The copy I'd made of Jonathan's letter from the *National Enquirer* as well as the printout of my e-mail murder threat were in that bag! Two pieces of hard evidence. I'd forgotten all about them. Now that I'd remembered, I desperately wanted to find out where the bag had gone. I eased past Ben as Father Doyle droned on through another decade, the Agony in the Garden.

Since most of the mourners' eyes were downcast in prayer, I moved through the room without much notice. Circling the room, I peered under each row of chairs. In the first row, my mother, Gypsy Rose and Linda held hands, crying more than praying.

Directly behind them, Caroline clutched her rosary beads—I'd have bet that she was Church of England—loudly dropping her haitches throughout the Lord's Prayer. Mrs. Madison, looking grim as the Reaper, stared straight ahead at the casket. Her right hand grabbed hold of Kate's left elbow in a viselike grip, as if supporting her in her grief. Ivan had squeezed into their row, no doubt stealing someone's seat when he'd gone to the john. The sounds—borderline bellowing—coming from Ivan could only be described as keening. If he didn't cut it out, Mike Rogers might throw him out of here; Mike would welcome any excuse to do so since he'd never liked Ivan from day one. Mike himself stood stoic with his three sons, next to Father Doyle.

Dennis, Bill and Jonathan had remained standing. All three were mouthing, "Forgive us our trespasses," as if they meant every word. Mrs. McMahon had shared the world's largest rosary with Too Tall Tom, and both were deep in prayer. Modesty, Ginger and Jane, united in sadness, sat huddled next to Too Tall Tom.

Dozens of flower arrangements lined the walls of the room and, as at Barbara's memorial, there was no escaping their scent. As Father Doyle began the Crowning with Thorns decade, I fled to the foyer. I had to pass right by Patrick, who still lounged against the same center wall, surrounded by a basket of roses on one side and a vase filled with lilacs on the other. His eyes were closed; so were his lips. Did his New Age spirituality preclude participating in the Lord's Prayer? Or did he mourn Emmie too deeply to speak? Or was he planning which area of whose body he'd uncover in his next repressed emotions, parts therapy treatment/seduction? His chiseled profile and rugged good looks were even more striking in repose. I tried to sneak by, but the space, between the last row and where he stood in silence, was small. I jostled his reverie. His blueberry eyes flew open, then he gave me a broad smile and a bold wink. The man infuriated me.

I found my bag, propped against the banister at the foot of the staircase going down to the rest rooms. The tote had been turned inside out, its contents spilled over Connelly's slightly worn carpet. And, no surprise, the copies of both the letter and the e-mail were missing. I'd never left the viewing room. Who'd pinched my bag? With all the milling about, hand shaking, lining up to say a prayer at the casket, heading outside for a smoke or downstairs to the rest rooms and lounge—where a mourner can sit and relax for a while in a room without a corpse—it wouldn't have been too difficult for someone to have walked off with my bag. Especially if the murderer were a woman. However, the weather-beaten, old leather bag was sexless. Its austere lines, more like a briefcase than a tote, could just as easily be carried by a man. As I tried to scoop up my belongings, the terror that had subsided to a nagging nervousness sent me reeling. I swayed, then flopped on the bottom step, my scattered possessions at my feet, my violated bag in my lap, listening to Father Doyle's drone, wafting down the stairs, dead certain that Emmie and Barbara's killer was, at this moment, completing the Sorrowful Mysteries. I wondered what book would enjoy fifteen minutes of revisited fame when used as my murder weapon.

. . . . .

Considering the dramatic transformation that most of Jackson Heights had undergone, 87th Street hadn't changed a whole hell of a lot since Mom and I had moved away, twenty-five years ago. Its stately trees and English Tudors brought back warm and fuzzy memories. My mother and Linda Rogers had grown up on this block and, after her parents had moved to Florida, Linda and Mike had raised their family in her childhood home.

Every Christmas Eve, for the past quarter of a century, Mom and I and, often Gypsy Rose, like the Three Wise Men, had traveled east. The Rogers's tree would be decorated with silver and red balls as well as Emmie's and my handmade Christmas cards from first through third grades at St. Joan of Arc, where we would all attend Midnight Mass.

Gypsy Rose had dubbed this past Noel "the dead celebrity Christmas," based on the gifts that all of us necrophile fans-of-the-deceased-rich-and-famous had exchanged. I'd given Emmie yet another commemorative, limited edition Princess Diana plate—all proceeds going to her charities; my mother had given me *The Last Will and Testament of Jacqueline Kennedy Onassis*; Emmie had given her mother the video *Diana* as well as two recent biographies of the princess. Mike, much to my mother's chagrin, had given Linda an audio tape of *The Dark Side of Camelot*, and Gypsy Rose herself had a touch of the ghoul, presenting Emmie and me with the Women Writers calendar. Nary a live one among the twelve calendar girls.

Tonight, I returned to 87th Street for Emmie's wake.

. . . . .

"You didn't tell me you had a copy of Jonathan's letter in your bag." Ben pulled into a No Standing spot on 34th Avenue, around the corner from the Rogers's house. He sounded totally annoyed.

"Jesus, Ben, I'd just had a death threat; I guess it slipped my mind! Last Friday night, I stood Emmie up at Elaine's; tonight, one week later, we're at her wake. So don't you dare raise your voice to me!" I screamed.

"Okay, okay. I'm sorry, Jake." Ben turned the ignition off and took me in his arms. I pressed my cheek against his starched, blue collar, inhaling the aroma of Irish Spring, and wept. Wailed. Ben patted my shoulders and rubbed my back, murmuring, "It's okay; it's okay."

Somehow, we shifted positions and his lips were on my forehead, bestowing small kisses that tickled. I angled my head back, settling myself into his arms; now his lips were on mine. This kiss didn't tickle, it tingled all the way down to my . . . I opened my mouth to protest and his tongue moved in. . . . If this kept up, we'd be making love in the front seat of an unmarked NYPD sedan. I shut my mouth and pulled away.

Linda, Ginger, Too Tall Tom and Jane were on the sun porch, going through the Mass cards that the Connolly staff had stuffed into two large shopping bags, with bold, black letters advertising the funeral home. I joined their sad circle.

"We can all attend this announced mass at St. Pat's," Too Tall Tom was saying. "Of course, it's not till next March 15, at seven o'clock in the morning."

Jane groaned, but Ginger smiled. "No problem. I'll cook up an Ides of March breakfast for all of us after the mass."

"And what would that be? Blood sausage and hemlock on toast?" Modesty had arrived.

Dennis and Mr. Kim were mixing cocktails and

pouring wine. The twin cousins from the Bronx, Dale and Roy, were drinking Manhattans as fast as Dennis could pour them.

None of the Connors crowd had come to the wake. I'd watched them all get into a limo as we left Connolly's. Bill Bernside had said his good-bye, too, saying he'd see me at the funeral in the morning; and he'd be leaving directly from there for Philadelphia. Patrick had passed, hailing a cab and, while he tried to convince the Pakistani driver to take him to Manhattan, Mrs. McMahon convinced Patrick to drop her off in Carnegie Hill.

Gypsy Rose waved me over. "Jake, darling, there was an overwhelming presence of evil at that viewing, and I'm afraid you're in danger. I want to channel my spirit guide, so she can contact Emmie and Barbara's guides. Then we'll try to summon the shades of Emmie and Barbara on my Ouija board, and we need to do it as soon as possible. Maybe after the funeral, tomorrow. You have to be there."

My mother appeared and took Gypsy Rose's arm. "Come help me arrange the fruit platter."

Ben overheard. "Is she the biggest flake in a blizzard?"

"I believe that she believes. Besides, Gypsy Rose has some very successful contacts within the world beyond. Some of her channelings have produced amazing results."

"And some not so?"

"Yeah, well that, too. But when her spirits are hot, you can bank on what they say."

Ben looked skeptical. As a less than born-again believer in Gypsy Rose's psychic prowess, I resented playing the role of her apologist. New Age was old hat as far as I was concerned, but Gypsy Rose had me convinced that sometimes she did chat with the dead.

Modesty, after three red wines, quoted T. S. Eliot: "The most heinous offense a writer can commit is dullness—all the other vices result in lesser offenses."

Jane and Ginger wanted to know if that included murder.

By midnight, most everyone had gone home. Jane, Ginger and Too Tall Tom had departed about a half hour earlier in Modesty's ghostmobile, a 1964 Beetle. Dennis had driven the tipsy twins to the Bronx, then returned to collect my mother, Gypsy Rose and Mr. Kim. Ben and I had stayed and served on the cleanup committee with the three of them. Linda had gone to bed, but Mike and his boys sat nursing beers and reminiscing. I was wiped out and weepy when we all finally left around twelve-thirty.

. . . . .

Ben double-parked and we were on our third kiss when his cellular phone rang.

"Yeah . . . No! . . . When? . . . I'll be right there." He hung up, breathing heavily. And not, I suspected, from my kisses.

"Who was that?"

"Headquarters. Go on up to bed, Jake. Double-lock your doors. I'll call in to get an officer over here. . . ."

"Why? Where are you going?"

"Sutton Place. To Kate Lloyd Connors. Jonathan's been murdered."

Twenty-two

After Ben had dropped me off, I couldn't sleep, pacing and sipping decaf tea, until he finally called at two-thirty in the morning.

"Wide awake?"

"Ben! Jesus! What happened over there?"

"Just the facts, ma'am. I don't have much time. The nuances will have to wait. But Jonathan did die by the book."

"An attempt at gallows humor?"

"Sorry, chalk that up to exhaustion. . . . Jonathan died from a skillfully aimed blow to the base of his neck."

"Which book was the weapon?"

"A brass-and-leather-bound volume, a folio edition of *The Picture of Dorian Gray*. And the killer used the solid brass spine of the book for a heavier hit."

"Base of the neck. Similar to the way Emmie died?'

"Yes. Hit from the rear, presumably by someone he knew and trusted. He'd been leaning over his desk, apparently reading or working on something . . . but that something disappeared, no doubt removed by the murderer. And, Jake, it turns out that Jonathan had been a ghost, too. That's how he started with Kate; we found an old contract in his desk drawer.''

''Who discovered the body?''

''Caroline. Says she heard a noise—like, maybe, the front door closing—she's not sure, but anyway, she got up to investigate, saw the door to Jonathan's office was open, his light was still on, and she decided to check it out. She went berserk when she found the body. The family doctor has her sedated.''

''Will she be okay?''

''Was she ever? I don't know, Jake.''

A kaleidoscope of Caroline careened through my mind. Caroline—arms wrapped around Patrick—her hands on his butt. Caroline—little girl lost—relating her orphanage days. Caroline—praying without any haitches—at Emmie's wake.

''Listen, Jake, I've got to go; I'll talk to you in the morning.''

''It is morning.''

''Right. Try to get some sleep. I'll call you before the funeral.''

Our conversation had been about as sleep inducing as a double espresso.

. . . . .

Ben didn't make it to Emmie's funeral. And as I stood in the steady, fine rain falling on her grave site at Calvary, I missed him. Mom, Gypsy Rose and I huddled under the big, black umbrella that the funeral director had handed to Gypsy Rose as we left St. Joan of Arc after the Requiem Mass. Her Armani silk ensemble, which included a black turban, had elicited an unctuous, ''Madam, we must protect that lovely outfit from nasty Mother Nature.'' Many of the other mourners, not provided with Connolly's complimentary umbrellas, were getting wet and growing weary, as Father Doyle droned through the Twenty-third Psalm. Of course, one of the funeral parlor's pallbearers had the good padre's bald pate well covered.

The Rogers's family plot was in old Calvary, a section filled with tombstones dating back to the early 1800s. Cherubs atop crypts and massive mausoleums complete with pictures of their occupants surrounded us and, with startling statues of androgynous angels seen through the morning mist, provided a gothic—and somewhat scary—setting for the funeral. Queens as *Wuthering Heights*.

The group at graveside was considerably smaller than last night's crowd at Connolly's or the congregation gathered earlier today for the Mass at St. Joan of Arc's. Dale and Roy Rogers had brought their own umbrella—red and yellow stripes—more Rockaway Beach than Calvary Cemetery—and stood with their mother, Aunt Veronica, next to Linda, Mike and their three sons. Emmie's parents had put up a good front so far this morning, but the last—and worst—part of the service was yet to come.

Our Ghostwriters Anonymous members had turned out in force, filling several pews at church, and all of them continued on to the cemetery. Across the grave from me, squeezed under one umbrella, Jane and Modesty had linked arms, while Ginger held tightly to Jane's other arm. Their truce still intact. Ginger lacked spice today, appearing wan, wilted and silent. Modesty, too, appeared somewhat more austere and miserable than usual, glowering at anyone who approached her. Her black shroud and high-top sneakers didn't help. Jane's serenity had vanished, and semihysteria—manifested in bouts of uncontrolled sobbing—had taken its place. Only Too Tall Tom, standing alone, seemed to be himself.

Naturally, Kate, Caroline and Mrs. Madison were among the missing. Nor had they been at church. Sutton Place would be under siege. Police, the coroner's team, hundreds of media—print and television—and the curious. Bill Bernside, probably grief stricken as well as a possible suspect, had not attended the funeral and, no doubt, wouldn't be leaving for Philadelphia today, either.

Patrick Hemmings, however, had been present at the Mass and now, at the burial, stood in front of a statue of Saint Michael the Archangel. I avoided eye contact with him. Ivan and my mother had competed for most-candles-lighted award before this morning's Mass started. As the funeral director offered a rose to each mourner, Ivan fell to his knees alongside the casket. Dennis, Mr. Kim and Mrs. McMahon, who'd attached herself to them, were among the many mourners who probably would have preferred an umbrella.

I asked myself: When Dennis had dropped the twins off last night, could he have detoured from the Bronx, over the Third Avenue Bridge into Manhattan, and bashed in Jonathan's head before heading back over the Triborough Bridge to pick up Mom, Gypsy Rose and Mr. Kim in Jackson Heights? God! Next, I'd be accusing Gypsy Rose of multiple murders.

The damp grass, mixed with dirt from the mound piled by the freshly dug grave, stained my shoes as I flung my rose onto Emmie's decending casket. The damn shoes still hurt. I decided to toss them, along with the DKNY dress, into the garbage when this day ended.

. . . . .

Mike Rogers dropped a handful of dirt over his daughter's casket, then Father Doyle sprinkled holy water and waved the incense over Emmie's remains, one last time, and we all turned away from the grave. Except Ivan. He said, "I vill stay vit my beloved Emmie a little more. This is our last date." Then he sat on the mound of dirt, defying the gravediggers, as if he were a student protesting police brutality.

We left him to his vigil. Everyone was far too drained to attempt to reason with him. Too Tall Tom said, "Maybe he'll jump in."

"We should only be so fortunate," Modesty said.

I wanted to go home. I'd had enough of death to last me a lifetime. Dennis offered to drive Mom, Gypsy Rose and me back to Carnegie Hill, and we said our good-byes to the Rogers.

"I'll never hear Emmie laugh again, Jake. Her loopy giggle used to drive her father crazy. That's what I'll miss the most." Linda held a rapidly wilting rose in one hand as she grabbed hold of me with the other. I couldn't think of a thing to say. "Remember, Mike, how you'd bounce Em on your knee, and she'd giggle, giddy with . . ." Linda gulped, then buried her head in Mike's jacket; the rose slipped through her fingers and fell to the ground.

My mother wrapped an arm around my waist and, as we walked away from Emmie's grave, the sun burst through the clouds: bright, glaring and intrusive.

"Jake!" Timmy Rogers, Emmie's youngest brother, called to me.

"Go ahead, Mom, catch up with Gypsy Rose and Mr. Kim; I'll be right there."

Timmy stepped away from a small group that included his two brothers and the Bronx cousins and led me to a quiet spot in front of an old mausoleum gaudily decorated with red, white and blue plastic flowers in Styrofoam vases. No doubt left there by the deceased's loved ones during a Memorial Day visit.

"My mom told you about her conversation with Emmie that last afternoon before . . . !"

"Yes. Your mother said Emmie had stumbled on some scary stuff at Kate Lloyd Connors's place and whatever she'd discovered had freaked her out."

"Right. I'd answered that phone call last Friday, and before Emmie spoke to Mom, she asked me a strange question."

"What?"

"Well, you know I plan to be a lawyer." Timmy, in his senior year at Columbia, was viewed by the rest of his family as a nerd. His older brothers, both jocks, scoffed at his double majors of political science and art history. "Emmie asked how she could find out who the officers of a corporation were."

"Did she say why she was asking?"

"Not really. She only said, 'Doesn't Aubergine strike you as a strange name for a corporation?' Then she mumbled something about things are seldom what they seem, and asked me to put Mom on."

"Think, Timmy, did she say anything else?"

"No. And I didn't make too much of it at the time. Emmie was always asking weird stuff like that, researching for a book or whatever, but maybe this 'Aubergine' is connected somehow to whatever she'd found out at Kate Lloyd Connors's place. Anyway, I thought you should know."

"You may be on to something, Timmy." As I kissed him, then dashed toward Dennis's car, an itch—vague and unformed—took hold in my subconscious and wouldn't let go.

. . . . .

The sun warmed us and, asking the ladies' permission, as we all settled into the cream convertible,

Dennis put the top down for our drive across the 59th Street Bridge. Mom, Gypsy Rose and I had climbed into the back, while Mrs. McMahon, who'd wangled a ride— sat, somewhat scrunched, between Dennis and Mr. Kim in the front seat.

Jonathan's murder had provided us with a common denominator for lively conversation.

"Reminds me of Ted Bundy," Mrs. McMahon said, "except this guy's bumped off three people in one week."

My mother squeezed my hand—the one with the burn on the pinkie—so hard that we both heard the crunch and she released her death grip. Mr. Kim, hampered by his seat belt, rescued today's *Post* from its resting place under the front seat and handed it to me. The headline screamed: SERIAL KILLER STRIKES AGAIN.

There were large photos of Jonathan and Kate in her Sutton Place mansion and smaller photos of Emmie and Barbara. The copy under Jonathan's picture read Murder By The Book. Jesus, the *Post*'s writer had used the same sick—and unoriginal—humor as Ben had. Would this be the byline for the duration of the case? The copy under Kate's picture identified her as the most famous mystery writer in America and Jonathan's employer.

Mr. Kim said, "Seems like the paper has accused Kate Lloyd Connors right on its front page."

"Yes," my mother said, "but in most murder mysteries, the obvious suspect is never the one who done it." Then she resumed her terminal grip on my hand.

Gypsy Rose said, "That may be; however, I hope you're giving up that editing job with that woman, Jake. Ever since Maura told me that you were working at Sutton Place, I've had bad vibes about Kate's house and all of its occupants."

"You're working for Kate Lloyd Connors?" Mrs.

McMahon smacked her forehead into Mr. Kim's chin as she tried to swing her black-bonneted head in my direction.

I glared from my mother to Gypsy Rose, the two blabbermouths. But they both ignored me, and Gypsy Rose rambled on, "A spirit—Emmie's, I do believe—is trying to communicate with me."

Dennis veered sharply to avoid a Ford Explorer's attack on the Roll's rear end. He grunted, as if in pain.

Mr. Kim said, "I'd love to talk to Emmie again."

"Stop by the tearoom around four-thirty this afternoon," Gypsy Rose said. "We'll contact my spirit guide and see what she can arrange."

My mother asked, "Via the Ouija board?"

"Oh, I'd love to come!" Mrs. McMahon squealed.

Dennis said nothing. But, like me, I'd bet he wouldn't miss it for the world. Not this one or the world beyond.

Twenty-three

I woke up screaming. A large blob of deep purple had morphed into a giant eggplant, chased me across Calvary Cemetery, then shoved me into a patriotically bedecked mausoleum. Exhausted, I'd dozed on the couch, falling into a fitful sleep, dreaming not of visions of sugarplums, but of an attack by dinosaur-sized eggplants.

Mom had served a late lunch of Campbell's Chicken Noodle Soup, rye bread and chocolate pudding. An Irish gourmand. I loved it but hoped that Aaron Rubin knew her culinary limitations. At Gypsy Rose's request, I'd called Ginger, Jane, Modesty and Too Tall Tom, knowing they wouldn't want to miss an opportunity to commune with the spirits of our dead ghosts. Modesty's ghostmobile had made better time than Dennis's Rolls. All four were at home and would be delighted to attend the séance. Then both Mom and I had napped, trying to recoup, before our séance at four-thirty and Mom's dinner date with Aaron at seven. I hadn't heard from his son since my early morning phone call.

. . . . .

Splashing cold water on my sleep-deprived skin, I heard a buzzer blare through my brain, interfering with a hazy piece of fuzz free-floating there. Why couldn't I download that memory fragment? Whatever it might be?

"Jake! Please answer the intercom!" My mother called from her bathtub where she was soaking.

Ben Rubin had been up all night and looked it. I kissed his bleary eyes, then reprised Mom's lunch menu. Ben finished the entire loaf of rye and two puddings.

"Did you spot your tail?"

"No. Damn it, Ben. I told you I didn't want police protection! Who was it?"

"An off-duty cop in a Ford Explorer."

"Oh. He almost rammed Dennis's Rolls's rear. Following orders?"

Ben grinned. "No, but accidents happen."

As annoyed as I was at Ben for assigning someone to watch over me, another part of me was grateful. Maybe there was something to this parts therapy. I poured two cups of tea and checked my watch. Two-forty-five.

"Do you want to come to Gypsy Rose's channeling session?"

"Take notes. I just wanted to fill you in before I go home and pass out."

"So, tell me!"

"Jonathan left Connolly's at nine, right?"

"Right. With Kate, Caroline and Mrs. Madison, in a limo."

"And the 911 call was logged in at twelve-fifty-seven A.M. The first cop, cruising by in a parol car, arrived at Kate's at five minutes after one. I've been filling in the whereabouts—a timeline, if you will—of our merry little band of potential book bashers—from nine P.M. to one A.M.''

''Where did Bill go after he left the viewing?''

''To Bemelman's Bar in the Carlyle for a farewell-to-Manhattan, dry martini—two, in fact. Then he went up to his room alone, around ten, and ordered room service.''

''Witnesses?''

''The bartender confirmed that Bernside had left around ten; and the room service waiter served Mr. Bernside a turkey sandwich, decaf coffee and a hot fudge sundae at eleven o'clock. That's not to say Philadelphia Bill couldn't have left his suite a little later and strolled over to Sutton Place.''

''Well, there you go. One motive. One opportunity.''

''Jake, do you have any more pudding?''

I pulled the last pudding out of the refrigerator and opened a box of Social Teas. Poor man, if he wanted to hang around with me, he'd have to appreciate kiddy fare.

''Kate, Caroline, Vera Madison and Jonathan had a large pepperoni pizza delivered at ten-fifteen.''

''No way! Just like real people?''

''Yes. Kate 'withdrew' . . . her word . . .''

''Pretty fancy for a pizza-eating person.''

''. . . to her bedroom at about ten-forty-five. Claims she was sound asleep by eleven o'clock and only awakened when she heard Caroline's frantic screams.''

''What about the Dragon Lady?''

''Mrs. Madison says she watched AMC— *Rebecca* . . .''

''Get out of here!''

''That's what she said—and it was playing—till midnight, then went to sleep. Kate had to bang at her door. Mrs. Madison, lost in the arms of Morpheus, never heard Caroline's screams.''

''And Caroline? What's her story?''

"She'd gone for a long walk after Kate and Vera had gone to their bedrooms; and Jonathan had gone to his office to catch up on some work. Got back at midnight or a little later. Says Jonathan's office door was shut then. In this murder, Caroline used the book alibi—*Oliver Twist*—what else? Read, then fell sleep, but thinks it wasn't too long before a noise awakened her."

"The front door closing?"

"That's her story. She told it dramatically, through bouts of tears, screeching like a banshee, gasping for breath and complete loss of control."

"How she is now?"

"She's been sleeping on and off for most of the day. In addition to the family doctor, Patrick Hemmings showed up, again, this afternoon to hold her hand."

"Again? Where did Patrick spend the hours after leaving the funeral parlor and before one in the morning?"

"Well, he dropped Mrs. McMahon at her door in Carnegie Hill, then continued downtown in the cab. He dined in a health food restaurant in Chelsea and walked over to Murray Hill, arriving home about ten-forty-five. Says he updated his files, then practiced yoga and meditation exercise, opening his mind and heart to receive messages from any souls he has known in this or other lifetimes."

"Oh, come on!"

"Could I make this crap up?"

"Then what?"

"Patrick received a call from Caroline and raced up to Sutton Place. But, get this, his phone records show Caroline's call to him came at twelve-fifty-two. The 911 call was logged in at twelve-fifty-seven."

"Why am I not surprised? I wonder what they chatted about before Caroline called the police."

"And I wonder if Hemmings the hypnotist had paid Jonathan an earlier visit, say between eleven-fifteen and twelve-fifteen? There would have been plenty of time for him to make it back down to Murray Hill to receive Caroline's frantic phone call."

"But if Caroline heard the front door close at twelve forty-five or so . . . ?"

"Jake, 'if' is the biggest little word in the English language."

My mother, freshly emerged from her bath and swathed in her chenille robe, but wearing full makeup— Mom's baths were influenced by old Betty Grable movies—waltzed into the kitchen. "Jake, did you offer Ben some vanilla ice cream?"

Ben accepted a large bowl and, to my total amazement, my mother left us alone, going to get dressed for the séance.

"She'll be back. And I don't want to talk about this in front of her. Ben, I'm sure that Jonathan's dead because someone at Emmie's wake took that letter from my bag. It's eerie. Knowing that we know a serial killer but not knowing who it is."

"Who might have known that letter was in your bag?"

"Jesus! Well, Kate, Mrs. Madison and, possibly, Caroline could have seen the envelope from the *National Enquirer* on Jonathan's desk and suspected that I'd copied it. And remember that Vera Madison almost caught me red-handed."

"Or the killer, fearing what you'd discovered, might have rifled through your bag on a fishing trip."

"Either way, that letter was Jonathan's death sentence. And Kate seems to have the best—or, at least, the clearest—motive. Though I firmly believe that Vera Madison would kill on Kate's behalf."

"The police report from Honey Bucket is inconclusive at best. The Hansen daughter did disappear the same day the father had drowned, but while it looked suspicious, she was never an official suspect. The cause of death remained a question, but no arrest warrant was ever issued for Sarah Anne Hansen."

"So if Kate had been blackmailed, the blackmailer, and her probable killer, had unearthed some further proof of her involvement . . . unless . . ."

"Jake, if you don't hurry up and change, we'll be late for Gypsy Rose's séance." My mother, in a soft gray linen blouse and matching linen trousers, stood in the kitchen door, dressed and ready to go. "We don't want to keep the ghosts waiting."

Twenty-four

According to Gypsy Rose, the afterlife is a blast. "Being dead is divine, dear!" She believes our spirits may not reside in a traditional heaven; however, she's certain that in the world beyond our dreams come true. We, who have served hard time here on earth, are rewarded when we become one with the universe.

I once asked Gypsy Rose how she conversed with the dead, "Do you hear voices? Does the spirit speak directly to you? A real conversation?"

"It's telepathy of a sort, Jake. During a channeling, I go into a kind of trance, and the soul's thoughts will leap into my spirit guide's mind. Then the guide borrows my body and my voice. I'm the medium, but the message comes from the spirit via my guide."

Beats MCI's best rates. "Can anyone do this?"

"We all have a sixth sense, Jake; everyone has experienced déjà vu. Walking down a block or into a room, *knowing* that we've been there before, then asking ourselves if those memories came from a previous lifetime."

"Could I contact my father?"

Cynic that I was, I also knew that some of Gypsy Rose's encounters with the dead and many of her accurate psychic predictions had been awesome.

"Try to talk to him in a dream state. Ask about when and how he passed. Did you know that the last memory of an earth life is the first memory of a newly arrived spirit in the world beyond?"

I definitely didn't, but took Gypsy Rose at her word. I still haven't reached my father either by thought transference or any other method of communication, not awake nor in a dream. It's crossed my mind to ask Gypsy Rose to contact her spirit guide, but I guess skepticism has overruled curiosity. So, today would be my first official séance.

My mother is acquainted with one of Gypsy Rose's spirit guides—Zelda Fitzgerald—and Mom has received word, indirectly, from Dad. He's taking dancing lessons from Fred Astaire. My mother had always been after my father to brush up his fox-trot. I guess he's getting ready to waltz her around the big ballroom in the sky when she arrives. I'd teased and taunted her when she'd breathlessly shared this revelation with me, so now my mother will not discuss my father's spirit's news bulletins with me.

However, I've noticed Mom's in no hurry to leave this incarnation to whirl around heaven all day. Indeed, she's doing everything humanly possible to hang in here, keeping her current body—host to her immortal soul— in great shape.

"How can you be such a good Catholic and still believe in reincarnation?" I'd asked.

"Religion and spirituality are not mutually exclusive, Jake. I only have one soul; it's just been recycled through several lifetimes. Eventually, my spirit will wind up in heaven . . . with all the saints . . . and your father!''

Hell would never be an option for my mother.

. . . . .

Ginger, Modesty and Too Tall Tom had arrived before us. Saturdays usually brought bustling business to the tearoom/bookstore. But Gypsy Rose had closed up shop for Emmie's funeral. Two tables were pushed together, a Ouija board strategically placed in their combined center. Several scented candles of varied heights and shapes were on the table and scattered about the store.

Modesty said, ''Jane's running late, but she'll be here.''

Mrs. McMahon, still dressed in her funeral attire, including the black bonnet circa the Civil War, helped Gypsy Rose pour tea, making no effort to hide her excitement.

''Milk, Jake? How about you, Maura? Isn't this thrilling? Why, I've never even had my tea leaves read! Of course, we're breaking one of the ten commandments—you know—the one: Thou shall not put strange gods before me. It's probably a mortal sin; I'll just stop at Confession at St. Thomas More's before I go home. Father will be there till six.''

''Let's hope you don't get killed by a car on your way to church, Mrs. McMahon. Remember, the road to hell is paved with intended Confessions,'' I said.

''Well, if I do go there, Jake O'Hara, you'll be right there with me.'' But Mrs. McMahon didn't sound annoyed. The idea of sin seem to stimulate her.

Dennis, seated next to his father, checked his watch. ''How long do you think this will take, Jake?''

"Well, you know how it is with the dead, Dennis, they have all eternity."

Mr. Kim chuckled. "Dennis is always in a hurry, but I don't think he'll leave before the show's over."

Gypsy Rose had changed from her Armani black to a bright tomato-red caftan and had placed an Egyptian gold amulet around her neck. She motioned me over to a quiet corner of the book section. "Jake, the energy filling this room is so powerful that even though Zelda should be able to handle any evil spirits, I don't know what to expect. Please sit between your mother and me, I want you to be surrounded by love."

I gave her a squeeze. "It's your séance, Gypsy Rose, you're in charge of place settings. I'll sit wherever you say."

Modesty moaned, "Oh, no!" Both Gypsy Rose and I turned to see what was wrong. Jane had arrived with Patrick Hemmings in tow. No doubt Patrick would be delivering a few messages of his own: reporting all the news straight from the world beyond to Kate Lloyd Connors in Sutton Place.

Ginger, standing across the table from me, said, "Wouldn't it be amazing if the spirits could tell us who done it!"

Jane caressed the Ouija board. "Shouldn't we pull the curtains and turn out the lights?"

"You want to do this in the dark?" Mrs. McMahon shrieked.

Gypsy Rose came across silky and soothing. "Please leave the lights on. Light speeds up energy. And please relax; this room is filled with tension. My spirit guide will prevent any evil spirits from crashing our channeling. We all want to reach Emmie, and I'm sure none of us has anything to fear from her."

Modesty, sounding like Mike Wallace interviewing a

television call-in psychic, asked, "Just what's going to happen during this channeling? How does this work? And how can you be sure that these spirits will talk?"

"Put your left brain on the back burner," my mother said before Gypsy Rose could answer. "The world beyond believes we all drag our left brains around with us, impeding our spiritual growth. I urge you to keep an open mind. Go with the right side of your brain."

Jesus, was my mother a closet New Ager?

"Okay," Gypsy Rose said, "here's how it works. I'm going to close my eyes, enter a trance, and channel my spirit guide. Once I reach her, she'll take over my body and speak to you in my voice. But I'll be gone—that is—I won't know or remember what happens while my guide talks to you and attempts to reach Emmie."

"You won't remember?" Ginger asked.

"All of you can fill me in."

"So, should we join hands and close our eyes?" Modesty, a stickler for details, wanted to know.

"No," Gypsy Rose said. "The spirits like it lively. Talk to each other and, when my guide arrives, treat her as you'd treat me. Ask her anything. She's your conduit to Emmie's guide and to Emmie herself in the world beyond."

"Who exactly is your guide, Gypsy Rose?" Dennis sounded jaded. "Just who will we be chatting with, while you're off only God knows where?"

He did not faze Gypsy Rose in the least. "I have three guides at the moment. The one who's most likely to show up this afternoon is Zelda Fitzgerald."

"For God's sake, who are your other guides?" Ginger asked. "Mata Hari and Mother Teresa?"

"You can ask to speak to Gray Feather, an Apache brave, who once scalped three hundred Union soldiers, and is now a Master, or to Lady Eleanor."

Patrick spoke up for the first time, "Who's Lady Eleanor?"

"A lady-in-waiting to Catherine Howard . . ."

My mother jumped in, "Henry the VIII's fifth wife. You know, he had her beheaded—his wife that is—not Lady Eleanor."

I hadn't been aware that my mother knew Gypsy Rose's other guides or—for that matter—that she had two other guides. All this fascinated me and, looking round the room, reading the faces . . . their expressions ranging from amusement to amazement . . . they all seemed as intrigued as I was.

"What's a Master?" Modesty asked, surprising me. I knew she'd attended several New Age retreats.

"A teacher in the spirit world," Jane, who'd covered New Age wisdom in her how-to books, answered. "Didn't you read *Many Lives, Many Masters*?"

"I write; I don't read," Modesty said. "The truth is that I don't have time to read nonfiction." With her gothic novel-in-progress, by today's count at 1,500-plus pages, I believed her.

"Not a charwoman among them," Ginger said. "I guess with our spirit guides as with our previous incarnations, only interesting lives need apply."

"That's not true." Jane banged the table and a candle, perching precariously between her table and the one abutting it, almost fell through the crack. "Patrick suffered as a leper in one previous incarnation . . . isn't that right, Patrick?"

"We're here to channel Gypsy Rose's guide and, hopefully, one of Emmie's. Barbara may put in a word. My past lives are not the issue." Patrick sounded pragmatic and professional. The way Jane used to sound before she'd become so enamored of Patrick's parts therapy.

Dennis glanced at his watch, again, and said, "I suggest we get started."

Mrs. McMahon, making the sign of the cross, said, "Hell, yes."

Gypsy Rose folded her hands in front of her—I focused on her well-manicured fingernails, the exact shade of her caftan. Next, she lowered her head and closed her eyes. Then, although I didn't know it, Gypsy Rose turned her body over to Zelda Fitzgerald.

The ghosts, Dennis, Mr. Kim, Patrick, Mrs. McMahon and my mother talked to, and over, each other. Continuous chatter. Nervous and noisy. "Look!" Modesty shouted. "Gypsy Rose's dropped her jaw."

I became a convert. Gypsy Rose's carriage was always picture perfect. If she were still in her body, her chin would never fall to her chest. With an open mouth, yet! Suddenly, her head raised; her eyes, wide-open, sparkled, and an impish grin seemed to lift her features.

"Gypsy Rose?" Ginger asked.

"This is Zelda. Did someone wish to speak to me?"

The group, dumbstruck, stared at her. Gypsy Rose's voice had taken on a youthful, flirtatious quality, with just a hint of southern accent. "Well, ladies and gentleman, I'm waiting."

"Zelda . . ." I sounded tinny, like an old phonograph record.

"Yes," Zelda said, her voice clear as a bell. "I've come at Gypsy Rose's request, and I'm delighted to act as your liaison with the spirit world, but I do have a date with the Murphys, so can we please begin?"

"We're trying to reach Emmie. Can you help us, Zelda?"

"Who's this Zelda, anyway?" Mrs. McMahon asked. "Gypsy Rose didn't go away, she's still here."

"No, Ma'am. I assure you, Gypsy Rose Liebowitz is gone. Zelda Fitzgerald is in residence." A spirited answer from Zelda, but delivered with great charm.

Dennis asked, "How's Scott?"

"Working on a comeback."

"A new book?" Ginger asked.

"A new incarnation. Now could we please discuss whose spirit you all want to reach?"

"Emmie Rogers," I said. "A ghost. She was murdered here in New York, a week ago, yesterday. Hit over the head with *Crime and Punishment*."

"We prefer 'spirit' to 'ghost' in the world beyond, Jake."

"No. No. Emmie was a ghostwriter. You know, she'd write the book, but someone else's name would appear on the cover as author."

"Not for Fyodor. He worked alone. Frankly, he's as deadly as his body of work." Zelda winked at me.

"I love Dostoevsky," Modesty said.

Zelda ignored Modesty and asked, "Now, please, where and when was Emmie born?"

"Jackson Heights, Queens. Thirty-three years ago."

"Did you know East Egg was really Great Neck? Long Island, but bordering Queens."

I said, "Yeah. Well, Queens has changed a lot since *The Great Gatsby*."

Zelda raised Gypsy Rose's arms over her head, as if reaching for the sky. "Emmie, is that what you called her?"

"Yes!" A chorus of voices answered Zelda.

"Well, Emmie's guide is here. I'm turning Gypsy Rose's body over to her. Good luck to you all. I have to skiddoo now."

In a split second, the sparkle left Gypsy Rose's eyes

and her body stiffened. "I am Emmie's spirit guide. How may I assist you?" The voice sounded starchy, low-pitched and British. "Please forgive me, I have not introduced myself. My name is Emily Brontë."

Twenty-five

Emily Bronte's guest appearance turned the séance into chaos and its participants into literary groupies. The ghosts behaved like crazed Grateful Dead fans, stepping all over each other's lines, trying to chat up Miss Brontë.

"Jesus Christ!" Modesty shouted.

"No. He's my spirit guide," Dennis said.

"Shut up!" I said to Dennis—then to Emily Brontë, "Thank you for coming. My name is Jake O'Hara."

"I am not familiar with the name, Jake. But American spirits are so sprightly, Miss O'Hara, it is a pleasure to meet a live one."

"Have you met our friend, Emmie Rogers—er—that is her spirit—since she passed over?"

"Indeed, she's right here beside me, aren't you, Emmie?"

Ginger let out a loud gasp, followed by Mrs. McMahon's, "Holy Mother of God, protect us!"

Modesty persisted, "Miss Brontë, can you take a moment or two to discuss Cathy's deathbed scene in relation to the wind howling on the moors?"

"Modesty, put a lid on it, and let Jake do the talking."
Jane was furious. "This isn't English Lit 101."

Ignoring Modesty, I asked, "Miss Brontë, will Emmie
talk to us?"

"Miss Rogers is such a recent arrival that she is somewhat disoriented. If you will permit me, I shall speak
for her as her thoughts flow through me."

Dennis said, "Well, I have a few questions for Emmie."

"Sir, I would prefer to address Miss O'Hara. And that
is Miss Rogers's request as well."

"Dennis, Miss Brontë's not in the witness chair." His
father scolded him as I gave Dennis a dirty look and
resumed my conversation with our dead author.

"How do we begin, Miss Brontë?"

"You have a Ouija board on the table. Miss Emily
Rogers would be comfortable with you and your mother,
Mrs. O'Hara, using the planchette to reveal the truth."

Jane clutched Patrick's arm; he caught my glance and,
with his other hand, gave me a thumbs up. Why did I
allow that man to grate me?

"We are ready, Miss O'Hara. You may ask your
question," Miss Brontë said.

My mother placed a shaky hand on the planchette, a
small wooden, pointed platform on casters, and gave me
a weak smile. I put my hand across from hers, my faith
in God, and posed my question. "Please know that we
miss you and we love you. We want to know, who killed
you, Emmie?"

The planchette took on a life of its own, spinning
crazily about the board, completely out of our conrol,
and stopping, after a final bumpy bounce, on the letter
W.

Miss Brontë spoke. "That initial is the answer. The
murderer's name begins with W."

God help us! There wasn't a suspect in the bunch whose name began with W.

"Are you sure, Miss Brontë?"

"It is not I who must be sure, Miss O'Hara," the spirit chided me. "The message comes from Miss Rogers. And she is certain."

"What else can she tell us?" I could hear the desperation in my voice.

"Miss O'Hara, the word 'aubergine' comes into my mind. I am not familiar with this word. Do you understand its meaning?"

The group muttered and mumbled among themselves. I never took my eyes off Gypsy Rose's features, which now reflected Emily Brontë's tense puzzlement. I didn't understand the significance of "aubergine" either, but I did understand that Emmie had sent me a message.

"Can Emmie explain more fully?" I asked.

"Skim milk masquerades as cream." Emily Bronte recited the words as Gilbert had written them to be said. "Do you understand, Miss O'Hara?"

"Emmie sent that quote to me in an e-mail last week." I wiped the tears from my cheek.

"I will have to inquire of Miss Rogers what an e-mail might be. But, for now, good day to you, Miss O'Hara. Miss Rogers and I must take our leave. Oh, my dear, here's a final thought: Be careful, Miss O'Hara, you are in grave danger."

"Wait! Don't go. . . ." But I knew my plea fell on Gypsy Rose's ears. She'd come back and the two Emilys were history.

. . . . .

My possible dire fate brought the séance to a dead end. When Gypsy Rose was herself again and heard what had happened while she'd been otherwise engaged, she made a judgment call: all channels were off. Barbara's spirit would not be appearing today, and everyone should go home. The show was over. But the ghosts and the rest of the guests proved hard to get rid of.

"Could we somehow be part of a mass hypnosis? Did we all just imagine this happened?" Jane asked.

Modesty, visibly shaken, said, "Ask your friend, Patrick. He's the expert."

"I don't know what to make of all this," Patrick said. "But I do suggest that you be on guard, Jake. Everywhere and with everyone."

"This is as big a mystery as the murders. I can't believe what I've heard." Ginger kissed me, then added, "Take care, Jake."

Mrs. McMahon dashed off, without a good-bye, presumably en route to St. Thomas More's to save her soul. Dennis seemed contemplative. As he and Mr. Kim started to leave, Dennis turned and walked back to where I stood, still holding the planchette in my hand.

"I need to check something out on Monday—before, if I can—then I'll call you."

"What's going on, Dennis?"

"This mumbo jumbo is all a big joke to me. I came for the laughs . . . now I'm intrigued." Dennis shrugged, "Listen, Jake, don't take any chances."

I touched his hand. "Maybe you should be careful, too."

"Maybe."

After they'd all left, Gypsy Rose said to my mother and me, "The next time it will be just the three of us and the spirits. And Jake, I want to warn you."

"What about?"

"While I was in my deep meditative state, I sensed that you could be the killer's next victim. And, there's something else—something to do with Jackie Kennedy."

Neither my mother nor Gypsy Rose had acknowledged Onassis. "Oh, come on!" I said.

"It's not all clear, Jake, but you must be very vigilant."

Then I had to listen as Mom and Gypsy Rose spent a full fifteen minutes on how frantic they were about my safety, suggesting various, sometimes bizarre, methods to protect me.

. . . . .

Mom's nerves hadn't improved any when we arrived home. "Jake, I'm canceling my date with Aaron—or you can come with us—you're not staying home alone, tonight."

"Look, Mom, I didn't want to tell you this before, because I knew it would upset you, but Ben's assigned someone to protect me."

"A policeman."

"Yes. So stop worrying. I'll be fine."

"Well, are you staying in? Double-lock the door when I leave."

"I think I'll give Too Tall Tom a call. If he's going to be at home tonight, I'll go down there for a while."

"Take a taxi. Call the livery service and have a driver pick you up here."

My mother felt guilty about leaving me, but I wanted her out of the house and out of my hair.

"Okay. Okay. Now go change or you'll be late for your date."

"Is it a date, Jake? Would your father like me to date? I think of it as having dinner with a new friend."

"If he's paying, it's a date. And if you're worried about Dad, have Gypsy Rose ask Zelda Fitzgerald to get his approval."

"You know, Jake, I think that's just what I'll do."
She went off to get dressed and I called Too Tall Tom.

The Carnegie Hill Livery Service had no driver
available. "It's Saturday night, madam. All our cars are
booked."

. . . . .

I walked alone over to Fifth Avenue to grab a
downtown bus, breaking my promise to Mom and
wondering if my unknown guardian was on my tail.
Inhaling the June evening's fresh air, smelling the still-
damp patches of grass in front of the brownstones, and
bird watching, "sparrows swift with a whirling of
wings" came to mind. Nothing like a morning and
afternoon with the dead to make you feel alive.
However, a caveat—fear—colored my mood. Like an
old man whistling as he passed the cemetery, my joie
de vivre seemed forced.

The Avenue's parade of people rivaled Easter Sunday.
The crowds, lining the sidewalk, waiting for a downtown
bus convinced me to walk a few blocks. Near Central
Park's 85th Street transverse, I joined a large group of
would-be passengers. A bus pulled in, filled up, and
departed, leaving twelve or fifteen of us behind to wait
for the next bus. The cars and cabs whipped by. I felt
two firm hands on my back, then I was pushed, headfirst,
into the traffic. A taxi barreled down on me, hitting me
on my thigh and spinning me around in the middle of
the onrushing Fifth Avenue traffic. Tumbling, I slammed
my elbow and forearm against the cab's bumper and
then hit the ground. The last thing I saw before I lost
consciousness was an address on a green canopy—
1040—the apartment house where Jackie Kennedy had
lived and died.

Twenty-six

I'd like to say I had a near-death experience that would provide fabulous fodder for future cocktail parties, but the truth is—I hadn't even realized I'd been hurt. Of course, I did come to in the emergency room of Mount Sinai Hospital with three nurses and two residents hovering over me, hooked up to a machine monitoring my vitals, and sporting a tube in my left arm.

"Is she going to be okay?"

Ben's voice sounded far away. "Ben?" My own voice was a hoarse whisper. I felt a gentle touch on my arm.

"Right here, Jake."

"What?" I asked, then drifted away.

. . . . .

When I next opened my eyes, I raised my wrist. Even that small motion hurt. The clock on the wall in front of me read nine-thirty. Could it still be Saturday evening? The cubicle, partitioned with white sheets—or drapes of some sort—was still well staffed. A cute, freckle-faced nurse who looked like a high school senior said, "Feeling better?"

Better than what? My head hurt worse than any too-much-red-wine hangover I'd ever endured, and my body ached from stem to stem. "Am I okay?"

"You're doing great, kid." Ben's smiling face appeared from behind a resident, who reminded me of television's Dr. Quinn. Where was the real medical staff?

I tried to smile back, but my jaw throbbed. "What's the damage?"

"Do you remember what happened?" This doctor sounded as if she really cared.

"A cab sent me flying. I came down in front of Jackie's O's building. Well, her former . . ."

"Good. That's right." Ben made it sound like I'd just split the atom. "Your head hit the ground, hard. We were concerned . . ."

"I guess I have a thick skull."

The doctor said, "Well, you're bruised—your entire body—and you have some nasty abrasions on your hands and knees. And your left thigh will be painful for a while. All in all, not too bad, though. You lessened the damage by landing on your hands after you'd been bounced around by the car's impact."

"My head hurts like hell."

"I've no doubt." She scratched an entry in a file attached to a clip board. "You eventually did hit your head—a lot of blood, but no permanent damage, possibly a mild concussion. I'll give you something for the pain."

My hands were red, raw, and seemed to be swelling. Last night's burn on my finger was now lost among my more serious scrapes. "Ben, someone pushed me in front of that taxi!"

"I know, Jake."

How did he know? Well, first things first. "Can I go home?"

The young doctor looked at me as if I were crazy. "I want to admit you at least until tomorrow."

"Please, can't I check myself out of here?" In a frenzy, I cried, "Ben, I want to go home!"

"Well, let's see if we can't convince the doctor." Then Ben brushed the hair out of my eyes, just like my mother always did.

Against the ER resident's judgment call and, two hours later, after signing a waiver granting immunity to Mount Sinai and its staff—I charged the whole episode on my OPTIMA card, rethinking a health insurance plan that my mother had been lobbying for, and I left the hospital. But I didn't go home.

· · · · ·

As our taxi sailed past 92nd Street and continued on downtown, I asked, "Just where are we going?"

"It's a surprise. You're in real danger, Jake. There's no question that someone tried to kill you this evening. Someone desperate enough to attempt murder in front of an audience."

"Who told you that?"

"Your tail, Hank Adams . . . an old pal of mine . . . on leave from the department."

"Why?"

"Why what?"

"Why is he on leave?"

"Let's say he had a major difference of opinion with the captain. He's on probation, but he's a good cop, Jake."

"Apparently not good enough." I rubbed my head with my gauze-covered hand.

"Hank feels like a piece of crap about what happened on his watch. He'd realized that you were about to board a bus—he'd left his car near your house when you took off on foot—so he hailed a cab to follow you. Then— zap—you were shoved into the street and struck by the very cab he'd hailed. The taxi driver had slowed down. Otherwise, the impact would have been much worse."

"Did your friend, Hank, see who pushed me?"

"No. However, two people waiting at the bus stop did notice a young man in a baseball cap, but after you went flying, he'd disappeared."

"What did he look like?"

"About five-eight or nine, dressed sloppy . . . baggy jeans . . . Nikes. Wore the cap pulled down over his face and dark glasses. Most of his face was covered."

"And he just vanished?"

"Into the park, one witness thought."

None of the suspects came anywhere near this description. "Ben, this makes no sense. If this guy did try to kill me, who the hell is he?"

"Seems strange, I agree."

We crossed 72nd Street. "*Where* are we going?"

"To a Duane Reade drugstore to buy you a toothbrush."

"Ben, take me back to Carnegie Hill! Jesus, did you call my mother? She must be totally crazy by now!"

"I did call, before we left the hospital. She wasn't home."

"What do you mean? Why wouldn't she be home at eleven-thirty?! She went to dinner with your father. What could they be doing?"

Ben laughed at me. "Jake, Dad's not Jack the Ripper."

"Well, this isn't like my mother . . . and I want to go home now!"

"Consider yourself in protective custody."

"Are you kidnapping me?"

We passed the Plaza on our right, the fountain aglow, normal people, all dressed up for a Saturday night out on the town. The hansom cabs were doing a thriving business.

"Yes, for tonight. I don't want you to go home. This killer is convinced you know too much. And he's someone you know, someone who attended Emmie's wake. He could be waiting for you to come home. Maybe ringing your bell, right now."

For just a fraction of a split second, I questioned if Ben was all that he seemed, considering and rejecting the notion. Then I asked. "But who pushed me? Patrick has gray hair. Would the witnesses describe him as young? And he's taller than five-nine. Bill? I guess it's a possibility. Wait, there is someone it could be. Ivan! His outfits are always black and too tight, but he does fit the general description. Or maybe the killer has an accomplice?"

"I don't know, Jake, but while I'm finding out, you're going to be in a safe place."

"What about Mom?"

Ben handed me his pocket phone. "Call your mother. If she's home, tell her Gypsy Rose is on her way over to spend the night with her."

"Did you call Gypsy Rose?"

"She's psychic, isn't she?" When I didn't even smile, he continued. "I've arranged for Hank to escort Gypsy Rose to your apartment—she says she has a key to your co-op—and if Maura isn't home yet, he'll wait there with Gypsy Rose. Then he'll work outside surveillance all night." I dialed my mom, wondering where I'd be sleeping tonight.

Gypsy Rose and Hank had arrived just as my mother

and Aaron finally returned. After dinner, they'd gone to the Metropolitan Museum of Art's theater to see a revival of *Breakfast at Tiffany's*. All four were waiting by the phone.

My mother was crying, "I said three Hail Marys, Jake, and I'm starting a novena to St. Jude at Mass tomorrow morning."

"I'm with Ben, safe and sound."

"Hank seems like a nice man, darling; he and Gypsy Rose said you're okay. Are you, darling?"

"Well . . ."

"Come home, immediately! Ben can protect you here. I'll get Dr. Brown to come over."

"I'm okay, Mom, really."

"I only pray you know what you're doing!" Me, too. "Jake, tell Ben that Gypsy Rose and I will be down to join you for a late brunch tomorrow." I guess everyone knew where I was going except me.

"Good. Thanks, Mom, talk to you later. I love you."

. . . . .

I shopped with abandon at Duane Reade's. In addition to a toothbrush, I purchased a comb and hairbrush, deodorant, Vaseline Intensive Care, shampoo, a few cosmetics, a large bottle of Extra Strength Tylenol, two Milky Ways and, even an I Love NY T-shirt to sleep in.

Ben said, "It's on the city." I added a box of Oreos, Lays Potato Chips and a six-pack of Diet Coke to my basket.

With Ben carrying my new possessions in two Duane Reade plastic bags, we walked around the corner and into the lobby of the Algonquin Hotel. At the desk, Ben gave his name and said, "I've reserved the Dorothy Parker suite." Wow! Mom, Gypsy Rose and I had toured the celebrity suites at the Algonquin, so I knew how posh the Parker suite was. Even Dottie herself would have loved it.

"Ben, you're a sport." I knew the City of New York wouldn't spring for this.

"Would Mr. Benchley do any less for his good friend, Mrs. Parker?"

We rode the tiny elevator to the second floor. The elderly operator and the bellman were gracious enough to ignore my bedraggled appearance, bloodstained hair, bandaged hands and, tackiest of all, the discount drugstore's plastic bags. The bellman showed us how to insert the card-key—always a real challenge for me—then opened the door for us. I crossed the threshold and stepped into another world.

Twenty-seven

"So, the scoop from the spirit word is that this ghost may be a dead duck." I finished my séance saga. Ben had listened raptly, laughing often and asking lots of questions.

"I don't get it." He shook his head.

"You had to be there. Scratch that. Most of us who were there didn't understand what happened, either."

"Could Gypsy Rose have been putting on a show? Maybe she used to be an actress?"

"Not in this lifetime, Ben."

"Well, I don't need Emily Brontë to confirm that you're in danger. That's evident even to a mere mortal like me."

"And what about this Aubergine business? I heard about it at Emmie's funeral and then, again, from her spirit guide. Whatever else is going down, that has to be a clue from the grave. Don't you think?"

"So it seems." Ben picked up the big, white, fluffy towel and continued to dry my hair—very gently. My fingers were not badly scraped, but my palms were so raw that I couldn't do much with my hands. Ben let me borrow his.

Strange, how comfortable I felt with this man. From the moment we'd walked into the charming suite, filled with Parker memorabilia and furnished in Edwardian splendor, he'd kept up a light banter and the charade that he was Robert Benchley and that I was his dear friend Mrs. Parker.

"Run a hot bath for you, Mrs. Parker?"

"Maybe lukewarm." How would I get out of these jeans? The freckle-faced nurse had literally dressed me.

But Ben had tugged my T-shirt over my head and pulled down the zipper on my jeans as if he were my mother. "Here, wrap this towel around you and I'll go check on the water temperature."

While he'd gone into the bathroom, I managed to get my Jockey-For-Her underpants off, using the tips of my fingers. The bra presented more of a challenge, but with much persistence and some pain, I'd unhooked it. I found Ben, with his elbow in the tub, testing the water.

"This bath water is so perfect that someone as special as you should bathe in it, Mrs. Parker."

"Thanks, I'll holler if I need help."

I'd gingerly washed myself without using my palms— or getting the gauze wet. Then I globbed some shampoo on my head, then flat on my back, stuck my hair under the tub's faucet and called it a wash. A trick I never want to repeat. Dried, I'd called for help and Ben had pulled the I Love NY shirt over my head, while I stood modestly wrapped in the towel. Then we'd shared the sodas and treats, me propped up like a princess in the pretty bed, my knight in a rumpled suit, sitting beside me in an armchair, as I recounted my long day dealing with the dead.

"Enough about me." I said, swallowing four Tylenols for dessert. "Tell me about your day. What's new on Jonathan's murder?"

"Not a whole hell of a lot. I did show Kate Lloyd Connors the Sarah Anne Hansen clipping."

"No! What did she say?"

"She claims she has no idea who the Hansen woman was or why Emmie had the clipping. And Kate's sure that Emmie didn't find it in her house."

"What about Caroline's birth certificate? How about her birth mother's name being Hansen? Did you ask Kate that?"

"Kate says it's just a coincidence."

"There are no coincidences." I love Ghostwriters Anonymous program speak. "I say Kate's a liar."

"Yeah. Well, Caroline's psychiatrist wouldn't allow her to be interviewed today. I'll try to get some straight answers out of her in the morning."

"It is morning." I glanced at the bedside clock: two A.M "I think Caroline's the key, here. Could you do a blood test? DNA—or something—to see if Kate's really her grandmother?"

"Not without some hard evidence."

"Like what?"

"Like a diary or revealing letters that Kate might have kept. Or Kate's own birth certificate, but so far our search of Sutton Place has turned up nothing."

"Well, I'm sure Emmie found something."

"I did talk to Bill Bernside," Ben smoothed out a wrinkle in the blanket. "He's going to accompany Jonathan's body back to England as soon as the medical examiner releases it."

"Thank God, that's one funeral I won't have to attend. Hey, as a suspect, can Bill leave the country?"

"There's not much of a case against him."

"I don't think it's Bill—he wouldn't have killed Barbara."

"Why? Because she was his sister? Think of your Greek tragedies."

"Mostly mothers, fathers or children are the ones getting bumped off . . . not siblings." A question came to mind. "Ben, how come you live with your father?"

"That's some segue, Jake! When my mother died two years ago, he fell into a deep depression, so I moved back home. He's much better now. Actually, my father's turned into a Jewish mother, wants me to get married . . . I guess . . . Why are you living with your mother?"

"Money. I love Carnegie Hill and our co-op. Mom loves having me live there. Neither one of us can afford to keep it on our own, so . . ."

"Well, if my father married your mother, maybe . . ."

"Ben, I'm totally sleepy."

He tucked me in, grabbed an extra pillow and blanket from the closet, kissed the top of my head, and opted for the couch in the living room.

"Good night, Mr. Benchley," I called to him.

"Sleep well, Mrs. Parker."

. . . . .

Ben was gone when I woke up at nine-thirty, as room service—at Ben's request—delivered juice, coffee and bagels. He had left a note, reminding me that Mom and Gypsy Rose would be here at noon, and they would be bringing me some clothes. He'd reserved the suite, again, for tonight: "Stay put, don't leave the hotel. I'll be back in time to escort you to the Oak Room for dinner at eight."

I struggled to get washed and to brush my teeth—even my gums seemed to hurt—and decided to wait for Mom to get dressed. I didn't have a thing to wear, anyway. My mother would probable arrive with half my closet. I put on a little foundation, trying to cover some of the damage, and added lipstick. Then I checked my messages. There were seven in all. Maybe I'd get lucky.

. . . . .

"Jake. It's Kate. Isn't it too tragic about poor Jonathan? Please come to work at ten on Monday. We'll just meet briefly. You can gather the material you need to work at home. Frankly, I'm far too upset to work on the book; but my publisher's deadline doesn't stop for murder. Thanks."

Her message had been left at eight-thirty last night . . . just about when I'd been landing in front of Jackie's. Well, good. I needed a reason to get back into that house as soon as possible; Kate had given me one.

"Jake! Where are you? It's almost nine-thirty. I'm growing more frantic by the minute. Call me!"

Too Tall Tom! Lord! I'd stood him up. With good reason, of course. But I'd never called him after the accident. No, attempted murder. I still couldn't accept that someone had tried to kill me. Someone I knew. I'd call Too Tall Tom as soon as I finished listening to the messages. Maybe, he'd reached Mom and she'd explained why I hadn't made it down to the Village.

"I should have figured that a girl like you wouldn't be at home on a Saturday night. But this lonely old bachelor is. Jake, it's Patrick . . ."

As if I didn't know.

"Can you stop by my office tomorrow afternoon or evening? I have some information that concerns me, and I'd like to share it with you. Give me a buzz to set up a time."

Come into my parlor, said the spider to the fly. Patrick had called at ten P.M.

"Caroline 'ere. Jake, they're trying to kill us. I told you so! I found a journal. We 'ave to talk—not at the 'ouse. 'Ow about . . ."

Caroline seemed to have been cut off in mid sentence—at two-fifteen Sunday morning—and she'd sounded either drunk or drugged.

"Jake! Hi, it's a beautiful Sunday morning. Jane and I are doing brunch at Tavern on the Green at eleven-thirty. Call me if you want to join us."

Ginger. She'd called about an hour ago. How I wished I could go meet my girlfriends. And wouldn't they have been impressed to know that I'd slept—in a manner of speaking—with a detective in the Dorothy Parker Suite at the Algonquin!

"This is Ivan. I vant to tell you somethink. I vill be by this afternoon."

Ivan the Terrible. He'd phoned at nine-fifteen. One of my possible pushers. But the truth was . . . as much as I couldn't stand Ivan, I didn't think he'd done it. When he arrived at my apartment, no one would be home. I wondered what he "vanted" to tell me.

"Jake. Dennis. It's nine-thirty or so, Sunday morning. I've been reviewing my files . . . how in God's name could that spook have known about Aubergine? I'm telling tales out of the office here, but I'm intrigued. Call me. Maybe, we can have dinner."

. . . . .

Well, well. It seemed I'd become the most wanted woman in Carnegie Hill!

Twenty-eight

My cosmetic camouflage proved less than effective. My mother burst into tears as she entered the suite, and Gypsy Rose suggested a trip back to the emergency room. "You're the walking wounded, Jake. You belong at Mount Sinai, not the Algonquin, charming as this suite may be."

My mother placed a careful kiss on my left cheek, a relatively unscathed area. "I do hope you feel better than you look."

"Ladies, we're going to the Oak Room for brunch as scheduled; I'm feeling fine," I lied.

Gypsy Rose opened one of the two suitcases that she and Mom had dragged downtown and pulled out a long sleeved, navy, cotton knit top and matching pull-on pants—the kind that those older women who have given up belts wear—and the outfit appealed to me! She added a cheery red, white and blue scarf, big Jackie O dark glasses and navy flats to the neat pile on the bed. "Voila! Come along, darling. I'll help you dress. Then we'll tackle your makeup. You'll be chic yet comfortable."

"For God's sake, Gypsy Rose, you sound like a Home Shopping huckster," my mother said.

· · · · ·

Before they'd stormed the suite, I'd made a few tough decisions and several phone calls.

The first decision had been the hardest: I couldn't spend another night in the Dorothy Parker Suite. Ben Rubin was too damn appealing to remain Mr. Benchley, and neither my tattered psyche nor my sore body was in any condition to start a love affair. Ben and I seemed destined to be more than friends; I wanted to be totally "present" when that transitions occurred. I called the front desk and canceled the suite for tonight. Why should Ben, or even the City of New York, be stuck with a hotel bill for a suite we wouldn't be sleeping in? Then, I'd called Ben.

"Can we still have dinner at eight?" he'd asked.

"Damn right. Pick me up at home," I'd answered. "And in the meantime, Ben, please don't assign another guardian angel to me."

Dennis was up next. His machine picked up. Telephone tag—the game we all play far too often. *"Dennis, it's Jake. I can't make dinner, tonight, but I do want to see you. Why not stop by the house at five-thirty? I'll have a batch of martinis mixed. Leave a message only if you can't make it. Thanks."*

Reaching Caroline would be tough, but by calling Kate, maybe I'd manage to chat with Caroline. Carla picked up the phone on the third ring. "Hi, Carla, this is Jake O'Hara. Is Kate there?"

"Miss Connors has gone to church. May I give her a message?"

"Yes, I'll see her in the morning." I felt guilty, ignoring Ben's warning. "Is Caroline around?"

"She is . . . but she's with Mr. Patrick . . . they're in a therapy session. Miss Caroline's been in a bad way, Miss O'Hara. We're all worried about her."

"Please tell Caroline I'd like to talk to her tomorrow."

"I will. She'll be happy to hear that."

"And, Carla, don't mention that I left a message for Caroline to Miss Connors. Okay?"

Patrick would probably be tied up with Caroline—not literally, I hoped—till this afternoon. If I could dump Mom and Gypsy Rose, maybe I'd just detour, drop by his Murray Hill office and surprise him before heading home.

I'd figured later for Ivan. Maybe Ben and I could dine at Budapest East—actually, I loved their food and on Sunday nights they had a strolling violinist—and talk to Ivan over our Hungarian goulash.

. . . . .

By the time we were seated in the Oak Room, my insides full of Tylenol, and my outside a Gypsy Rose fashion statement, I felt well enough to order the eggs Benedict. I *had* missed dinner last night. Too Tall Tom had reached Mom last night and, after inquiring about my missed appointment, she'd invited him to join us for brunch.

"I'll have the French toast with sausage and the basil and tomato omelet. Oh, and a bagel . . ." Too Tall Tom had a lot of space to fill. "Jake, this serial killer is a madman! We need Alec Cross! Why you could be dead. Thank God, you . . ." he caught the departing waiter's eye—"Waiter, could you bring cream cheese and strawberry jam for the bagel? Thanks a bunch"—then turned his attention back to me " . . . escaped this time!"

"This time?" My mother asked. "Jake, that killer

must be caught. What's Ben doing to find him?'' My mother fiddled with her cup, spilling coffee onto the saucer and the sparkling, white linen tablecloth. ''It seems as if you're in a witness protection program. Next, they'll change your name and send you to Madison County, Iowa. I want action! Now!''

Gypsy Rose, perhaps to change the subject, asked, ''Ben didn't become too—um—romantic, did he? That suite's quite conducive to seduction.''

''Jesus, Mary and Joseph!'' My mother said, more in prayer than anger. ''Of course not.'' Then she turned to me, ''He didn't, did he?''

The waiter arrived with our mimosas.

Ignoring my mother's question, I said, ''I've canceled the suite. As soon as we finish brunch, we're going to get the bags; then we're out of here.''

''Jake, it's after twelve. Won't you have to pay for another night, even if you don't stay?''

A good diversion. Now my mother was more worried about money than sex. ''No. I arranged for late checkout.''

''But who'll protect you, if you don't stay here with Ben?''

''Mom, a minute ago, you were trying to protect me from Ben.''

Gypsy Rose hoisted her champagne glass. ''To health, happiness and finding out the identity of the killer!''

I drank to that.

. . . . .

Too Tall Tom and I loaded Mom, Gypsy Rose and their baggage into a taxi. Then, on the pretense that I was going to Too Tall Tom's—over much noisy protestation from Mom—he and I shared a second cab, downtown. ''Let me off on Lex and Thirty-first,'' I instructed the driver as we passed 32nd Street.

"What are you doing, Jake? You promised your mother you'd let me take care of you this afternoon. Where are you going now?"

"We're going nowhere. I have to make a quick visit to Patrick Hemmings. Then I swear, I'm heading straight home to mother."

"But . . ." I started to ease out of the cab while Too Tall Tom continued, "I just hope you know what you're doing. You could be dropping in on a serial killer!"

The cabbie turned around, "So, you going or coming, lady?"

"Gone," I answered, closing the door as the driver pulled away.

. . . . .

"Jake O'Hara! What a pleasant surprise. Come in." Patrick wore a shirt the exact color of his blueberry eyes, jeans and boots. But his handsome face looked grim. "What happened, Jake? Were you in an accident?" Gypsy Rose's repair job certainly hadn't covered the damage.

I decided to tell him the whole truth; maybe I'd get a little of it from him in return.

Patrick's living quarters were adjacent to his office. We now sat in his open, airy kitchen–sitting room, the sun streaming through the louvered windows, sipping Irish Breakfast tea. The cups were Belleek.

"I'm not surprised, Jake. I've been concerned; that's one of the reasons why I called you. You're a very verbal inquisitor, and we're dealing with a most determined murderer here."

"What were your other reasons? Why did you think I needed to be warned?"

"It's a long sequence of events."

I poured another cup of tea. "I have all afternoon."

Patrick sighed. "Kate Lloyd Conners's years of regression therapy have revealed some unsavory stuff that I shouldn't discuss with anyone. But with people I know being murdered with such regularity, I have to do something. Do you realize that all of the victims have been Kate's former ghosts?"

So Patrick *knew* that Jonathan—and Barbara!—had been Kate's ghosts. I guess that shouldn't be a surprise. "And you believe that I'm the next victim?"

"Don't you?"

"Hell, yes. Ethics be damned! Go ahead and break your client-hypnotherapist confidence. The life you save may be mine."

Taking a sip of tea, Patrick, seemingly with great difficulty, began. "Kate's regression released memories of childhood trauma—so ugly—she'd buried it in a subconscious grave that she never wanted to have dug up. Her father was a real bastard."

"Do you have any reason to believe that Caroline might be Kate's blood granddaughter?"

Patrick blanched. "How could you know that?"

"So it's true?"

"Caroline's discovered a journal that she says proves her mother was Kate's illegitimate daughter. But she left it in its hiding place. Caroline's afraid of Kate; the last thing she wants Kate to know is that she read the journal."

"Where is this journal?"

"Caroline claims it's in Vera Madison's room. Jake, the problem here is that Caroline suffers from delusions and more than a touch of paranoia. She's heavily medicated—has been for a long time. I'm frantic. It's a tough call with Caroline. I never know if she's in real or imagined danger. And why would Kate be lying to her all these years? To all of us?''

''Patrick, on that first day I came to Sutton Place, why did you tell Caroline that there was cyanide in the sour cream, then eat it yourself?''

''I'd warned Caroline to be careful. My suspicion that day had been vague and unformed . . . but growing. Something just didn't seem right, you know?''

Oh, yes, I knew.

Patrick continued, ''Caroline decided that Kate was trying to kill her. A delusional patient's therapist walks a thin line; the poisoned sour cream was one of Caroline's fantasies . . . that's why I ate it.''

''What's your real relationship with Caroline?''

Patrick squirmed in his chair, but he answered me. ''Sometimes I ask myself that question. She's my patient, and I'm worried about her well-being; however there's no doubt that I'm very fond of her. It's complicated because I'm also Kate's hypnotherapist. I'm torn professionally. I never should have taken Caroline on as a patient.''

Or maybe the conflict came from Patrick's wanting to stay on the well-heeled mother's payroll more than he wanted to help her stepdaughter.

Patrick walked me over to Third Avenue and attempted to hail a cab. ''One more thing, Jake.''

''Yes?''

''I never slept with Emmie. I guess one more broken confidence won't matter. Em was my patient, as you know, and she was drinking too much. Were you aware of that?''

I felt ashamed. ''I should have realized that she was in trouble. Ginger and Jane both mentioned her drinking to me.''

''She wanted to end it with Ivan, but there was

something else bothering her, too. Something she hadn't shared with me; she'd hidden whatever it was deep inside, and she seemed in denial. Anyway, she got roaring drunk one night at a local bar, then wound up in bed with the bartender. And he fathered her child. The last time I saw her—late morning of the day she was murdered—Emmie was frightened and confused. I only wish I'd reached that secret part. I might have saved her.''

A taxi deposited a passenger, and Patrick held the door open for me. ''Yeah, me too. And, Patrick, thanks.''

. . . . .

When I arrived home, my mother fussed and fumed, and I escaped to my bedroom to check my e-mail. Only one: ''Is *To Kill a Mockingbird* still your favorite book?''

Twenty-nine

The second threatening e-mail, like the first, had been sent from an uptown mail service franchise, arriving at four-ten P.M. An hour ago. I called Ben, leaving a rambling, highly charged and frustrating-to-me message on his voice mail. Then, I called Mail Boxes Etc. on First Avenue and 78th Street. When a loud, unfriendly "Yeah?" hurt my ear, I introduced myself as Detective Bea Rubin of the Nineteenth Precinct. It worked. The gruff tone took on a more helpful quality, and I learned that the e-mail in question had been a cash transaction, that the sender—a youngish man in big jeans and a baseball cap, wearing dark glasses and a denim jacket—had given a New Jersey address and telephone number, both probably phony.

· · · · ·

Patrick had been pouring the last of the tea when the threat had been transmitted, pretty much putting him out the running as the ghosts' book-bashing serial killer. Unless he had an accomplice. Part of me regretted crossing him off the list. He'd been so easy to hate. Even today, when I'd asked him what he'd done before becoming a certified hypnotist, his response scratched my soul. "The health field. I worked as a personal trainer and offered private classes on a seaweed and chocolate nutrition plan."

"Quite a career change." I hadn't even tried to hide my disdain.

That didn't stop Patrick. Into true-confession mode, he seemed to need to purge his past and to offer proof of his salvation. "Then I got in touch with my spirituality during a hypnotherapy session to stop smoking. And I found my path in this incarnation would be in service. You know, helping people to cope, and to live in the now, by regressing them to confront their long-ago problems during past lives."

"This—er—profession requires no degree, in say, psychology, or any medical training or licensing?"

"No, I earned my certified hypnotherapist's title through the mail. A study-at-home program. Now I'm in a theology course, where I'll become the Reverend Hemmings. I'm getting straight A's. The Divinity Center's based in Fort Lauderdale, Florida."

Naturally.

"It will be the perfect combination for counseling souls in distress." Patrick the apprentice preacher.

. . . . .

My mother appeared in my bedroom door and broke into my reverie. "Jake, Dennis is on his way up." As I limped into the john, I called out, "Entertain him for a few minutes, will you, Mom. And try not to arrange an engagement while I'm in the bathroom."

"You'll die an old maid, Jake, if I don't do something." My mother could be right.

For the third time today, I decided that my face was

irreparable—at least for the short term—but I valiantly applied more base and blush, then combed my hair over my bruised forehead and cheeks. With great anticipation, I then tottered into the living room to learn what Dennis Kim knew about Aubergine.

But first I had to get rid of my mother. "Mom, I promised Dennis a martini or two. Could you be a dear and make a pitcher of them? You know yours are as good as Nick and Nora's must have been. And maybe some Cheddar cheese and crackers?"

"Dennis and I will have martinis. You're on drugs; I never should have allowed you to down those mimosas at brunch. I'll bring you a club soda."

I waited till she'd gone down the hall. "Okay, Dennis, tell me about Aubergine!"

"What I don't get is how Emily Brontë or Gypsy Rose Liebowitz, or whoever the hell had use of her body, or, for that matter, anyone else in that room, could have heard of Aubergine."

"So, I guess you'd be surprised that I've heard of it."

Dennis sank into the sofa. "How? When? Who told you?"

I debated if I should go first, then figured—what the hell—he wouldn't be here if he wasn't going to tell me what he knew. "At Emmie's burial . . . her kid brother had talked to her on the afternoon of the day she'd been murdered. And Emmie'd asked him about Aubergine, even indicated that she thought it was an odd name for a corporation."

"Funny, I'd thought the same thing when I heard the name."

"A Kate Lloyd Connors company, I presume?"

Dennis smiled. "Jake, you're always one step ahead of me. But then I've known that for twenty-five years. When Kate decided to form the corporation . . ."

"When was that?"

"Less than two weeks ago. Anyway, I referred her to a colleague of mine in corporate law. A Larry Helms. And I reached him this morning. I've not been involved in the details, but I did know it was all very hush-hush, right down to the name of her silent partner. Who that might be was my first question to Larry."

"A silent partner . . ."

My mother came in, carrying her best silver tray, holding stem glasses, a pitcher of martinis, a arrangement of cheeses, crackers, nuts and olives, and a club soda for me. "Who has a silent partner?" she asked.

I poured a martini into the tall glass that she'd intended for my soda water. Then I poured their cocktails. My mother grimaced. "Not a word, Mom. I'm having one while Dennis and I finish our chat."

"And may I stay for the denouement? Or shall I go to my room?" She actually pouted.

"Sit down, Mom. But, like with Bond, this is for your ears only."

"That was 'eyes,' darling, but not to worry, my lips are sealed." My mother sat, obviously delighted to be part of the action.

Since Mom knew how Aubergine tormented me, it took no time to bring her up to speed.

"Who is this silent partner?" I asked Dennis.

"One V. Woolf. That's the name listed in the corporate papers. Larry's never met this mystery man or woman in person. Kate gathered up all the papers and the contract, then had V. Woolf's signature witnessed— I'd assumed at Sutton Place—by Vera Madison."

"W. The murderer's initial on the Ouija board," my mother said.

"That's right. Jesus!"

"That's spooked me since I left the séance," Dennis said. "And when Larry Helms cried, 'Woolf,' I became a believer. I'd go buy some spirituality if I knew where it was sold."

I chuckled, then asked, "Could Vera Madison be this V. Woolf?"

"Not legally. Then she'd have witnessed her own signature. But who knows, Jake? This case gets curiouser and curiouser." Dennis took a good swing of his martini. "Excellent as always, Maura."

My mother raised her glass, "To you and Jake, Dennis. To a happy future."

I choked on my drink. When all this is over, I might murder my mother.

Dennis just grinned and changed the subject. "Hey, Jake, what happened? You look like you've been run over by a Mack truck."

"No, just hit by a New York cabbie." It took a little longer to fill Dennis in on last night's murder attempt. He absorbed every detail, then said, "I'm hiring a private investigator, tonight, to watch out for you, Jake."

"Don't you dare!" I envisioned my designated tails watching each other while the killer closed in on me. "The NYPD has taken care of that, but thanks, Dennis."

"I suspect that Detective Rubin would like to snare more than a murderer in this case." Dennis leered at me. "And how does the fair maiden feel about that?"

Like a schoolgirl, I thought. "Listen, Dennis, let's get back on track here. Do you have any idea why Kate formed a corporation now? She never had one before, did she?"

"No. She didn't." Dennis accepted a Cheddar-topped cracker from my mother. "And I only found out today—

from Larry—that Kate wanted to incorporate because she's going into show business."

"Show business?" My mother sounded as surprised as I felt.

"Yes," Dennis said, swallowing the cracker. "It seems that Kate's become an enterpreneur. When I called Larry, he'd been ready to call me to handle the business end of the deal. As Kate's literary and entertainment attorney, I've been doing those kind of contracts for her for years . . . movies, audio rights and all that jazz. But this is the biggest deal yet."

"What kind of deal, Dennis? You're not in court. Don't make me cross-examine you."

"Sorry. Must be an occupational hazard. It *is* a big deal, Jake. Kate and her silent partner are going to buy a cable television station."

"Totally mind-blowing! Does Kate have that kind of money?"

"More money than you can conjure. Kate's one sharp cookie." Dennis turned his attention to my mother. "May I pour you another, Maura?"

"No, thank you. Now tell me what are Kate Lloyd Connors and her oh-so-silent partner planning to do with this station?"

"I don't know." Dennis seemed stumped. "Maybe an all-mystery channel featuring her works. God knows enough of them have been turned into movies. She could write the teleplays for the rest of her books and create new ones, as well. That's just a wild guess."

"Kate couldn't write an excuse good enough to get her out of school. How the hell could she develop a scenario?" I started to pour myself another drink. My mother glared at me, and I put the pitcher down.

"Well, she has plenty of ghosts." Dennis looked a bit guilty as he admitted that.

"Not at the rate they're being bumped off," I said.

"Stay turned," my mother said.

Thirty

I sat across the table from New York's finest detective—in my opinion—at Budapest East, the room filled with red tulips and the strains of a strolling gypsy's violin, thinking how handsome Ben looked. And how lousy I felt. All my aches and pains had magnified as the day had waned and now, at eight-thirty Sunday evening, I hurt. Popping three Extra Strength Tylenol into my mouth, I washed them down with a sip of Diet Coke. Listening, for a change, to my mother's advice.

. . . . .

It had been tough getting out of the house. As soon as Dennis had gone, the buzzer rang again. Ginger, Modesty and Jane trooped in. Too Tall Tom had told Jane that someone had tried to kill me and how I'd wound up at Mount Sinai, then in the Dorothy Parker suite at the Algonquin. I'd also made the late editions of both the *Post* and the *Times*. Modesty clutched a copy of each. However, there had been no mention in either paper that my being shoved in front of a cab had any connection, however tenuous, to the book-bashing-ghost-serial-killer.

"So, who done it?" Modesty asked, as my mother went to freshen the martinis and replenish the cheese and crackers. I checked my watch. Six-forty-five. I still had time before Ben would arrive.

"Too Tall Tom and the papers say some young man tried to kill you," Jane said. "Anyone we know? From the description it could be Ivan the Terrible, but his last name doesn't begin with a W."

"Don't believe everything you see or hear at a séance, Jane," Ginger said. "Isn't that right, Jake?" Ginger knew and shared my skepticism of things arcane or too New Age.

"Well, I certainly believed that going in, but neither Mom nor I moved that sucker round the Ouija board; so my guess is the spirit moved it."

"You see!" Jane said. "I'm convinced that Emmie sent Jake a message from the world beyond, and it's only a matter of time before Jake solves these ghastly crimes and catches the killer."

"Unless the killer catches up with me first." A nervous laugh escaped, rumbling from deep in my throat, and I felt foolish and melodramatic. My mother came back with the tray, and Ginger helped her serve the drinks.

Modesty drained her martini in two gulps and reached for a refill. "I had lunch with Bill this afternoon."

"So that's why you couldn't come to brunch with us," Ginger said. "More interesting fish to fry . . . What did he have to say?"

"Bill's leaving for Philadelphia this evening. There's some family business he has to take care of. But he'll be back later in the week, probably Thursday, to

accompany Jonathan's body to London. And guess who
wants to go along for the ride?''

"No contest," I said. "Kate Lloyd Connors."

"Give that little lady a great big cigar," Modesty said.
Then lit one herself, dropping the match in her saucer.
Ginger jumped on Modesty. "Lettuce head, you're
giving us cancer!"

Modesty put it out as Jane opened a window. My
mother carried its smelly remains to the kitchen.
Ignoring the commotion she'd caused, Modesty
continued, "Bill's a wreck. Barbara had warned him
about Jonathan Arthur; she had bad vibes from the get-
go. But Bill had not taken her advice and Jonathan broke
his heart and borrowed his money. Almost fifty thousand
dollars . . . never repaid. Now I guess it never will be.
Bill says Jonathan—greedy and less than gentlemanly—
had sold his soul and Kate Lloyd Connors's secrets to
a tabloid. And he was murdered just as he'd been ready
to deliver an even dirtier story. Do you think Kate killed
him to stop the presses? That's what Bill believes; he's
worried about you, Jake. Three ghosts are dead. All
somehow connected to Kate." Modesty drank her
second martini in one fell swoop, then pointed her index
finger with its lacquered black nail polish at me. "You
could be her next victim!"

"You've been accusing Kate from the beginning,
Modesty . . . and with no proof," Ginger said. "Why do
you hate this woman so? Could it be you're jealous of
her?"

"Jealous?! Of those bilious little cozies that
America's great unwashed Babbitts devour. They should
be sold with a PEPCID AC chaser. My work is literature.
She's a hack and so are her ghosts! How dare you accuse
me of envying that talentless tramp?''

My mother returned to the living room just in time to

prevent mayhem. I excused myself, saying I had to lie down for a while before Ben arrived, wondering if Kate really was a tramp, but certain she was a killer. Almost certain. Had I ever told her that *To Kill a Mockingbird* was my favorite book?

When I reappeared forty minutes later, all the ghosts were gone and my mother was entertaining Mrs. McMahon. She'd read the *Post*'s late edition and decided that her homemade chicken soup would cure my injuries as well soothe my nerves.

"Oh yes, Maura, I'd be delighted to have a martini." Mrs. M seemed to have squirreled in for the evening. Ben's arrival saved me. Only a miracle could help my mother.

・ ・ ・ ・ ・

Ben brought my fingers to his lips as the gypsy stopped at our table and played "Fascination." Enjoying the romance of the moment and the music of the violin, I looked into Ben's kind, dark eyes, asking myself: Could this be the look of love? Or would I even recognize that look if it bit me on the nose?

We'd asked to be seated in Ivan's section and the owner had taken our drink orders. Now Ivan, in all his pale flesh, stood before us, menus in hand. "Jake, you are vit the police?"

"That's not a crime, Ivan." I smiled at him, resenting his tone but wanting his cooperation.

"You vere shoved in front of car, no? Someone tries to kill you, Jake. Vat do you know?" With a flare, Ivan opened the menu and, with great drama, placed it in front of me.

Ben reached for his before Ivan could repeat the performance. "Say, Ivan, where were you last night at eight-thirty?"

"Right vhere I stand tonight, Detective Rubin. You not believe, I call owner over."

"I believe you, Ivan. It's just that you fit the description of the man who pushed Jake."

Ivan shrugged. "Is the look of every man." What the hell did that mean? With Ivan you never knew.

"Vell, I vant to tell you somethink. Emmie, I love too much, she vanted to end our love. I think I frighten her." How perceptive, I thought. Ivan scratched the side of his generous nose, "So, vhen Emmie tells me she is having another man's baby, I tell her ve marry, anyvay."

"But . . ." I said.

"She vants to keep baby, but not me. Emmie says she will raise child alone. This is vat ve fight about that last day of her life." Ivan sounded stricken.

"And?" I prompted.

"Emmie had been drunk; she sleep vit married man, but he no vant her or their baby. This man has no morals. You know him, Jake."

"I do?"

"You do. Is bartender at Elaine's. Joe Vynn."

"Joe Wynn is the father of Emmie's baby!?"

"Vat did I just tell you?" Ivan said. "He's a no goodnik. Don't tip him, ever again, Jake. Now, do you both vant the goulash?"

Ben ordered the trout "I have an Hungarian grandmother . . . the world's worst cook; I haven't eaten goulash since I left for college."

When Ivan left, I shook my head. "Joe Wynn told me all about Emmie's last night at Elaine's, what she'd done while she waited for me, even scolded me for not showing up. He'd spoken about her as if she were just another customer. Boy, for sure, people seldom are as they seem."

"This is one strange case, Jake. When I called the

mail services store to check out the e-mail, I learned that a Detective Bea Rubin had already called. Impersonating an officer, lady?''

"Sorry, Ben. I'm so nosy and I was so scared. I couldn't wait. Am I in trouble?''

"Yes . . . the killer wants you dead. Don't run the police investigation, Jake. We'll get him.''

Chastened, I changed the subject. "Let's assume that Kate is Sarah Anne Hansen and someone had been blackmailing her . . .''

"For killing her father?''

"Or standing by and allowing him to drown . . .''

"There would be no crime in that.''

"What do you mean?''

"Watching a person drown and not saving him may be morally reprehensible, but it's not against the law.''

"Do you mean to tell me one person can let another die, doing nothing to save him, and that's perfectly legal?''

"Absolutely. Unless the first person was responsible for the second person. For example, a parent for his child.''

"But not in reverse? A daughter for her father?''

"Nope. We have no Good Samaritan law here like they do in France.''

"So, if someone shot my mother, I could let her bleed to death, and that would be okay with you?''

"No. And I'm sure it wouldn't be 'okay' with your mother. But it wouldn't be a crime.''

Ivan arrived with the food.

After tasting the goulash, I decided that I should have ordered the trout, but what little appetite I'd had was gone anyway. Knowing it wasn't appropriate dinner-date conversation, I forged on. "Well, if Kate killed her father—or allowed him to die, crime or not—either way would leave her open for blackmail, and if Emmie had found out, then told Barbara, and if Kate killed them to keep her secrets, and if Jonathan added those two murders to Kate's blackmail tab for his silence, well, then Kate would have had to kill him, too."

Ben swallowed a bite of fish. "That's an awful lot of ifs."

"What if I can prove it?"

"How?"

"Caroline left me a message in the middle of the night. She says she's found Kate's journal. She told Patrick the same thing."

"When did you talk to Patrick?" Ben seemed bothered. By my playing detective again, against his advice or by my talking to Patrick?

"He'd called, too. I stopped by to see him on my way home from the Algonquin. For what it's worth, Kate seems to be his first choice for serial killer, too."

"Where is this supposed journal? Our guys went through that place with a vengeance."

"Hidden in Vera Madison's room. At least that's what Caroline says."

"Okay, I have an appointment with the medical examiner in the morning; I'll drop by about one and have another chat with both Vera and Caroline."

"Good, I'm going over at ten . . ."

"Listen to me, Jake, you are not to play cop again. Not tomorrow, not ever. Do you understand?"

A plot hatched in my aching head. "Yes, of course, I do," I said.

We ordered apple strudel a la mode for dessert.

Sipping espresso, I asked about Emmie's computer. "Did your expert crack the code?"

"Yes, today, in fact. 'Rachel' was the password. Most

of the stuff was drab routine. There were notes for a new book she'll never get to write.''

I bit my lip. ''So, nothing then?''

''Just one odd thing. In big, bold font, she'd typed over and over: WHO'S AFRAID OF VIRGINIA WOOLF? Any idea why she'd have done that?''

I told Ben about Dennis's visit and Kate's silent partner. ''You see, that proves Emmie had discovered something.''

''Yeah. But what?''

''Ben, did you ever try to recall something, like the name of an old movie star or your second grade teacher? And you just can't retrieve it? You know you know it, but the name's escaped to some unreachable corner of your mind. That keeps happening to me in this case. First with Aubergine. It reminds me of someone or something. Same with Virginia Woolf. Not the writer or the movie—something else—that name rings another bell. Just not loud enough to reach the memory.''

''I hated that movie,'' Ben said. ''I'm a sentimental slob, I guess. My favorite movie is *It's a Wonderful Life*.''

''That's okay, Ben; I'll tell you a secret that I've never told anyone.''

''I'm honored. What?''

''I cry at most Hallmark commercials. I turn my head or pretend I'm blowing my nose so that my mother doesn't notice, but I suspect she's crying, too.''

''And here I believed you were a hard-hearted woman, Jake. Maybe we are . . .'' Ben reached into his jacket and handed me a pocket phone, leaving his thought incomplete. ''This is programmed. Hit #1, you'll ring into my pocket phone. Hit #2, you'll reach my office, and #3 is 911. You'll have Hank tagging along starting in the morning, but I wanted you to have this . . . just in case.''

''Thank you, Ben. It's the nicest present anyone has ever given me.'' I reached over and kissed him on the lips as Ivan brought the check.

Thirty-one

I stood in front of Kate's Sutton Place house on Monday morning, hesitating before ringing the bell. God, could it only be a week since the first time I'd stood here? Now three ghosts were dead, I'd had two death threats and one very real attempt to kill me and, today, I would be alone with Kate in her library, where the serial killer's choice of weapons lined the walls.

Hank's Ford Explorer was parked across the street. Taking comfort from that, I pushed the bell, hard. Carla opened the door as if she'd been waiting behind it. "Miss O'Hara, come in! I have coffee set up in the library. Miss Connors is in conference." Carla gestured down the hallway, toward the Conservatory. "She suggests that you have a bagel, then start gathering what you need to take with you; it may be an hour or so before she can join you."

I glanced up the stairs and spotted Caroline, peering down at us, from between the rungs on the banister. "Okay, Carla. I'm in your hands." By the time Carla turned and we started to climb the staircase, Caroline had vanished.

Eating my bagel, I thought what a beautiful room. What an awesome way to live. This woman has it all: rich, famous, looking as marvelous as money can buy, an international best-selling author's acclaim, and ghosts to do her grunt work. If someone . . . Jonathan? . . . had threatened all that? Certainly people have killed to protect far less.

The doorway to Jonathan's office was still draped with yellow crime tape. I was surprised that I'd been allowed into the library. Wouldn't the killer have come through here to get to Jonathan's office? Or through the bathroom door as I once had? But, unless Carla had polished them away before the night of the murder, my fingerprints would have been all over the library, anyway, as well as the bathroom and Jonathan's office. I added more jam to my bagel, poured another cup of coffee, then sank into a big armchair, fumbling in my briefcase for Tylenol; the pain hadn't lessened. I wished I were home in bed. Where had Caroline gone? And where was Vera this morning? If I could get rid of her, I could search her room.

Impulsively I pulled the pocket phone out of my briefcase and dialed Dennis. Thank God, he picked up. "Dennis, can you get Vera Madison out of Sutton Place and over to your office on some excuse? Like, maybe, you need to check her signature on that contract . . . or something?"

"Well, good morning, Jake. Plotting a little conflict, are you?"

"You said you wanted to help. I need to get . . ."

"I don't want to know what you're about to do . . ."

"But you will help me?"

"Now that you mention it, Jake, I would like to ask Vera what the V in Kate's silent partner's name stands for."

"Try 'Virginia.' See how Vera reacts. You'll call her right away? Kate's tied up with someone, but I don't know for how long!"

"Just as soon as we hang up."

"I'm sorry I bit you twenty-five years ago."

"Hell, I was hoping you might take another nibble."

I laughed, feeling flattered by his flirting, but got back to business. Something still scratched at my subconscious. "If you find out anymore about that cable station or Kate's partner, let me know." I gave Dennis my pocket phone number. "Thanks and bless you, Dennis."

I put the phone in my denim shirt pocket—where it belonged—as Caroline, looking thin and pale, walked in. "Jake, I'm so glad to see you. 'Ave you come to save me, luv?"

"Maybe, Caroline. Maybe I have. Sit down; have a bagel and some coffee while we go over our game plan."

"Oh, jolly good, we 'ave a strategy, do we?"

"Well, sort of . . . but before we get to that, tell me, quickly, what you discovered in Kate's journal."

"Jake, it's 'ot stuff. According to Kate's own 'and-writing, she's my grandmother! My blood grandmother . . . God 'elp me! And Kate's father is Lily 'ansen's— my mum's—father, too! I guess that makes 'im both my grandfather and my great-grandfather. No wonder I'm tetched in the 'ead."

"You're not crazy, Caroline. I suspect Kate has influenced your doctor to prescribe too many drugs and that she has you overmedicated."

"Well, that witch, Vera, is always 'anding me a fist full of pills, and 'alf the time I don't know what they're for."

Today, Caroline's attire bordered on normalcy: black jeans, tee, and sneakers . . . no socks. With her scrubbed face and her long hair in a ponytail, she could have passed for a world-weary fourteen. I saw the hurt in her eyes and put my arm around her skinny shoulder. "Maybe, when this is all over, you can come and stay with Mom and me. She'd love to mother-hen you." I could see Mom outfitting Caroline at Polo.

Staring at the floor, Caroline whispered, "I'd like that."

I gave her shoulder a squeeze. "Okay, what else? Just hit the high—or low—points. We don't have much time!"

"Well, ages ago, Kate killed 'er father. Says she laughed as she 'eld the bastard's 'ead under the freezing water. Lovely values in the family tree, don't you think?"

Carla rapped on the library door and came in. "Can I bring you anything else, Miss O'Hara?"

"I wish you'd call me Jake. No thanks. Oh, I guess you could bring more cups and plates. I gave Kate's to Caroline."

Carla grinned. "Okay, Jake." She paused. "Mrs. Madison has gone to Mr. Kim's office. She said to tell Miss Caroline that she wouldn't be long." Long enough for Caroline and me to succeed in our mission, I hoped.

. . . . .

Vera Madison's room turned out to be a sick joke. The country French, white four-poster bed, topped with a pink and white gingham comforter that matched the Cape Cod tieback curtains, was strewn with stuffed animals. All pink or white or some combination of that color scheme. A rocking chair's cushion matched the checks as did the seat pad on Vera's desk chair. All the furniture was white and, here, the elegant, old hardwood flooring had been covered in pale pink shag wall-to-wall carpeting. Posters of James Dean and Elvis added to the teenage time warp . . . a room straight out of *Grease*. The dour Mrs. Danvers's exterior covered Gidget's soul. Weird and somehow sad.

"A regular Rocky 'orror show, ain't it?" Caroline asked.

"You've got that right. Now where's this journal?"

Caroline reached into Mrs. Madison's top drawer and pulled out a large, pink leather jewelry box. "In 'ere." She tossed it to me. God! I held Pandora's box in my hands. It scared me more than I would have thought. I opened it and lifted out a book, about five by seven inches, covered in brown alligator . . . not Vera's taste . . . but definitely Kate's.

"How come the police never found this journal, Caroline? I understand that they did a through search."

"But not a strip search. Mrs. Madison 'ad this tucked away in 'er knickers. I 'appened to pass 'er room as the old witch made the switch from 'er drawers to 'er dresser."

Now that was more information than I felt I needed. "Come on, Caroline. We're on countdown."

In this caper, Caroline would serve as lookout while I copied as much of the diary as I could. We agreed that she should be stationed outside the library, on the second-floor landing, with her eyes on the front door and her ears tuned in to hear if Kate's door might open. If either door opened, Caroline would scream—"Someone's trying to kill me!"—then dash down the stairs. Kate and Vera, as well as Carla, were used to Caroline's hysteria. Still, the ensuing commotion should give me the chance to stash the copies, turn off the machine, and either hide the journal or get it back in the jewelry box. Okay, it wasn't as well thought out as D-day, but then I hadn't had as much time as Eisenhower.

· · · · ·

Forty-five minutes later, I'd copied most of the diary, when I heard a bloodcurdling scream and footsteps thundering down the stairs. Caroline's choreographed "Someone's trying too kill me!" routine. My fingers flew, shoving papers into my briefcase; I managed to press the OFF button and close the top of the copier as I heard Mrs. Madison's voice as she stomped toward the library doors. "If there is someone, he could be hiding in here."

Then Caroline's weak objection, "I don't think 'e could be in the library; Jake's been working in there."

"And I think this is all a figment of your imagination, Caroline!" Mrs. Madison shouted, as she flung open the door and I, aping her ploy, stuffed the journal down my jeans, then pulled my briefcase in front of me, as I turned to face the dragon.

"Where is Miss Connors?" Vera Madison demanded.

Good question. I'd forgotten all about her. "Haven't seen her. I guess she's still with her visitor." Struggling, I juggled to cover the journal's bulk by carrying my briefcase like a six-month pregnancy.

Mrs. Madison stared at me. "What have you been doing all this time?"

"Gathering my material to take home with me as Kate requested. What's wrong?"

"Nothing. Caroline's thinks someone wants to kill her She's just overdue for her medicine. That's all. I suggest you check in with Miss Connors. I know that she strongly believes you should start working at home, immediately."

"Caroline, why don't you come downstairs with me? There's been one murder in this house and, if there's a intruder, I'm sure your mother would want to know." I gave Vera a nasty smirk as the book shifted, slipping toward my crotch. She left in a huff. I retrieved the contraband journal, shoved it in my bulging briefcase and, slinging its strap over my still-sore shoulder, went downstairs with Caroline to the Conservatory.

I knocked on the door three times. "Do you think we should just barge in?"

Caroline giggled. "Yeah, let's see what the old girl's been up to all morning."

I went in, Caroline on my heels. Kate was alone. Her head lay on the desk, her glorious gray hair awry, her neck twisted to the left at a hideous angle, her eyes open and staring. Somehow, a vase of white roses had been knocked over, its spilled water now a puddle, running through her hair. I had no doubt . . . either that she was dead or that the serial killer had struck again.

Thirty-two

Kate **had been** killed with the first edition of an abridged anthology of her Suzy Q murder mystery series. A book heavy enough to split the thickest skull. The murderer had placed it to the right of her head, the spine facing the door. I'd admired its cover—burgundy leather and gold lettering—last week when I'd started work; the book had been on display upstairs in the library. Who'd brought it down to the Conservatory?

Back to square one. This blew my theory to hell and back. If Kate wasn't the killer, who was? Just as I began to feel ashamed of myself, for my lack of sorrow—but abundance of curiosity—about Kate's death, Caroline let out a wail that made me jump and brought Carla running into the Conservatory. She stood frozen. Mrs. Madison couldn't be far behind. Even Hank might have heard that shriek, sitting outside in his parked car.

"I'd wished 'er dead a thousand times," Caroline cried, her eyes opaque, her shoulders slumped. "Just this morning, I told 'er to sod off. Now she 'as, forever. My wicked stepmother . . . who's really me old granny . . . is dead!" As the thought seemed to sink in, both Caroline's expression and her tone changed. "Jake, I'm rich as Fergie. I'm not crazy anymore; I'm a wealthy eccentric! Bloody grand, isn't it?"

"Caroline, shut up," I said, as Carla spun around and fled from the room, crashing into Mrs. Madison as she came charging through the door.

Vera Madison sized up the situation and crumpled to the floor. Jesus! Whatever happened to her stony stoicism? "Carla," I screamed, "come back here, bring a glass of brandy and a wet cloth." I thought for a second, then added, "But first call the family doctor. And hurry up!"

Shaken, I pulled my phone from my pocket and wound up pressing all three programmed numbers. I left two messages, one on Ben's pocket phone's tape recorder, the other at his office, then explained, at some length, to the 911 operator who—and where—I was and what had happened.

Stepping over Mrs. Madison, I crossed the room to the desk and, timidly, touched Kate, checking her pulse. None. Her arm was still warm. This was my first corpse, other than those already laid out in a casket. At a wake, the body's been painted and perfumed, before the mourners arrive to kneel at the bier to say good-bye or a prayer. The close encounter with Kate's corpse revealed the naked truth: Death is ugly. A warm breeze fluttered a few papers on the desk, and I realized that the French doors positioned to the right, behind the desk, were open. The killer could have exited through them, into the garden, then out the side gate to York Avenue. No one would have known, not even Hank, who'd parked in the street in front of the house.

Suddenly Caroline was next to me, reaching for the phone on Kate's desk. "I must ring up Patrick."

"Don't touch, anything. Not till the police arrive! You understand?"

"But," she started to wail again. "I want 'im with me."

"Here, call him on this." The irony, that the first three calls on my new phone had been to Dennis, Ben and Patrick, did not go unnoticed . . . even as Vera Madison's moans rose from the floor and Carla returned with the requested items.

Between us, Carla and I propped Vera on the couch and encouraged her to sip the brandy, while holding the damp towel to her forehead. All of her style and any aura of assurance had vanished. Vera Madison appeared grief-stricken and disoriented. She sat sobbing, saying nothing, simply staring at Kate's dead body.

"Carla, who visited Kate this morning? Who was she in conference with for so long?" I asked, as Caroline, who'd carried my phone to a far corner of the room, whispered to Patrick.

"Why? You think he killed her, Jake?" Carla sounded confused and frightened, but at least she was on her feet and functioning.

"Looks that way. He didn't leave by the front door, did he?" I gestured to the open French doors and watched as comprehension covered Carla's face. Then I asked, "Had you ever seen him before? Can you describe him for me, Carla?"

"No. I never saw him till this morning. A young man. Medium height and kind of skinny. A mustache. He wore those droopy jeans and a baseball cap. Dark glasses."

My pusher. "What color mustache? What kind?" No other witness had mentioned a mustache.

"Blond. Just a plain one, Jake, nothing special about it." Maybe Carla could work with a police sketch artist.

"What did he say?"

"He just asked to see Miss Connors. He'd laughed and said to tell her the wolf was at the door. I thought that was pretty funny."

God almighty! "Carla, this is important. How did Kate react when you told her that?"

"Well, you know how she is—er—she was..." Carla choked up for a second. "Always in control."

"Yeah, I know. So what did she say?"

"She said, 'Jesus H. Christ!' I'd never heard Miss Connors say anything like that before. Then she kind of sighed and told me to tell you that she'd be in conference for an hour or so."

"Then what?"

"I showed him to the Conservatory, but he opened the door and went in alone. That's all I know, Jake. Honest." I could hear the stress in her voice. I patted her hand.

"That's fine. You've been a big help." I reached into my bag and retrieved my Tylenol, swallowing them neat. Would my head ever stop aching?

Compounding the pain, an annoying little ditty went round and round my brain. To the tune of "Who's Afraid of the Big, Bad Wolf" Who's Afraid of Virginia Woolf? Who's Afraid of Virginia Woolf? Who's Afraid of Virginia Woolf?... played over and over. I couldn't turn it off. Why couldn't I connect the dots? What a nagging nuisance... both that name and its importance to this case! The answer seemed to be buried in some cubbyhole in my mind. Didn't I want to remember?

Caroline walked over to me, still on the phone. "Patrick's with a patient. He'll be here as soon as he can." I grabbed the phone from her hand and took it into the garden.

"Patrick, this is Jake." I spoke in a low, but firm

voice. "I'm on my way to Murray Hill. Stay put! We have four murders to solve, and we can't do it here. Listen, that's the police siren. They're here now! We'll return to Sutton Place, together, after we finish. Regress me, Patrick! Free my repressed memory."

"Come on down!" I hung up before he could change his mind.

Ignoring Caroline and the still mute Mrs. Madison, I shouted to Carla, "I'm heading out through the garden gate. Tell the police that the guy in the Ford Explorer is one of their own. And when Ben Rubin shows up, tell him I'll explain, later." This last, I yelled over my shoulder, as I exited the gate, turned left unto York Avenue, and tried to hail a cab, heading in the wrong direction.

As I settled in the taxi, I told the driver to take Second Avenue downtown to Patrick's office and took stock of my screwy behavior. Like a Robin Cook heroine allowing the mad scientist to inject her with a three-days-and-you're-dead virus, I could be willingly wading into troubled waters. Granted, Patrick might be able to dredge up my missing memory, but he also had a multimillion-dollar motive for Kate's murder. As Caroline pointed out, she had just come into a bundle of big bucks. Kate's death would also free Caroline to marry, and Patrick would seem to be her most likely groom-elect. Kate Lloyd Connors's royalties alone could keep the happy couple in Rolls Royces for the rest of their lives. Patrick could have killed Kate, wearing a fake mustache.

The noontime traffic frustrated both the young Israeli driver and me. There hadn't been time to read any of Kate's journal as I'd copied its pages, so I only knew what Caroline had told me. I flipped through a few entries, written before she'd murdered her father. Kate—

Sarah Anne—spoke of a bleak, dreary life, a childhood with little love, and that ending when her mother died. Sarah Anne was ten. Her father began abusing her the following summer. The way Sarah Anne described the freezing, cold day that she'd drowned her father in Lake Superior, I felt as if I'd been there with her.

Dad jerked back as if he'd felt a sharp tug on his line. Somehow he lost his balance—he'd been kneeling on the edge of the hole, a foolish way to ice-fish—screaming, "Help me, Sarah Anne!" And I screamed louder. "I'm pregnant, you bastard!" As he desperately clawed at the breaking ice on the sides of the fishing hole, I lay down on the ice, carefully stretched out into the freezing water, put both my hands on top of my father's plaid woolen cap and pushed him under the bitter cold water. I held him there, laughing, as he squirmed for a few seconds, then sank. When I pulled off my soaking-wet gloves, my fingers were red and raw. My only regret was that he'd died so quickly . . . I hope it hurt.

I ran home, threw some clothes in our one old canvas suitcase, took the three hundred dollars hidden under the mattress, Dad's total nest egg, and walked two miles in below-freezing temperatures to the Honey Bucket bus station, where I caught the bus for Detroit, vowing I'd never look back.

Wow! "Hurry, driver, please!" I fast-forwarded through the diary to Detroit.

My landlady's turned into my fairy godmother. Vera Madison likes me so much that it's scary, but

she always has an answer for my problems, start-
ing with my new identify. An absolutely creepy
friend of hers is a forger, so I bought a birth cer-
tificate from him for fifty dollars, then applied for
a social security card as Kate Lloyd Connors. I
love my new name. It reeks of elegance.

I'm proud of myself. Not only did I get my GED
while working two jobs, but I'm earning an A in
Creative Writing at the Community College. And
I was smart enough to give my baby away. I used
my real name for the last time. That way no one
will ever link her to Kate Lloyd Connors. I'm go-
ing to be a famous writer someday. Vera believes
in me. My biggest fan! Total devotion. It's kind of
nice to have her waiting on me hand and foot.
She's going to pay for the move to Manhattan. Of
course, she's coming along.

"We're here, lady." I put the journal back in my
briefcase, but Kate Lloyd Connors's words lingered in
my mind.

Patrick greeted me with a professional manner and a
twinkle in those deep blue eyes. "I never expected to
have the pleasure of hypnotizing you, Jake."

"Yes, Patrick, four murders can drive a potential victim to unexpected measures. Now, how does this regression business work?"

After I'd explained how I'd lost a name that could
help us identify the killer, in what might be a repressed
memory, Patrick nodded. "It happens. Sit here, Jake;
we'll give it a try." He indicated a sleek leather recliner.

I sank into its comfort, my aching body somewhat
eased, but my spirit shaky.

"There is nothing mysterious or threatening about
hypnosis, Jake. No one will ever do anything under hyp-

nosis that would be against his or her moral or ethical code. Most people tell me that they're never more aware than when they're in a session with me.'' Probably realizing that his last remark might be construed as vain, he added, ''Or any certified hypnotist.''

I closed my eyes as suggested and tried to relax, also as suggested but not as easy to achieve. Patrick helped. ''Picture a beach: white sand, blue skies, aqua ocean. You're all alone, drinking in the warm sun.'' He paused, and I thought: He forgot to put a color before the sun . . . then told myself to get serious about relaxing. ''Start with the toes on your right foot,'' Patrick was saying, ''and relax each one. First the big toe . . .''

By the time he reached my forehead, I was putty.

''Jake, you are serene; you are completely relaxed. Let's go back a bit—to a younger Jake. Can you picture yourself in your late twenties? Maybe in a special outfit? Perhaps at a party or a dance? Is there a special song being played?''

I was in a splendid salon, surrounded by beautiful women in formal gowns and fussy hair styles. I, however, wore pants and some sort of a tailored, old-fashioned man's jacket. A handsome young man sat at a piano, playing a polonaise.

''Where are you, Jake?'' Patrick sounded far away.

''In my home, in Paris.''

''Did you ever live in Paris? What's your name?''

''George Sand,'' I answered.

''Oops!'' Patrick said. ''We went back too far!''

Thirty-three

·

Patrick brought me back to the present. I told
him, "My misplaced memory seems fairly recent—
maybe from a conversation I had a few years ago—
certainly not from one that took place in the nineteenth
century!" Although I'd enjoyed my cameo as George
Sand and hoped to replay that incarnation during some
future regression, I asked Patrick to hypnotize me again,
concentrating on the last decade of this lifetime.

"I'm off my game, Jake. All I can focus on is Caroline coping, all alone, with the police at Sutton Place."
Patrick frowned, shaking his head.

Oh God! Was he changing his mind? He really did
seem concerned about Caroline. "Patrick, please, if we
don't do this right now, the killer's name may escape
me forever."

My pocket phone rang. "Jake, it's Ben. I just got here.
Where the hell are you? Come back here, immediately,
and bring that goddamn journal with you!"

"Don't get so testy, Ben! I'm at Patrick's, trying to
recall an important memory, the Virginia Wolf con-
nec . . ."

"You've left the scene of the crime and you've taken stolen evidence with you! Get in a taxi, this minute!" He hung up.

I looked at Patrick "Er . . . do you think we could do this regression in the cab, while we're heading up to Sutton Place?"

. . . . .

The Haitian cabbie seemed to feel at home with what, from his point of view, could be two certifiable weirdos practicing voodoo, American style. Patrick said, "Put your head back, close your eyes, lift your arms and splay your fingers. Now reach for the sky—um—well, the top of the taxi, anyway. Slip off your shoes, wiggle your toes, then stretch your feet out as far as possible in front of you." Good thing we'd caught one of the few big Checkers left in the city. "I will count backward from ten; at the count of three, you will be totally relaxed, opening the portals of your mind and ready to retrieve your memory." If only I was as sure as Patrick sounded. He'd agreed, quickly, to this journey down memory lane, during our trip uptown . . . probably just doing it so he could get to Caroline.

On the count of seven, my phone rang again. "Dennis! What have you learned?"

"Where are you, Jake? Everyone from your mother to Ben Rubin is on your trail. I can't believe Kate's dead! Are you on the lam? You didn't do it, did you?"

"Very funny. Do you have any news for me?"

"Yes, and some advice: Get your butt back to Sutton Place."

"I'm on my way. Hurry up, Dennis! Tell me what you know."

"The cable station is an international, twenty-four-hour cookathon."

"Cooking???" I flexed my bare feet. And, turning away from the phone, I whispered to Patrick, "I'll be right with you."

He frowned at me, muttering, "We're already at 39th Street. How many years do you think you can travel back with less than a mile to go?"

"A mile can turn into years in New York traffic, Patrick."

"Who are you talking to?" Dennis asked.

"Patrick," I said to Dennis. "He and I are in the middle of a regression, about to release my repressed memory and we're almost there!"

"Well, I'm very happy for you both!"

"Dennis, please! Just finish what you were saying!"

"Seems the show's akin to *Lifestyles of the Rich and Famous* meets *Geraldo*. Only here, the viewer will visit the celebs as they cook in their kitchens, pull vegetables from their gardens or host their formal dinner parties . . . while revealing their secrets. Live! Round the clock! In the treatment for the pilot, Sophia Loren trades recipes with Elton John in Nelson Mandela's kitchen."

"Bizarre," I said.

"There's one other thing . . . for what it's worth. I just found out from Larry Helms that 'aubergine' is French for eggplant. Seems to all tie in, somehow, doesn't it? And, Jake, call your mother; she's frantic!"

My brain buzzing, I turned to Patrick. "Let's do it! Now!"

. . . . .

Ten minutes later, as the cab hung a right on 52nd Street, forging east to Sutton Place, and missing a roller-blader by inches, I'd retrieved my memory and had my answer. An answer I hadn't expected and didn't want to accept. Horrified, I tried to work the steps of the

Ghostwriters Anonymous program. Just as we ghosts couldn't control our anonymity, but had to accept it, I couldn't control the killer's identity and would have to accept who done it . . . even though I'd hate it.

Funny how my lost memory had become all mixed up with lost identities. Since we ghosts never had our names on the book covers, using a pen name would seem to be an oxymoron. Even our program's suggested use of the first initial of our last name—just like in AA meetings—reeked of irony. I now thought of Modesty as Modesty M; however, her last name was Meade. We always referred to Jane as Jane D, almost forgetting that her last name was Dowling. And Ginger S had a last name, too. Smthye. But that *was* a nom de plume. And that was what I couldn't—maybe hadn't wanted to—remember. When we'd co-authored *Cooked to Death* all those years ago, Ginger had said, "My real name's the same as a famous writer, but I've been using Smthye in preparation for my own future fame." When I'd asked Ginger which well-known writer shared her real name, her answer had been: Virginia Woolf.

Patrick shook my shoulder. "I don't know what's the matter with you or why you refuse to reveal what you've remembered or even talk to me. I know a patient can't fake a recovered memory! But why would anyone pretend she hadn't reached her repression? I heard that, 'Oh, God!' I know you got there!"

"Patrick, would you please shut up? I'm trying to think!"

The clues added up. Who but Ginger would be a silent partner in a corporation with a French name that translated into "eggplant"? Who but Ginger would be crazy enough to want to host a round-the-clock, international cable celebrity cooking channel? Certainly not Kate Lloyd Connors, who was even less creative in the kitchen than she was at the computer. And since half the ghosts in New York seemed to have worked for Kate at one time or another . . . why not Ginger?

If Ginger had found that journal—or some other evidence regarding the revered Queen-of-Murder-Most-Cozy's lurid past—and, having proof that Kate was a killer, had been blackmailing her, the cable station might have been Ginger's big payoff. Then, when Emmie had discovered Ginger's scheme and shared her secrets with Barbara, Ginger would, as a dear friend and fellow ghost, have had no problem getting into either of their apartments to "explain" things.

More ghastly memories—ones I would have preferred to forget—surfaced. If my theory proved true, then on that Saturday, a little over a week ago, when Ginger had supposedly searched all over the Upper East Side looking for Emmie, she'd already killed her the night before. Actually, that day, Ginger had been busy murdering Barbara! And, of course, Jonathan had signed his own death warrant when he'd tried to sell Kate's secrets to the *National Enquirer,* infringing, unknowingly, on Ginger's blackmail territory. And, after Emmie's wake, when Modesty had dropped her off at home, Ginger had popped over to Kate's and book-bashed Jonathan to death. Then this morning, dressed as a man, she'd killed Kate. There you go! Motive, means and opportunity for each of the four murders.

But . . . still . . . Ginger was my friend and I loved her. So did Mom. And Gypsy Rose. We'd shared ghost stories, holidays and hope. How could sunny, funny Ginger be a murderer? How could Ginger have fooled so many people for so many years? Not Ginger. Impossible. It couldn't be Ginger. How could this woman I knew so well be a sociopath? A serial killer?

My God—if this is true, Ginger shoved me in front of that taxi . . . She tried to kill me!

There had to be some other explanation! Unbidden, Arthur Conan Doyle's quote from *The Sign of Four*— "When you have eliminated the impossible, whatever remains, however improbable, must be the truth"— assaulted my brain and chilled my soul.

Patrick said, "Driver, let us out here; we'll walk the rest of the way. Come on, Jake, get out of the cab!" He pointed to the police cars piled up between York Avenue and the East River and the ambulance parked in front of Kate Lloyd Connors's house, the block a mass of media who'd flocked like homing pigeons to the fresh homicide.

"Wait, I have to call my mother. I won't have a chance once we get into that mess at Kate's."

I dialed. Ginger answered on the second ring.

"What are you doing there?" I screamed. "Where's my mother?"

Patrick stepped out the cab, pulling bills out of his pocket to pay the driver. "Are you coming, Jake? Caroline needs me!"

"I've given your mother a nice cup of tea." Ginger said in her Lauren Bacall voice. "She can't come to the phone at this moment. But you'd better come home. Alone. Now."

"Ginger!" But I spoke into a dead line. She'd hung up.

The driver handed Patrick his change, and I grabbed the door's handle, shouting, "Patrick, tell Ben to get to my house, immediately. Tell him Ginger's there. That she's Virginia Woolf! And I need him!" Then I pulled the door shut, before Patrick had a chance to stop me. "Please take me to 92nd and Madison Avenue, driver, just as fast as you can," I said, as Patrick sprinted toward Kate's.

. . . . .

Ginger stood in my living room, impeccably groomed, as always. Pale green flowing pants, and matching cotton-knit, ribbed sweater were covered with a crisp white apron. Her sandals were a shade darker than her outfit, and her blonde hair was swept away from her face, secured with a green ribbon. She had one hand behind her back, holding something. "Come into the kitchen, Jake. I've brought peach pie just out of the oven; I know how you love it. And there's fresh coffee, too." As she turned, I slid the lock back open.

The afternoon sun flickered through the white shutters, and the apartment seemed as golden and gracious as Ginger. As we passed through the dining room, Ginger laid the book she'd been carrying down, cover up, on the dining room table. *To Kill a Mockingbird.*

My mother's head was on the kitchen table. I shrieked, "What have you done to her?"

"Just a shot of chloral hydrate in her English Breakfast tea. She'll wake up in time for your last good-byes. So, have you figured it all out, Jake?" Ginger asked, as she poured the coffee.

"Jesus! Please let my mother go. You can't hurt her!" Even in my terror, I smelled the fine aroma of Ginger's fresh-ground brew.

"I'm afraid I can't do that. And it's all your fault, Jake," Ginger smiled. "You always were too good at solving puzzles and guessing who done it before the second reel." Ginger crossed the kitchen and held up her goddamn perfect peach pie. "Would you like a piece, Jake?" she asked. Speechless, I shook my head.

I might never be able to eat peach pie again as long as I live . . . if I lived. "Well, drink your coffee." Ginger handed me a cup. She could have been playing hostess at a Ghostwriters Anonymous meeting or a brunch at her house. "The beans are imported from a remote plantation in the Argentine outback. You'll never enjoy anything like it again."

"Ginger, for God's sake . . ."

"I hope you understand, Jake. An international cooking cable channel will allow me to bring good taste to the world. Nothing can stop me. Not even you."

Then, in one swift movement that I almost missed, Ginger put the pie down and removed a long, sharp knife from the cutlery rack standing on the counter. In her deep, sexy voice, she said, as if pondering her options, "I could kill you in the kitchen."

Déjà vu! I ducked as she lunged at me, dropping the coffee cup, and throwing my hands in front of my face. The blade made contact, nicking my right wrist. Christ! Ginger was going to kill me. George Sand flitted like a firefly through my brain, accompanied by Chopin's music. A previous life flashing through my mind before I died? I wondered if my next incarnation would be as good as that one must have been; however, I had no complaints about this time around and really didn't want to depart. Then I screamed, as Ginger loomed large above me, the knife thrust in a downward motion, aimed at my heart.

"You killed Kate!" Startled, both Ginger and I swung around to face the archway leading into the dining room. Vera Madison stood there, looking completely disheveled, but in total command of the compact pistol that she had pointed at Ginger. "You greedy, blood-sucking blackmailer. You got your TV station and Kate became expendable."

I heard a moan and turned back to the table. Mom held her chin propped up in her hands and gave me a silly smile, looking like someone who'd just downed four martinis. Then her head flopped down again.

Vera ignored my mother and continued talking. "I overheard Patrick tell Detective Rubin that you'd gone to Jake's. So I slipped out the garden gate. This is payback time for Kate. I'm going to kill you, Virginia Woolf!"

I screamed again as Vera shot Ginger in the chest, then aimed the gun at me. I watched Ginger crumple to the floor, then closed my eyes, starting a Hail Mary, wondering how Gypsy Rose would get along without me and Mom. George Sand and Chopin returned.

Ben's loud and clear "Jake!" brought me back to my kitchen. I opened my eyes and, over Vera Madison's shoulder, I glimpsed his wonderful face. Then he shot Vera in her left leg, bringing her to her knees and sending her gun flying across Mom's highly polished floor.

Epilogue

While the cleaning crew was sopping up the splatter, scraping bone fragments from our kitchen appliances and scrubbing bloodstains from the walls and floor, Mom and I had moved into Gypsy Rose's third-floor guest suite. The three of us sat, sipping tea and sharing our shock and sadness.

"Even Zelda never suspected Ginger." Gypsy Rose shook her red curls in disbelief. "So it's no wonder that we didn't have a clue!"

"Oh, but we did. On that first Saturday, at the Ghostwriters Anonymous meeting, I'd asked Ginger why she'd missed Mom's lesser-literary-lights cocktail party. She never had before, you know . . . but she'd been murdering Emmie that Friday night. And Ginger kept insisting Ivan was the killer, while trying to keep the focus off Kate. Then Ginger disappeared from the receiving line at Barbara's memorial—to avoid coming face-to-face with Kate—and only returned, claiming that she'd been in the bathroom, throwing up, after we'd all been seated."

"That's when I felt the killer's presence!" Gypsy Rose said.

"And, if I'd remembered either my high school French or Ginger's real last name . . ." I knew tears were coming, so I changed the subject. We'd all been doing that a lot. "Listen, thanks to Dennis, I still have my assignment . . . and that big advance. Mom, I think we should buy a beach house in the Hamptons. I'll even let you invite Dennis and Ben out to visit. Of course, not at the same time. Gypsy Rose, why don't you close up shop for a month or so and come with us?"

My mother's blue eyes widened, as a light missing from them since that sunny afternoon when we'd entertained two killers in our kitchen, returned. But then she crossed her arms and hugged her shoulders, shaking her head from side to side.

"Come on, Maura." Gypsy Rose sounded firm. "We have to accept what happened and get on with our lives. The Ginger we loved was gone long before she died. Her spirit guide tells me she'd suffered both a mental and a spiritual breakdown. Some day, she'll have another chance in a future incarnation. Let's all go to the beach."

"You're right, Gypsy Rose. The truth is painful, but not only can I accept it, I can live with it." A small smile lifted my mother's lips as she nodded, sagely. "Ginger snapped."